Levitation

Levitation

Sean O'Reilly

Stories

The Stinging Fly

A Stinging Fly Press Book

Levitation is first published simultaneously in paperback
and in a special casebound edition (300 copies) in September 2017.

Copyright © 2017 by Sean O'Reilly

FIRST EDITION

ISBN 978-1-906539-63-4 (casebound)
ISBN 978-1-906539-64-1 (paperback)

The Stinging Fly Press
PO Box 6016
Dublin 1
www.stingingfly.org

Set in Palatino

Printed in Ireland by Walsh Colour Print, County Kerry.

Earlier versions of some of these stories appeared in *The Stinging Fly* and in *All Over Ireland: New Irish Short Stories* (Faber and Faber, 2015).

The Stinging Fly Press gratefully acknowledges the financial support of The Arts Council/An Chomhairle Ealaíon.

Contents

hallion #1	3
Free Verse	16
Rescue	24
The Cavalcade	40
Downstream	58
hallion #2	79
The Three Twists	92
Scissors	105
Ceremony	119
Critical Mass II (*Abandoned Work*)	145
Levitation	161

'He suited the action to the thought, and went to a barber.'

The Legend of the Holy Drinker
by Joseph Roth
Translated by Michael Hofmann

Levitation

hallion #1

... aye if the army were spying down on us from the watch tower on the walls the scum would have thought I was one of the gypos going door to door with a swanky red pram / the big long-range binoculars zooming in to check what's under the hood / oi Lionel flipping heck mate one of the paddies is trying to flog a nipper in a stolen pram

    all afternoon in this sleet too / how many doors in the Brandywell did we knock on and no joy even though I had the money right there in my hand / will you mind the wee man for me for a couple of hours it's an emergency / you'd think people were afraid of money around our way / Mrs Hughes going I'm expecting an important visitor and the coffin lid leaning against the hall wall / Mrs Walters going I only do wee girls now only the blonde ones / or shy Leonie O' Brien with the bow in her hair smiling at you through the gap in the sandbags until her da appeared and we had to make ourselves scarce off the Lecky Road

    catch that r-a-t for me and I'll keep an eye on him for nothing Mrs O' Connell says and holds out the brush pole with the sharpened edge / spear or no spear that's one thing about your da he'll run a mile from even the mention of that word / my own da bit the head off one and threw it into the middle of us wains on the bed / he did / last one out gets to

LEVITATION

stay off school he said / I still have to check under the covers at night before I get in / it drives your mother round the bend / stop acting the corny weakling and lie down beside your shivering wife she tells me / she'll have a field day to herself with new names for your da when she finds out I have you out here in the good pram up a back lane / at night too / and this fog now around the bins like it wants a head on a plate

so where's those two sluts of sisters of yours and that communist you tricked into marrying you Mrs Match writes down in her notepad and shows it to me / you see her around the town handing out messages to people / some of them are right too ones say / I wrote back the truth that your mother's stuck in the sit-in in the council offices and your two aunties won't speak to me because of what I have coming to me tonight and my ma your poor granny's still in the hospital / but she can't read my handwriting / and she tears it out and burns it and wants me to write it again and my hand starts to shake like I'm back at school / your da never did great at school either Neil / that's your mother's territory / up and down the road to Belfast to the university / always a book in her hand whether she's warming your bottle or cleaning her big teeth / she'll let one fly at you too if you annoy her / a book on the nut you'll feel if you get her goat

thought that was him there arriving the man with the bazooka / Mulhern you call him from Pilot's Row / and he's bound to keep us waiting to make himself feel big / nearly half seven it is now / we'll hear him first with his bicycle bell he rings in his pocket thinking its scary / here I come ready or not / dring dring / dring dring / a bottle of vodka in the other pocket and the sweaty bald red head your mother says would put you off your dinner / mind that woman we kept seeing everywhere earlier with the ladders on her shoulder and I didn't want to talk to her that's his wife / she does the windows / I could tell you a story or two about Ladders / if she takes a shine to you ones have moved across the border to avoid her / she can't help it though / but Mulhern's not all he's cracked up to be not any more anyway / he's slipping / they'll have to replace him soon / in the past few months there's three knee caps he's managed to make a balls of / look what happened to me right here in this exact same spot only a fortnight ago right over there in the corner where Camel it must be has written we know too much / Camel is off his head

it was a nicer night than this none of this fog / Mulhern turns up half an hour late and he's in bad form because he has a toothache and he's necking the vodka which makes me even more nervous that it'll affect his aim / you have to do it properly or your da won't be kicking a ball around with you or badminton which is my favourite game did you know that / badminton on the beach in the sun that's the way it should be every day / Mulhern can barely talk with the pain and he's pointing the gun at me to lie down over there by the corner / we're still waiting for somebody else to turn up with the bullets and hold me down too / that's the way they do it / keep the bullets separate so if you're caught with the gun it's unloaded which is not as bad / hold on I'm telling Mulhern and trying to take off my jeans / they're the only pair I've left and I don't want a big hole in them or blood either / what the hell are you gawking at I say to him / he's staring at me like I'm a brand new perfect bike for his bell / then he has the lighter out and he's kneeling down in front of me and starts inspecting my skinny white legs in the flame / it was right over there

your mother hates my legs / girly legs she calls them / cover them up before I heave she says / but Mulhern must think they're nice because you see that crooked yellow back gate he's banging his head off it and the butt of the gun and whinging / I can't hurt those fine alabaster legs I can't hurt

LEVITATION

those fine alabaster legs / alabaster Neil / I was checking for it in your ma's dictionary / I took it into the toilet with me but she caught me on the way out and thought I was looking up dirty words / and that got your da another clout and a night on the sofa

now don't you be telling anybody / that's a secret between you and your da / I didn't mean to lie to your mother about it / mind how happy she was when I came back and told her I had a reprieve / you and her were round at your other granny's / the gun jammed I told her and they can't hang you twice / I really thought I was off the hook / mind how delighted she was / it's all over she thought / when she's happy like that who cares about anything / we got fish and chips on the way home and she told us about when she was a girl and broke her ankle up Mount Errigal

only Mulhern to save his own neck went and told the boys I hadn't showed up the sneaky f-u-c-k-e-r / and they believed him and not your da / and they commanded I turn up again or else and so here we are / the Quinns father and son / two legs and four wheels and a stretcher with my name on it

I didn't have the heart to tell your mother Neil / I tried a few times but it never felt right to upset her again / hasn't she been in great form the last few days / passed her exams and talking about a holiday / just take me anywhere I don't care she was saying / nobody could have told her / look how she reacted when she found out the first time / you were there kicking your legs on the sofa and your ma was reading at the table with her curlers in and the doorbell goes / I went to answer it and four hours later I came back / who are you she says who the hell are you you useless drip of a man / five days she wouldn't let me back in the flat / and his name is not Neil she's shouting after me down the street and holding you way up in the air with her two hands / his name's not Neil any more / your father was a thief and a hood and you're

hallion #1

another bloody thieving hallion / shouting it all after me on the street

    sorry about leaving you with Mrs Craven / I was out of options son / run a few messages for me and I'll think about it she roars at me the deaf bat / over to the barber's with a bag of her famous mothballs and pick her up some soap powder and a bar of Turkish Delight from the People's shop on the way back / fair enough I thought / you could choke with the smell of chemicals in her hall but I was getting desperate and the sleet was worse and it was dark nearly / you'd be dry and warm and have a rusk and no need to see your da rolling around in the muck / the barber's on Nelson Street and then the shop and back / wee buns / I shouldn't have believed it / some days are not like other days son / some days nothing happens and you think it's because the people are nervous / people are quiet / the clocks seem slow / people wonder what might happen / other days they're greedy as hell

    we were trapped in there in Vinnie's Big Time Barbershop about a hundred of us / a hundred and fifty maybe / we had to bloody dig our way out through the old tunnel that's why my hands are so stiff I can't undo the button of my jeans / Mulhern will have to do it for me I'm not joking you

    straight away in the door of Vinnie's I meet my da's brother Boo and I have to stop and talk to him / and right beside him Sinclair the journalist / and then I have to talk to Querney and Dunne and then Mollock and Henri and Camel and Buckle and loads of them and * and all the time there's things dropping on your head worse than sleet / tons of moths / and the smell of their burning wings and

*REDACTED

7

the lights blinking in the smoke / I've a delivery for Vinnie I keep telling them but you have to stop and join in or ones take it thick / I've a delivery for Vinnie / it must have taken me about an hour to make it through the faces to the other side of the shop where Vinnie's trying to hypnotise this wee lad in the chair ten maybe eleven with long blonde hair like a girl's down to the floor / two men holding him down / and he's screaming away and choking with the moths probably stuck right down in his throat / and Vinnie swinging his special red stone on a lace and roaring at him you are feeling sleepy you are feeling sleepy

    you've some nerve coming in here he eventually says to me / our Iris is weeping a river / that's his daughter Iris he means / I didn't touch her I said but he carries on blanking me for another half an hour / you see I saw Iris in the People's shop on the way over / she took one look at me and started weeping because probably I remind her of Faze / your godfather Faze / where's Faze she grabs hold of me / tell me where Faze is the tears soaking the free cheese

    I didn't know where Faze was

    your mother made me swear I wouldn't have any more to do with him after we got caught again / and I stuck to it too didn't I / avoiding places / staying in at the weekends / but he was waiting for me one day outside the bru / I have a gun he says / I got us a pistol

    there's this chemist in Glenowen with a new safe / he had it all worked out / one last dance he said doing one of his tricky shuffles in his new white boots / when he's in that state he's a hard man to refuse / he spins you round / you say no and you may as well have punched him in the guts out of the blue with the shock on his face / disbelief / that's just how it happened / Faze in his white boots and the hair slicked back / the very next day we did it

    I always had a weakness for your mother from the first

time I saw her waving a flag on the barricade / hair flying in the wind like she was falling / the big teeth / but I never had the balls to talk to her

we don't need the noose Faze shouts at me out the back of the chemist's / why did you bring the noose you moron / call me that again and I'll hang you myself I said / I should have walked away there and then and told him to shove his excuse for a gun / it was only half a gun he had / the top bit only / just the barrel no handle or trigger / Faze had it cellotaped along his finger / and we didn't need it anyway because the noose scares people more / drag a chair into the middle of the room and show them the rope and they will give you the combination to heaven / the chemist man nearly fainted / we were in and out in no time / scot-free / clean and pure / and we thought we got away with it until that knock on the door you kicking your legs on the sofa and your ma reading one of her books / dring dring I hear before I open it and Mulhern says get in the car pronto / a Cortina estate / then I see Faze in the back seat in his pyjamas and I know we are for it / no way out / we were screwed son

leave town or take your oil that was the deal / we already had our last warning after we were squealed on over those magazines from the house in Prehen / Faze couldn't keep them to himself / wanted to show them to people / a big box of stupid bloody blue magazines / that was his fault / someone grassed us up / but how were we to know there was a man lying under the floorboards in the chemist's / a man on the run hiding under the floorboards who saw the whole thing / up through the cracks in the floor after we took off our scarves

and where is he now how should I bloody know / Liverpool / Coventry / what do they call it Holland / Faze blew the roost

poor Iris in the People's shop won't believe me though /

she obviously doesn't know Faze too well if she thinks he'd stick around for a pair of crutches / not Faze / he'd be more worried about what to wear with them than the bullets / whether he could get his good shoes on / what suit / mind him at your christening dancing with every woman there / some mover / and dancing with your mother too who never casts a shadow on the dance floor / three songs she danced with him / and those two were never supposed to get on / a fire in a bin she calls him / I only got the one at our own bloody wedding sure

but Faze is your godfather don't you ever forget that however many hearts he breaks or what people say about him

you'd think Iris was the first the way she was crying / take that poor girl home for god's sake the women were saying / nobody can stick seeing that type of crying for long / I felt bad for her / so we got her coat and I gave the invisible man his fags at the door / you see that's why I went into the shop in the first place / the invisible man was outside as I was passing and he asked me to buy them for him and I owed him a favour so I could hardly say no / he's barred from everywhere so he is / he winds people up the wrong way standing around listening in on their conversations and following them around claiming he's invisible / your ma says he's a cod artist but he may as well be invisible now / I tend to believe him / you have to believe people at some stage that's what I say no matter what line they're spinning you / you have to believe people Neil there's no other way

but poor Iris / mind the day she had you in her lap and you wouldn't let go of her million curls / and her pointy eyebrows / two birds in flight your mother calls her / if she had seen the way I had to practically carry her up the steps of the high flats and her sobs echoing so much it was like a choir of dying angels I'd never live it down / I'm too soft according to your mother a walkover / but I believed Iris / she was upset / it

hallion #1

wasn't her fault / and then hey presto she slips out of my arm and runs for the fourth floor landing and throws her leg over / what's she doing I'm there wondering / what the hell is she up to / only her long denim coat gets caught in the railings or she would have went right over / that's heartbreak for you / may it never know your name Neil / she would do anything to make it stop / but she's tangled up in her coat and the railings and she looks at me and you know what she says like it might even have been her last words / how can anybody be such a cretin / and me who had been nice to her / why the hell was everybody calling me stupid these days that's what I was thinking and so out of spite I ran over and grabbed her and started pulling her back on to the veranda and shouting for help / help / help / somebody help me here / down in the courtyard there's one of the foreign visitors giving a speech to the crowd / don't give up the struggle against the imperialists / the people united will never be defeated / and the crowd cheering so nobody can hear what's happening on the fourth floor and Iris is scratching the face off me with her nails / which your mother will be more annoyed about than the holes in my knees and having to bring me breakfast in bed for a while / and you know what else / Mulhern is just going to have to look after you if they don't let me take you in the ambulance with me

a strange thing happened next though / three wee boys appear and they've all got broken arms / five broken arms in plaster between them / they'd come out of one of the empty flats / three wee mummies on the fourth floor landing / at least I would never treat you like that / experiment on you with plaster the way their father does / he was there too / the bath full of plastery porridge inside / and arms and legs lying about the place / these white shells / crusts of arms and legs piled up in the corner / I nearly have the mixture right he tells me staring into the bath / one of the Smullens

LEVITATION

from the Wells / for the plaster to set right he means / then he was taking the wains down to the bru and making a claim against the government for injuries / everybody would be doing it once he had perfected the mixture he promised me / the entire town staggering around in plaster of Paris and suing the British state / break the bank he was saying that's all they'll listen to a nation of shopkeepers remember / Iris was there too now / like nothing had ever happened / the tears probably still hadn't hit the ground below yet / and she orders me to give the wains the Turkish Delight to cheer them up / I tell you I was so fed up by this point I nearly went back and got you from Mrs Craven and not showed up here at all / blow down over the border and live in a caravan / play badminton on the beach / live on candyfloss and milk from the cows in the fields / but they'd call me a coward and that's not what I am / your da's no coward Neil / they can run me down all they want but I'm not a coward / or a dope right / I know what's going on your da has his eyes open

twenty to eight now / I'm no grass either but if Mulhern doesn't show his bake very soon me and you are waltzing straight round to the house of you know who and spilling the beans that he's a has been

people aren't the worst though / ███████████ ██

you warm enough

I was always a bit scared of your mother to be honest and the whole lot of them / the McGerrigans / her crowd were always political / I think your mother only ever noticed my existence after my da bit the face off that RUC man / your granda would take anybody on it didn't matter how many / no law could hold him / one of youse slaves to the scumbag queen is not leaving here unchanged he was shouting at the top of the stairs when they kicked down the door / one of you will be altered / this is the house of Lockjaw Quinn /

and he pointed at the biggest of them and locked on with his teeth / they must have broke every bone in his body but they couldn't get him off / the two of them were taken away still stuck together / and that was the first time your mother spoke to me outside in the street afterwards / a riot started / I was sitting on the window ledge and thinking/ and thinking / and she must have seen it / she squeezed in beside me and took off her real balaclava and lit up two fags in her mouth at the same time and gave me one and you know what she said / don't be a dope Ricardo / my name's Richard I said / and she said don't do what they want you to do / who I said / them and you it's the same thing she said and I suddenly understood what she meant / them and you it's the same thing / you remember that too Neil because there's always somebody more than glad to order you about

three wee mummies on the fourth floor veranda as if that wasn't enough / as if I had more to learn today / I'd say by the point I'd left the flats Mrs Craven had already taken you with her round to her daughter's who bakes the cakes in any shape you want / you got a nice bit of meringue to suck on I hear / the funny thing is I saw Oodles her husband on the way to the barber's / Mrs Craven's son-in-law I mean / and guess who had him pinned to the wall only Ladders / he's shouting over at me and waving like he's a drowning man show her your legs show her your legs / how the hell does he know about my legs I'm wondering but I do it anyway because I believed him on the spot / pulled up my trousers / and when Ladders is distracted he makes a run for it and I pile into the barber's / into the jungle / it was like a jungle must be with the moths flying about in the smoke and the steam / an infestation it's called / and their bodies cracking open under your feet among the butts / and forty different arguments going on and Ladders at the window with her sponge and bucket / you are feeling sleepy you are feeling sleepy

LEVITATION

    this is what I've been meaning to tell you though the exciting bit / quick before Mulhern arrives / down in the tunnel underneath the barber's / ones in front and ones behind you / packed tight in the dark and not moving and the air running out / I'd always heard there was a tunnel down there and then today Ladders starts banging on the window shouting raid raid and the scumbag squaddies come charging in searching for you know who who might have been in there / and the next thing I know I'm being forced down the trap door under the chair / on your hands and knees is the only way to move your face forced up against the backsides of the ones ahead / we don't seem to get very far before it all stops / we're all stuck / underground / wedged in / and then word comes down the line they found a kind of big nest / and we all knew right away that it had to be the nest of the lonely thing / remember I told you about the lonely thing and your ma got up from the table in a huff / like a badger low to the ground it is but with the coat of a poodle and the weird long tail and some kind of horn between the lizard eyes / well we found the nest so she can eat her big words / my da claimed he saw it twice and gave it a feel of his boot / so we all had to back-track anyway but there was a kind of junction and another tunnel went off in a different direction until we saw some light and up we went one after the other into the world again and would you believe it there was you in your pram and Mrs Craven and her daughter and the other woman up near Bull Park

    where's Faze where's Faze they were all asking / anyone would think it's my real name the amount of times I get asked / where's Faze / oh hello to you too / and then it's how's Margot how's Margot and the sniggers / or it's watch your purses ladies this hallion here would lift his own mother's skirt / don't mind them though Neil / they were only slagging me for crawling out of a hole in the ground / that's why I'm covered in dirt / and Mrs Craven won't believe me about giving her Turkish Delight to the three wee mummies / you saw her almost take a swing at me / nobody believes a word you say in this town that's the problem / we're lost if we don't believe each other and the Brits will be laughing all the way to the bank

   ten to eight now / that fog is doing a dance for us

   your mother said his name one night in her sleep you know / Faze / the same night he was leaving / the very same night / I had said cheerio to him you see earlier / but you see and here's the hard part I'm sorry about / I was supposed to be leaving with him too / I needed to tell you that son / that's what's been on my mind all day in the sleet / I had a suitcase with me I took off one of your aunts and I was supposed to be getting on that bus as well / your mother had thrown me out and I thought she'd never speak to me again / or you either / head to London and send money back and maybe one day one fine day who knows that's what I was thinking / then Faze stops on the Diamond and says I should stay and look after Margot and you / you have to be his da he says / I'm just looking at him / you have to be his da he says and I realise he's right / your da shouldn't run away / it was clear to me suddenly / you hear me he said and put his hand on my shoulder and then he glides away across the square like it's just another dance floor in his white boots

   you hear that

   dring dring coming near in the fog

   I don't believe in the good sound of bells forever after this

Free Verse

Monday mornings were generally quiet in the shop, a trickle of three-legged habitués mainly, fading old dandies who enjoyed the unhurried attention of the barber. So far there had been a judge, a hotel owner, a stuttering bigamist and a Korean scholar with dense white hair coarse as wool, a first for Clyde. And meantime, through the rain, a kaleidoscope of umbrellas floating by the window. Clyde happened to be making himself a quick cup of coffee, hoping for a few minutes peace, when the door opened just enough to allow a woman to slip inside who, without removing her hood, perched herself on the arm of the Chesterfield.

Georgina McGoldrick, Clyde said, carefully.

Mute, the woman took a rapid measure of her surroundings, the three big chairs, the mirrors, the chequered tiles, and then the wall behind her lined with photographs of men who had caught a dose of brotherhood under the bib in the Scullery down the years.

The rogue's gallery, Clyde said. Some of them are fake obviously. Sinatra's never been in. Or Crocodile Dundee. And Brendan Behan was—

Georgina stood up again. She kept her back to him, hands deep in her pockets. Short boots, red tights and culottes under the wet military parka. The time he had followed in her wake along the river bank, carrying her clothes like a votive, as she waded through the shallows in search of a spot to swim. Now, he thought about moving closer and a moment before he did she seemed to sense it and took a step towards the door.

Don't, he said, and she paused. I won't speak, he said. You talk if that's what you want.

Her left hand appeared to turn the sign on the door to Closed and then it was hidden away again as soon as she had resumed her position on the arm of the Chesterfield and the hood turned towards him. The spokes of an umbrella scratched along the window.

Do you want a cup of tea? he asked her.

Wasn't it typical he hadn't aged at all. The big female eyes. The same heavy ponytail. Didn't they have to get it cut short incarcerated. She pulled the book out of her pocket, smacked the pages out of her way until she found the part she wanted and began to read aloud.

Forgotten in the exercise yard, sunburned, dissolving in the vast, precious solution, our vice is loving knowing seeing nothing is more dangerous than clarity. We have defected—

She raised her hand to halt him when he moved towards her. She wasn't done yet. Another page got shown who was boss.

Bla bla… the ounce of Ben Bulben glowed in me, the extra ounce, I was reinforcement, painful bronze, heal brother.

He said her name and she said, sweeping the hood from her head, How dare you? Apart from it being sordid and embarrassing and infantile, that's a crass and a seriously twisted attempt at a justification.

Look, he told her, it helped me to write it down.

Her eyes narrowed to a squint. And what about helping me? Haven't you done enough damage to my life with your violence? And now you want applause for it as well. Would it never occur to you to try helping me instead of helping yourself?

I never thought you would see it, he said.

Well why did you dedicate it to me then? She opened the ridiculous book again. For Goldie, lost by my own hand.

His volume rose as he said, You knew I was always trying to write.

It's a psycho's act of self-justification, she said. That Ben Bulben business was about the trip to Sligo, the fist-fight in the carpark with that other sinister Englishman. One of his jealous rages she shouldn't have let pass. His face stuck to the pillow with blood. You know I had a journalist come to the door to tell me, she went on. Are you aware your husband's killer has published a book of poetry? Would you like to make any comment? It was her who gave me it. She dropped it through my letterbox. You think I would have went out and paid money for it? and she threw the book at him, saw it strike his abdomen, weak as justice.

In a blank voice, he said, There was a writing group inside and the tutor pushed me to keep going with it and it's only a small unknown publisher.

Stop blaming everybody else. Take some responsibility, she said.

He faced her now. I had eight years to ponder the claptrap of responsibility.

You might think you're free, but you're not, she said. Never.

I know that, Clyde said, and then, more quietly, I am still your prisoner.

Georgina's laughter. He used to fear it more than losing her body. Her eyes when empty of all other truth but lust. Her bit of rough. This was not how he had imagined seeing her again. The shop, Christmas-time rain, pretentious and drab. And her a brunette now too. The sable rinsed down the plug-hole.

It's the truth, he insisted and immediately, she moved straight in for the attack with, You turned me into a single mother. And a widow. Her secret lover did away with the husband. That's me now. Everywhere I go. The black widow. Do you have any idea how small this town actually is, you pathetic British prick?

He held her bubbling dark gaze for as long as she needed. Then she released him and walked blindly in a circle until the mirror seemed to trap her. The hood was flipped again.

If anyone even knew I was here, said in sad bewilderment to her reflection.

In the lull, they each changed position. Georgina put her back to the window near the radiator. A pony and tinsel-trimmed carriage waited in the traffic as Clyde, palms displayed, stepped over the book on the floor and shorted the distance between them. Georgina, arms folded, brushing her cheek on the fur of her hood.

Clyde said, He came in here and I was convinced he knew. You and me had that blazing row and then he came in here for the first time in his life and he sat in that chair there.

I had to wash his hair, he went on when she refused to look at him. I had to trim those mad eyebrows of his. The way he was talking to me, full of innuendoes, I was convinced he knew. I thought he was gloating. I got it into my head that he sounded like he had won. Then you wouldn't answer your phone so I—

I'm not a prize to be won or lost, she said.

He waited a moment before continuing. So I made a line for your place to find out once and for all. Nobody was in. So I waited. The neighbour said that in court. She said I was friendly. Then I came back into town. I had a few pints and I felt relieved, Georgina, like I had avoided the worst. It had moved on, I thought. Then there he was in a group of his work buddies.

Savagery, she said, taking a step towards him. That's how the eyewitness described you, remember. Is it my fault now, is that what you're saying?

The last thing you said to me was you wouldn't leave your husband for a third-rate comedian who writes bad poetry and works in a barber shop.

Clyde thought he saw the flinch of a smile at the corner of her mouth before she said, It was just sex.

And I still want it, he gave her right back.

Good. I hope it eats away at you like a fucking…

It does, he assured her. Do you remember walking the river and the sun—

Shut up. I don't fucking care, she said. No one else suffers like you do, isn't that what you tell yourself? The poor battered son of the drunken emigrant father, raised in a London tower block. And back the young delinquent comes to the homeland to find his roots. What I ever saw in a cliché like that I'll never know.

You wanted it as much as I did, he said and saw her bright hand in flight and felt it meet his face. And seep into the hot bog of him. And he fixed on a photograph on the wall, pointed at it, and said, Remember that night? Ginsberg September 1993. Taken in here a few hours before he went on stage at City Hall. Where we met. Where I first saw you applauding Hum Bomb. What do we do, you bomb, you bomb them, what do we do, you bomb, you bomb. You were jumping up and down when I first laid eyes on you.

So Scully gave you your job back then, she said, indifferently.

Clyde had to catch his breath before he was able to say, Who else would?

You ran in here after stealing some woman's handbag, she said, rolling her eyes. A guard was chasing you and Scully hid you out the back. Nineteen years old. Isn't that the legend?

Seventeen.

And he's had his clutches on you ever since.

He's getting old. Tanning salons. That's his biggest vice these days. Yesterday he—

My mother died on a train, Georgina said, cutting him short. She would have been mortified. So shy and meek and she goes and dies in public on the train from Longford. They treated it like a crime scene. The poor woman had to sit there for hours in the carriage by herself. And then there was the funeral. Ellie read a piece she wrote herself.

How's Ellie? Clyde asked, eagerly.

Thirteen and fatherless. It was a detective came to tell me you were getting out by the way. He's no fan of yours. Or Scully for that matter.

I was warned not to contact you, not to even see you by chance, Clyde said.

And since when have you ever listened to what people told you?

When I got to my feet and the jury gave their verdict.

I hope some huge randy ogre took a shine to you in there, Georgina said, a hint of a smile again. Her old habit of gleeful cruelty. Stroking her cheek with the fur again. Pixie nose in the rabbit belly. He picked up the book, cast it on the counter top and confessed that he had seen her about a month before.

She knew he would. She knew he would be watching. In the car behind, from across the street. She had never realised how many English accents there were about the town. He had waited for her outside work, he was saying. He had followed her into town. Clanwilliam Terrace. Grand Canal street. Right into the pub where she met a man, a black guy.

Coloured, she said.

Does he love you?

He's the first man I've ever known who seems happy

in himself, she said. He's calm and decent. And he sleeps well. And I don't need him pawing at me every hour of the day. That's what I learned in counselling anyway. Cut out the drama. Breathe. Live. I should sue you for five years of therapy by the way. I suppose you got it for free.

Where's he from?

And Ellie adores him, she went on. They go to t'ai chi together. Life is good.

Can he even speak English? You used to say it was all in the voice for you.

Stop whining, she told him. I was addicted, I admit it. It was an addiction that's all it was. And I overdosed on it. And somebody else died instead of me. I have to live with that.

Jargon, thought Clyde and he said to her, proudly, I'm no chemist, sister, but I tell you I would do it all again.

Georgina shook her head slowly and said, Some people are more afraid of regret than anything else.

You and me will never be a mistake, he said.

Do you love me, Clyde? Her face had turned pale, like he had shocked her and her red hand flew to her mouth, touched her lips.

Like a nest, he said.

And will you do anything I ask?

Again, he saw her soft-focus transit along the course of that river, starkers, knee-deep in the dazzling, jigging gore, a stolen vision in the sun. Somehow he had managed to lose her favourite knickers in the nettles. He waited a moment before he assured her.

It's Ellie, she said.

In a whisper, he asked, You want me to meet Ellie?

Last week I opened her computer and you know what she was watching? Georgina went on, the smile breaking through now. A video of one of your old comedy gigs. No, don't speak.

I want you to do something for me. This is serious. This is why I came here today.

Name it, he said. And he watched as she seemed to be releasing all the air from her body, two red hands joined under her chin.

I want you to leave, she said. Leave Dublin. Ireland if you can, and he reeled away from her across the shop and buried his head in his hands on the counter.

Do this one thing for me, Clyde heard Georgina saying, Go live somewhere else. Go back to London. You never belonged here anyway. Then, I promise, I will never forget you.

After she had gone, Clyde, down on his knees, tore the little book to pieces. That's how Scully found him when he flung open the door and exchanged the wet pavement of Capel Street for the green and black tiles of his own establishment.

Rescue

After the show, the young daredevils were drinking cans on a ramp at the back of a horsebox. Tiernan wanted to go right over and tell them that their stunts on the scramblers had really blown his mind, Portia wasn't keen, she put her arm in his and pulled back off the grass onto the matting. All four of the daredevils, in unison, whistled their appreciation of his wife, and Tiernan said to her, They know a good time when they see it. Portia led him across the road, in the opposite direction to the car, and up the steps to the old promenade. The sea was quiet in the bay. Not a single star. At the end of the promenade when he thought they would turn, she took the steps down to the shingle. To reach the soft sand was a relief. A fraction of a second off and there would have been a disaster, he said. I bet you liked their costumes. Her silence seemed to be deepening as they moved beyond the last traces of light from the promenade. She took his arm again and they walked for a distance around the bay. Then she kissed him, a real urgent one, almost hostile, pushed him down on the sand and knelt astride him, the hem of her skirt in her fist. He knew not to speak. Portia took off her coat, then her blouse, everything came off in the darkness. She seemed to orgasm almost as soon he got inside her, and carried on for more. And more, even after they heard the same wolf whistle from the dunes behind them, and the voices of the daredevils.

Two months earlier, on a Sunday afternoon at the end of June, about four o'clock, there was an incident at a barbecue in the back garden of Tiernan's older brother. Tiernan and Portia weren't planning to stay long, they would do their duty for an hour at most, and then take the dogs for a walk in the woods nearby. After a few beers and skewers of spiced meat in the sunshine, Tiernan was beginning to enjoy himself; the people were friendly, even his brother seemed glad to have him there. Portia made a big deal out of carrying bowls of water out to the dogs in the back of the car. Eventually, his brother's wife, who was obsessed with allergies, gave Portia permission to bring the dogs in. People had finished eating. There was a perfect stillness the length of the table at some point, all the conversations seemed to finish at the same time, and each person looked from face to face united in the pleasure of being there, under a cloudless sky, with their glasses full on an ordinary Sunday afternoon. A little later, Tiernan was inside with his brother, trying to persuade him to change the music when they heard screaming from the garden and then Portia appeared on the deck, dragging the eldest dog Misty by the collar. Portia's face was scarlet, the way it went when she was embarrassed or angry. She didn't look to Tiernan for help. The other two dogs came behind her, side by side. He heard the front door open, the doors of the car closing and, lastly, the car driving away.

It would be late the next evening before Portia got in touch. She wouldn't tell him where she was or even where she had spent the night, in the car he supposed, which she often did if they had a row and she took off, parked by the sea or up the mountains, the three dogs asleep on top of her. She was only ringing to find out about the child, she said, how serious it was. The dog had taken a bite out of the boy's cheek, the wound needed a tetanus shot and seven stitches and there was mention of scarring and skin grafts. Somebody claimed

LEVITATION

the boy had taken food off another kid just before the dog went for him but everybody was drunk, he reminded her. I wasn't, Portia said. Tell them I'll pay, will you? The guards were here earlier, he said. With the dog warden. They wanted to know where his wife was. Search the house, he said. You don't know where your partner is, a guard asked.

And you know what I said, I said, Guard, it turns me on not knowing where she is. You should try it.

Another time Portia might have found it funny. She told him she was heading down to her father's but he had already guessed that's what she would do, where else would you go with a mad dog than to your crazy one-handed father's house in the middle of nowhere in County Waterford. She had to be thinking of leaving Misty with her father, otherwise the animal would have to be put down as soon as his brother and his wife got wind of it. I'll be back in a couple of days, she said. It would be two months, the heart of the summer, before he saw her again.

Misty was the first dog Portia brought home. This was years before when she worked for the magazines, the glossies, a stylist on the photo shoots. They were doing a spread on lingerie in a castle near the border. Old beams and lace. Stone and pearl, garter belts on the staircase. Portia combed and set the maiden's hair. During a break, she went for a walk in the castle grounds, through long grass towards a stream where she saw a dog on the other bank, a wretched looking thing, drinking from the stream. She said the two of them stared at each other for a long time until the animal turned and fled for no reason. Portia thought no more about it until, her hamper of brushes and powders stowed away for the day, and travelling at no more than a crawl along the castle drive in order to peek at the damage to the trees from a recent storm, she heard a weak thud against the side of the car, against the passenger door to be exact. Instead of the branch she guessed she would find, there was the wretched dog, arranged perfectly on the driveway, gasping believably, staring up at his ticket out of there. She laid him out on her favourite velvet jacket on the back seat and was first in line with him at the vets the next morning. All this she told Tiernan on his release from prison. Ten months for possession and distribution was the people's will. After four and a day, he came home to her cold arms and the lurid eyes of a grey and white mongrel called Misty.

That first week Portia was in Waterford, she would call him early in the morning and before she went to bed, always from the landline because the coverage was weak for her mobile. She would talk without a pause until she decided it was time to go, giving him an account of everything that had happened either during the night, her father's insomniac wandering, or over the course of the day, right down to what they had eaten, the taste of the vegetables from the garden, the weather, and of course the behaviour of the dogs, and Misty in particular who had started running off by himself for hours on end, and remember to ask how things were with him just before she hung up. It was as if, Tiernan thought, she didn't want to give him a chance to ask her when she was coming back. It was an old trick of hers, keep talking and the thing you fear can't happen. He let her away with it, Portia had been very wound up the last few months before this business with Misty, thinking that she could do with the rest, the time away in the countryside, to readjust to leaving Misty behind her, and so the days passed.

Will you come down, she asked him during the second week and he knew from her voice that she was saying it only because she felt she should, knowing full well also he was busy with work, that he was a stage manager and had to take the work when he had it, and him, I'd love to but I'm up to my eyes, knowing he didn't want to either, the company of her father was never appealing, Francis, the one-handed depressive.

Some of their biggest rows were over the amount of time she spent down there with her father. If she had no work on, a break in her schedule, she automatically got on the road out of the city. Where her father lived, his bungalow in the fields, wasn't even where she had grown up. We never do anything together, here, in Dublin, Tiernan was sick of hearing himself complain. You used to love the city. She was her father's only child. Her mother had gone on to have another family but Portia had little to do with them. Her face would swell and redden even at the mention of them.

After the play finished he went on a night out with the writer and some of the cast. They were still in town when the clubs were closing and then they went back to the writer's house. She had a bag and weed. The next morning, a beautiful summer's morning, they were still celebrating. Tiernan fell asleep immediately when he got home. When he spoke to Portia again, she didn't ask what he had been doing, not right out anyway. First he had to listen to all that had happened on the shopping trip to Waterford city for glasses for her father, his first pair. When are you coming home, Tiernan said, cutting across the description of the father's eye test. I'm getting sick of this.

You've been using, haven't you, she said. I can hear it in your voice.

Using? Listen to yourself. Stop dramatising everything.

Stop avoiding the question.

Avoiding the question? Me? You want to talk about avoidance. My wife has run away with a savage dog and she won't tell me when she's coming home. Seventeen days and nights.

Is this your I need a shag or I'll start using drugs again routine?

Yes, it fucken well is. I miss you. It's desperate. Come home, will you? To our bed. We'll sort all this crap out.

Tell me you're not using.

I'll tell you to your face.

Come down here, she said and it sounded worse than before. In the silence he knew she could hear it too. In reply he told her about the visit to his brother, to see how the kid was doing. They have him in counselling for the trauma, he said.

She's a stuck-up snob of a bitch with a mouth like a cat's arse, Portia said, meaning his brother's wife. You know what I'd like to do to her. Sometimes it flashes before my eyes like it's happening, like I'm actually doing it to her.

Leave the dog there and come home, he said.

Daddy doesn't want him. Daddy would forget all about him.

Tough. What are you saying to me here, Portia? You have to come home, no two ways about it. You can see the dog whenever you want. Will you just do what I'm telling you for fucken once?

It was never a good strategy to order Portia around. She didn't call the next day, or the next. Tiernan would ring and her father would answer and repeat the same message that she wasn't there and hang up immediately. Tiernan could have rushed down there to have it out with her face to face but he was getting angrier by the day and refused to do what she wanted him to do, or expected him to do, it was hard to tell the difference. He took another job, a last-minute offer. The more he thought about Portia, her beehive and long skirts in the summer lanes, the more furious he felt, what a bitch she was sometimes, what a crazy bitch to exclude him like this, and he stopped trying to reach her. He went out more in the evenings, the nights long and soft in the city, there was always somewhere to go.

Not for the first time either, Tiernan's brother rang to ask him for a favour. Some colleagues from the States were in town and he wanted to show them a good time. The cost didn't matter. Tiernan tried to brush him off, claimed he didn't have the contacts any more. You owe me, the brother said dismissively like he said it everyday to somebody. Tiernan arrived into the bar of a hotel and spotted his brother with a group of men in bright silk ties and trainers gathered around a champagne bucket on the veranda. A glass was put into his hand before he could get away quickly, and his brother with an arm around Tiernan's shoulder, introduced him as Damo, my man, my fixer here in Dublin. That same night Tiernan talked a girl into coming home with him, a young one who started hallucinating before he could enjoy himself.

Portia rang in the morning, and said, I'm lying in a field. But there are no birds. There should be birds, shouldn't there?

I don't give a damn about birdsong. What the hell's going on?

Nothing. Just lying here in a field all alone.

Some muck-savage will be along soon. That's why you need those bloody dogs. The constant attention.

Someone's in a good mood.

I'm not taking any more of this.

He was sure he heard her giggle. What are you going to do?

Bite some child on the face and maybe my wife will let me fuck her.

That meant to shock me, is it?

You're thinking about leaving me aren't you, he said, and all this stuff with Misty is just an excuse. The bitch wouldn't answer him. Aren't you? he had to ask again, and again and again, until he was shouting down the phone at her, answer me you cruel-hearted bitch. He thought he could see her laid on her back in a sheltered meadow, touching herself. Right, you asked for it, he said.

The early morning train across the country, then a two-hour wait for a bus to the nearest town on the coast, a taxi journey to the turn-off for the long lane to the house. The dogs were barking as he came up the blue gravel drive, opened the kitchen door without knocking and there she was in a disposable apron and gloves, her father seated on a chair in front of her, putting dye in his hair again.

That animal is being put down if I have to do it myself, he said. And then you're coming home with me.

The argument continued for the rest of the day, inside and outside the house where there was a table and chairs in the lee of the house with a view south west of pasture fields bordered by trees. The father kept to himself as usual, out in the greenhouse or digging his vegetable lines with his own one-handed technique, only showing his face and his darkened hair once his daughter had cooked the dinner. Steak and spuds and peas was the fare, Portia serving in a crisp white apron, the beehive undisturbed by her temper. The two men ate in silence while she talked about chefs she had known on film sets, the stars who wouldn't eat this or that, organic farming, about the way people treated their pets in the city, doing her best, Tiernan thought, to imitate someone who lived there permanently, in the country, a small town lady, until he couldn't listen to another word of it. In the living room, as he lay on the sofa watching the high clouds travelling towards the coast, a wet nose touched his hand. Misty wanted some attention. The trouble you have caused, Tiernan said, holding the dog's face up to his own. The eyes were rheumy he thought and one of the animal's teeth was broken. The last silver stud was missing from the collar.

Francis took up position in his chair for the evening, wearing his new glasses. It was game-show time. From the kitchen they could hear Portia doing the washing up, then what sounded like her cleaning out the fridge and mopping the floor from the metal bucket. She called the dogs and the front door slammed behind them. It was about eight in the evening, the colours in the trees still luminous beyond the window. If she was expecting him to follow her, she had another thing coming. He had done the night walk with her and the dogs in winter and summer, year after year, every twist and turn in the lane was familiar to him, the last long stretch downhill to the trunk road and the spooky ruin of a one-pump petrol station, about a three-mile journey there and back.

Francis, I thought you were a man liked your own company, this after he had gone outside to escape the game show, and come back in with the idea that maybe he had been thinking about this all wrong, that maybe Portia wanted to leave the men together for a reason. You really want your daughter here full time, day and night, because I tell you, Francis, she'll rescue a lot more than dogs if you give her the chance, you'll have donkeys and ponies, monkeys if she can get them. I'm not getting involved, Francis said, waving the idea away with his arms, the left cuff of his suit jacket sewn closed by Portia so that his stump didn't shoot out and scare people. Don't play the gombeen dope, Francis. You want her to stay. You're looking for a nurse, aren't you? Francis said, quietly, She'll make up her own mind when's she good and ready. Not knowing what Portia had told her father, Tiernan thought it might be useful to fill him in with the true facts of what had happened at the barbecue, and afterwards, the poor little kid with the scar on his face, about his brother's wife who wouldn't let this one pass, walking up and down the living room while his father-in-law studied the everyday folk on the box. Do you have a gun, Francis, just show me where it is and leave the rest to me, he said and only then was there a response from Francis, Her mother never had any time for animals, any type of creature at all, two legs or four, no liking for them at all. Children were no different. Tiernan, looked at the old man with his black quiff and said, But you forced one on her is that what you're saying? You knocked her up like a real man. You saying something to me here, Francis, are you? About kids. Portia hates kids. She doesn't want them. They say the past's important, Francis shrugged. Tiernan went up to the man's chair and stood in front of the TV and said, Your past you mean. Not your daughter's. I'm not letting you suck her into nurse-maiding you while you mope around with your broccoli because your wife ran off with an insurance salesman fucken decades ago. Yes, come on, Tiernan said, and took a step back while the old man got out of his chair and measured up to him. The quiff and the sideburns and his daughter's big eyes in the weathered face. The stump pointed at him. It's got nothing to do with me. And even less to do with you, Francis said and began to move through the cluster of furniture for the door. Tiernan said, Why don't you just cut off the other hand and lock her up here for good.

Once upon a time there was a poor and fabulous young beauty from rural Waterford who hid her withered hand under a shawl or a cloak or whatever they wore back then. One by one the men from the neighbouring townlands came snooping and courting and one by one they had the hovel door slammed in their faces. Who the hell does your one think she is, people began to say, she should be grateful for the first decent hand offered her. She will end up an old maid, a mad one dancing in a ditch. Until one gloomy young man came to call, and came back again and again no matter how many times he was met with the door and the pitchfork or her brothers. A blood moon hung in the sky the night the gloomy young man had his idea. After guzzling a sheep's bladder of the local poitin by the side of a river, he broke into a shed, found himself a hatchet and cut off his left hand. It must have been an anxious walk across the fields to the door of the proud beauty for the umpteenth time, where it is told he announced, look, now we are equal. And thus they were wed, Tiernan was telling himself as he hurried down the lane in search of

Portia and the dogs that evening, drunk on angry oaths in the narrow corridor of fuchsia and berries, the long shadows lying in the fields, determined to win his woman back. He smoked a couple of cigarettes at the old petrol pump but there was no sign of her. A half-moon appeared on the return trip, a few stars, and the darkness seemed to be moving down the lane to meet him, brushing past him like a silent crowd. He ran for short bursts. It went through his mind he was on the wrong road. Seeing the lights of the bungalow, he felt his heart begin to beat again, and the raw, sweet human warmth spread through his body.

He lay down on the bed as he was, Portia turned away from him towards the wall with the curtained window. There was a small knot in the thin red strap across her shoulder. Where did you go? she asked him, after a long silence, a softness in her voice. I went looking for you, he said and heard the crack in his own. It's a bit strange out there. That'll be the drugs, she said, and then, as if she wanted to take it away, she said, Misty's still out. Don't say it. I wasn't going to, he said. What's going on, Portia? There was another long silence he found hard to endure. He had to ask again.

I don't know, she said. All I know is I don't want to go back. Not yet anyway.

The dog will be fine here with your father, he said, a spell that didn't work any more. Is it your father you're worried about?

Did he say that?

No. You want to move out of Dublin, is that what you're saying? What about work? The house. Us?

Then, Portia, turning to face him, Can you not just give me this? Is it too much to ask for you to do this for me?

As long as I know what the hell's going on.

I don't mind if you stay here too.

You don't mind? he had it said before he could stop. Another silence followed, the two of them watching each other closely, waiting for the right words to come.

I don't want you to leave me, he said, finally.

I'm not happy, Tiernan. I need to figure out why not. I don't know if it's me feeling lost or trapped. And I feel so angry sometimes. I don't want anybody else if that's what you want to hear.

It is, he said, and kissed her mouth. She received it without responding, eyes wide.

Can you handle me staying here for a while? Will you just try to handle it and not fight me all the way?

He nodded and slid his hand under the sheet and inside her slip. Then he pulled the strap off her shoulder with his teeth. Tiernan, she said, I'm sick of fighting. And no more drugs, please. We're over all that, aren't we?

Me too, he said and kissed her breast, just above the nipple where she liked it. She said he stank, that he needed to take a shower. He did as she ordered, passing through the dark kitchen to the bathroom along the hall on the other side. From the shower cubicle, he could see the vegetable patch in yellow electric light, a shovel stuck in the ground. He hurried back through the kitchen, naked and wet the way she liked it, and there was Francis, playing solitaire at the table. In the bedroom, he found Portia sound asleep.

It was late in the afternoon the next day before he got even five minutes alone with Portia again. There was a pair of almost identical elderly women in the kitchen in the morning, neighbourhood watch as it turned out, a visit which Francis was delighted to have interrupted by the sound of the paw at the door—Misty was back. A little later, in warm rain, father and daughter shampooed and hosed the dogs out the back and it was time for lunch again. They ate fish and a salad made with beetroot from the garden. Portia seemed to know to keep the conversation going herself; when she wasn't slagging her father about being so awkward around his lady admirers, and women in general, she was slagging Tiernan for the brand of insinuating charm he used on them, and on women in general. After that, the dishes done and the floor mopped, and the windows washed, and every room hoovered, Portia and her father were off to Kilkenny to a wake for somebody Francis claimed was already dead. You'll believe any old shite just to avoid seeing people, it's in the paper, Daddy, Portia said, and Francis, I'm telling you I was at the man's funeral a half dozen years ago, it's a different man. On their return, and having taken great pleasure in describing to Tiernan the look on his daughter's face the moment she was proven wrong about the corpse, Francis told them both to sit down at the table and produced and envelope from his pocket. Somebody at the wake had given him tickets for the circus. We're going to the circus tonight in Tramore, he said. The three of us. My treat. And it was time to eat again. Tiernan made burgers on the concrete barbecue and they ate them outside, Francis doing the talking this time, a story about Portia and boarding school which was interrupted by a sudden heavy shower passing across the house. Inside, as he lay on the bed and watched Portia stack her hair into a beehive using only a little round mirror on the window ledge, a few pins and expert blasts of hairspray, he thought he was listening to the rest of her boarding-school story until he heard his name called and opened his eyes to find himself alone in the room, the late sun in his eyes and the taste of hairspray on his mouth.

When it came time to get going, Francis had changed his mind about the family trip to the circus. He was in his bedroom with the door locked. Portia told Tiernan to wait in the car and from there, for another fifteen minutes before she appeared, he could hear her shouting through the door at her father, her face red as her lipstick as she got in behind the wheel and sent the wheels spinning in the gravel as they took off. He had done this all her life, she was saying, making plans and changing his mind at the last minute. Tiernan had heard this before. You see why I'm afraid to leave the dog here, she said, you see why I don't trust him. They talked more about Misty and this new habit of running off by himself, or what Tiernan thought was a new habit until Portia said, as if she was reminding him, that it had started before the barbecue incident, once or twice he hadn't come back for hours when she had them out in the forest, how she'd started to go to the beach because he couldn't go far. You didn't tell me that, Tiernan said and she glanced over at him to check if he was being serious and laughed. Then, as they were coming into Tramore, past the fishing boat lodged in a roundabout, she wanted to know where he had gone last night when he claimed to have rushed out to find her.

Down the lane as ever, Tiernan said. Down to the pump and back again.

No you didn't Tiernan, she said, a sadness in her voice which made him strangely afraid.

I bloody well did, he said. And there was no sign of you. On the way down the lane or coming back up to the house either.

Unconvinced, Portia continued to move her head haughtily from side to side.

Quit that, he said. You were the one who wasn't there. I would have seen you on the lane. We would have passed each other.

But the beehive was implacable, and like she was forgiving him, she said, You weren't there, baby. You weren't.

The seats they chose in the big top were on the end of a bench in the tier furthest back from the ring and the noise of excited children. When the circus is in town it means summer's over, Portia said. Tiernan pointed out the tech platform above the entrance to the ring, faces in the glow of computer screens and a large woman with a short bleached bob leaning into a microphone and a male voice with an exaggerated Italian accent was heard announcing the start of the show. The clowns swarmed the ring with their buckets and ladders. Next, the acrobats, lean expressionless girls scuttling up ropes as lightly as spiders and spinning by their ankles or their teeth and one seemingly by her hair. Portia stiffened, a pack of white Chihuahuas were next up. They danced on their hind legs through hoops of fire and made a canine pyramid on the back of a piebald pony and the animals had not quite made it out of the ring before the lights went out, the tent was dark, pitch dark, there was a long silence, the smell of damp soil made it seem like they were all underground, a kid bawled, and a blast of a death-metal guitar initiated the main event.

In wild twisting lights, the guitars at full throttle, smoke swirling, a massive black globe descended from the heights of the tent. It was made of metal mesh. A ramp was pushed out into the ring by the clowns to meet it. They heard the revving of a motorbike engine and a small scrambler appeared, ridden by what had to be a teenager in a purple and yellow jump suit. He was doing a lap of the ring on his back wheel when Tiernan felt Portia take his hand and her mouth at his ear, But I came back up the lane the same as always, and, so you couldn't have missed me. Tiernan gave her a look to say what are you talking about and pointed to the ring where the kid on the scrambler had driven up the ramp and inside the sphere. The first tricks were predictable enough, 360 spins, but then another bike entered. A third bike joined and things started to get exciting, three of them traversing the inside of the metal ball, north to south, east to west, north-west to south-east. Tiernan was drawn to his feet as they went faster and faster, he was roaring and punching the air. Then he sat down again beside Portia and said, This is unbelievable, because a fourth rider was waiting to go up the ramp.

The black orb, carrying the four riders and their bikes inside, ascended high over the ring and the audience. The music was cut. Spots lit the ball from different angles. Off the first one went, north to south, and one by one, like an instrument picking up a tune, the others went. As their speed quickened again, the globe began to open and separate into halves. The crowd fell silent. Eventually, there was a clear gap between the two hemispheres, the four bikers still doing their laps, and then the globe began to spin like a disco ball. Tiernan got back on his feet but his voice seemed to have left him. When it was all over, Portia nudged him with her elbow and handed him a tissue.

In the car going home, the sand in their clothes, they were laughing at each other squirming and scratching like dogs with a dose of fleas. Wait, I need to say something, said Portia as she switched off the engine but it was only a ruse to be first into the house and into the shower. Tiernan had a cigarette on the bonnet, under the stars, thinking that all this might work out. He went inside. Portia was sitting at the kitchen table opposite her father. Between them on the table lay Misty's collar.

She didn't know it then but already inside her that night a new world had been formed. Ivan his name is. Four dogs and a kid now, a house in Dublin, and the days just keep coming.

The Cavalcade

Tuesday afternoon became Bernard's time to call on his slaves in Blessington Row. He liked us to be waiting in silence for his big arrival. He had to teach us how to wait, so he thought, the right positions around the house, posture, costumes, all that. Caitlin already knew more about waiting than was good for her.

My body is in way too much of a hurry, she said when I found her pills in the cutlery drawer. Ever feel you have a totally different sense of time than all the other fucked-up losers?

The colours of inside a tree trunk, those fresh yellows and ambers and the winding darker strands, her hair was always long enough to cover her little hypersensitive breasts. She generally wore only a bikini top. And bandages on her hands when the eczema was bad.

Alexander was the handle he gave us to use for him if we ever got the chance of a word in. Before I heard proof on that altar in Chapelizod that he was officially a Bernard, we had also known him as Tully, Wadham, and Marvin100. Parked outside the house in his grey two-year-old Yaris, elbow out the window, he would suck his way down a frugal spliff, a man in two minds about coming in, a man steeling himself, examining his tongue in the mirror. But it was the car doors we listened for, first the driver's, then the back door after he had stowed the taxi sign, and some afternoons the boot lid, hollow as the judge's gavel.

Bernard didn't like to knock, so one of my jobs was door-opener. Caitlin in position at the bottom of the stairs in some scrap of a costume, a man's denim shirt, a pink sari, a polka-dot bikini, her beautiful hair up or down or sometimes still wet from her bath. As soon as he was over the threshold she would take his shoes and socks off and hand them to me. Then it was time to follow him into the living room where he might warm the weird bulging red balls of his feet over the flames in our small grate for a minute or a lot longer before the recap began, where we were at, what had happened the previous week, who was being good and who was slacking. Some days he had notes with him on strips of paper from the car's receipt machine—Caitlin used to keep them to stick in her book.

This kind of thing: It occurred to me during the week, kiddiewinks, and I made a note of it here, that this is a snakes and ladders sort of landscape we are ushering through. We push and push, individually and collectively, we keep rolling the dice and maybe if we're lucky something gives and we surge forward and we're skipping along across the squares and the walls are coming down but then (checking his notes)—Bollocks, I can't find it. Bollocksville. I wrote the fucker down. And what the fuck do I mean by a glass catapult? Underlined and everything. Look. Glass catapult. Bollocks. Anyway, it's not about the ladders it's about the dice. The bones. Not just the muscles, the bones. So today, and I've put some thought into this, here's what we're going to do.

That was the kind of thing. He could be very serious about it all. He got better in my opinion, more instinctual. One Tuesday she was sucking him off and he switched to me suddenly, let me have a go with my mouth for the first time, and made a competition out of it. Who's the best? Who will Mr Alexander give a treat to? Like somebody had told him it was the easiest way to get under Caitlin's skin. She pushed me out of the way, left a scratch across my face when I stuck my head in again.

For a boss he was over-critical of himself and hard to follow but, as Caitlin put it, that didn't make him hard to fathom. She's a smart one, with her very own brand of the stuff. And she was probably bored with me a lot of the time, running rings around me, exasperated by that blush on my face of excitement and pride in how much I thought I was changing.

Did you learn absolutely nothing in juvie? No wonder they threw you and your grateful face out early, she said to me once after we had been to see her father, and walked off.

It was her who clocked Bernard wasn't too fond of the stairs: Why you ask? He's a bungalow man, are you blind? He's stuck on the ground floor with his hair-brain porn and we're stuck here with him until he finds a way to get us up there in the right order—who goes first, you, me, him, who goes second round the bend in the stair? He hasn't figured it out yet. He's more of a novice than you, my very own streak of tattooed jealousy.

She was always questioning me about my tattoos and rarely happy with my answers. I'd be telling her about the trip into town on the bus and the feel of the money in my pocket, who would be on the gun for the last session, the type of thing I remember, but Caitlin would wave it away like I had wandered off the subject. Go back to when you had the inspiration, she'd say, what gave you the idea for a flying fish? Why thorns around your ankles? Was it from a dream? It used to drive her mad when I just shrugged and said I didn't remember any of that.

One day I took her to see where I had hit my teens in Inchicore, a plain five-up block near the football grounds. She had made me tell her a lot about the people and the sounds and smells and now there it was in front of her. Caitlin has a face that looks cross most of the time, scowling, like she's always scoring out some line in her book but at that moment, she was looking over at the flats like they were very disappointing and in the wrong place altogether, they couldn't possibly be the place she had forced me to describe to her, where I had loved and lost and taken what I wanted anyway.

Was I just plain stupid or was I trying to mess with her head? Why was she wasting her time with a conniving scumbag dosser? Was I after her money and couldn't even do that properly? This was said only hours later in town. I thought it might be because the old flats were boarded up now but the real reason was I had moronically failed to mention the high-priority detail, and that was the flats didn't have verandas. They're as flat-chested as I am, she said. It took many more trips to the taps for me to understand that she had written about the building in her book, the hours I had killed on the balcony, dreaming of escape from the poverty and the drugs, seeing fantastic shapes in the lights of the city I knew I had to draw on my skin.

But it was all wrong.

No lies went into her book. No junk.

Now it was stained and poisoned.

And it was the same with the sex we had together. The way I kissed her and touched her and what I whispered to her, it couldn't be made up. I had to be more honest with her than I thought was allowed. Sometimes, I didn't dare chance anything more than putting my hand on her stomach or her long thigh and leaving it there until she began to moan. Caitlin was a thin-skinned over-heating lie-detector and if she caught me being false, I was thrown back into solitary.

LEVITATION

*

It wasn't easy to leave the bed in the early mornings for work. I knew only too well the danger in needing to know someone's whereabouts at every minute of the day. In the kitchens, in a white apron, I cracked open the cream gun cartridges, inhaled the nitrous oxide and stuck my head into the back-draft of steam from the big pot washers—trying to stop myself imagining the worst. Any chance I got, it was straight out to the fire escape with the phone. Whatever we found to talk about, I was more tuned into the background noise, wanting proof Caitlin was where she said she was.

The first time I met her father, it was because I had persuaded her to let me come along, otherwise I knew I would follow her. Some days it was easy to believe she would slip away from me into thin air. I took the day off work. Her father had a turn in his left eye and sounded posher than his daughter. She pushed him against a wall in the public gallery on a tour of the Dáil. He was patronising you, she said, amazed that I had to ask why. We were outside the gates on Dawson Street. She waved down a taxi with the envelope of cash he had given her and we went to buy some good weed. I'm nearly sure it was Bernard behind the wheel that day too, but he claimed he'd never had a beard.

He was more interested in Caitlin than me then too. It was me who sat on the stairs in the early days. As part of the initial deal struck between the three of us, I was denied the right to ask questions. You go through this on your lonesome, bumfluff, Bernard said. So I went through it. The one time I put my ear to the door they were talking out in the kitchen, their voices low, chairs creaking in the long pauses, a slow spoon stroking a cup.

It's like an interview, she told me. But he thinks he has come up with these trick questions to catch me out. And he's so proud of them, I can't bear to disappoint him. But do you know he has his own meanings for some words? He thinks poignant is something seedy and illegal.

Caitlin had more experience than me, a lot more—it was an easy one to win. Me, she let into her life by reading from her book, her novel about the girl in the private mental hospital. And her memories of being dragged around the country by her parents, the furniture wrapped in blankets, the new uniforms, the beds. And the search for more and more sex. Removal men, teachers, neighbours, lots of doctors, strangers, underage boys and two old poets at a wake, but never any mention of what you would call a boyfriend. That's where I came in I suppose. A boyfriend experiment. One pair of hands with pictures on the back. One forked tongue.

She's a posh poignant bitch, this one, Bernard said the first Tuesday afternoon I was invited into the living room. Caitlin over his knee, he was spanking her, making her confess what a spoilt slut she was, and Caitlin played along. She had Bernard and me hanging on her every word. I was made to stand by the window to keep an eye on the car because there were a few dodgy wetbacks on the street. Before that month was out, October, I had permission to watch her sucking him off or whatever was on the menu. So I went through that too, the new feelings you get, the suffocation, the smallness and the huge unbelievable surges.

I produce a lot of unnecessary skin, Caitlin explained about her eczema.

It's all in your head, Bernard said. Have you always had it?

Not consistently.

You get time off?

Sometimes it vanishes completely.

But not consistently?

So far never.

Whores ask too much of the world.

By the time he bought Caitlin the wet-look gold bikini and the coral necklace, Bernard was turning his attention to me more. His ideas were changing, finally, Caitlin said, and it was her turn to watch now, giggle, sneer, egg him on, the foul-mouthed lazy beach girl on the sofa smeared with hydrocortisone, masturbating, her eyes sinking deeper under her frown. Me on my hands and knees over a dog bowl of tap water—a punter left it in the taxi he claimed, a sign, he said, never ignore the ordinary—then me spreading my own asshole for them while they discussed which dildo to use.

I began to like her bandages scratching the skin off my back in the morning. Or pressing down on my chest like two big paws. I was on my last warning at work.

Caitlin was licking his balls the first time he found the nerve to go into me. After it, we lit the fire and got stoned together—another first because Bernard insisted we should be clean for him. Maybe some night I'll come round and stay over, he said.

Wow. Upstairs? Caitlin laughed.

What's the opposite of vertigo?

She thought for a moment and said, Gravity. Fear of gravity.

But he shook his head sadly. Vertigo is about the past. You two are too young to even know what the past is yet. Live in the moment for as long as you can, that's my advice, kids. Forget about the past. Do you think I should shave my balls?

You have the eyes of a child with three mothers, Caitlin said.

Those very same eyes in the driver's mirror the first time we got into his cab. We had been unlucky with the drivers the first few times we tried it. They generally tried to interfere and warn Caitlin of the risk she was taking. One country man stopped the car and told us to get out. It was always after she met her father, her allowance in her bag. She would stop a cab and get in and act the chatty, spoilt new pair of heels in town. I would be waiting further up the street, looking for a cab also.

Caitlin tells the driver to stop, leans out the window and says something like, Want to share a cab? I'm going northside, really I am. Do you know Blessington Basin?

I sham surprise for the driver's benefit. Sure why not, I say, and dip in beside her.

Hi there, I'm Pam. One hand out to mine and the other pressed to her chest, high on her own boldness.

There's no need to tell me your name, she says to stop me. It's simpler that way don't you think? I saw you there and thought you were cute and a little different somehow. Are you different?

I shrug, playing it cool.

Well I think I am, she says. Or I want to be. I really want to be. Which is why I came to the city. Actually, I haven't made many friends yet. I have to put myself out there more. So this morning I decided, today's the day, Pam. If you really want to be different then you have to take a chance.

It takes time to meet people, I say.

She laughs at herself and says, But I'm so impatient, you've no idea. It's unbearable. And biting her lip, she puts her hand on her long, bare thigh. What would you say if I invited you in?

And I give the driver my best lucky day grin and slide my hand under her little yellow frilly skirt.

I remember she was wearing the same skirt the day we took the helicopter ride over Dublin with her father. Tail up, surrounded by blue, we followed the motorway in towards the city, tracked the river and then veered off into the sun over Phoenix Park. Our shadow came and went over

Blanchardstown. We found the river again at Leixlip reservoir and made a stab for a rainbow over Rathcoole, Caitlin flirting with the pilot on the headset until the mountains silenced her. We saw deer and kestrels and the shaven side of a valley where a forest had been logged and carted away. Then the coastline, the blunt broken edge, slowly crumbling into the sea. Victorian Greystones to the docklands' mirrored glass towers. I'd never been up in the air before—there was so much ahead of me if I could get myself right for it to happen. Lines of rooftops like razor shells. Mossy patches of park. Mineral roads. Little caves. Crevices. Hollow carcasses. Miles of seaweed wires. Everyone gliding about like water-skating insects. Dublin was an ancient rock pool and the next tide was always the first.

At the lunch afterwards in the airport VIP lounge, Caitlin's father realised he had left his sunglasses on the helicopter. His bad eye made him hard to read. He worked in mind-control, according to Caitlin, owned part of an advertising company. He was just back from New Zealand where he'd met an old Maori woman who told him a story but only after he had promised that he would pick one person in his life to tell it to, and no more, a random stranger or a loved one, it didn't matter, and that he would make them promise the same thing. Tell that man over there, Caitlin said, pointing to a black guy with a mop and a bucket on wheels. Her father refused and she called him a snob and the fight developed from there, and security was called. Still, she got the money from him and we went out that night and right through the next one, blew every red cent of it.

One Thursday afternoon, nearly dark, Bernard turned up at the door on Blessington Row without any arrangement. There had been bits of snow that day but he was only wearing a

T-shirt. He said he had parked the car on the next street and there was somebody else in it who wanted to meet us. He made it sound like a threat. He was angry. New dice, I was thinking. Then he forgot about it, started barking orders, eyeballing the walls, stamping on the floor. Before the shoes were off, he had his cock out. He wanted it done in a hurry, No talking, you pair of dossers. Bernard was a big fucker in more ways than one. I was even wondering what we had in the house if he got out of order.

Caitlin wasn't fazed at all by the aggression. The threat in his eyes didn't worry her. In fact, she gave him more attention than usual. She actually managed to let herself go. It disappointed me to feel the jealousy as bad as ever seeing her engrossed like that, sitting astride him on the sofa, Bernard glaring over her slim shoulder at me. I waited my turn, impatient for what he would do to me after.

Caitlin had always said Bernard would run out of ideas for us one day. She saw through him. I don't remember him asking for what happened that afternoon. It wasn't an instruction. I can see Caitlin cross-legged on the floor and she's rubbing Bernard's lower back. He's lying belly down, his head in my lap. Caitlin and I have been staring at each other for a long time but it's as if our faces are masks, smooth, expressionless. It seems to be the end of the road.

Then I realise Caitlin has a finger or two in his ass.

It had always been out of bounds. It didn't even exist.

Bernard gasps, gripping my knee.

Then Caitlin has switched position, his head is at her chest now and I'm kneeling up behind him, holding his strong stiff hips, going in carefully, a touch and a touch more, patient, staggered, fierce.

It seemed to take hours.

Bernard roared and sobbed. An hour later he was lying in

the same spot, a broken man in a pool of tears. Caitlin and me stayed out of the way in the kitchen. Something important had happened—it was a first time for me too—but Caitlin played it down so much so I wondered if it had been what she really wanted all along. To see me take another man. I had so many questions: Did she think Bernard had been secretly after this all along, the boss dragged out of his office and raped? Or was it me, waiting and plotting my revenge on him? Caitlin acted as if she was more interested in whether we were going out later.

I went in to talk to Bernard. He wouldn't get up off the floor. He was still crying, choking on his snot. It was getting worse.

We didn't go out that night. Caitlin threatened to go by herself but she stayed upstairs in the end. Bernard grew quieter but he didn't know where he was or who I might be some of the time. He was scared, cornered. I managed to move him on to the sofa and threw a blanket over him, forced some of Caitlin's sleeping pills into him. Then I went to bed. Caitlin was pretending to be asleep, her breathing was too shallow and fast.

I'm sorry, I said, in case I was supposed to.

I had one of my bad dreams, woke up and her side of the bed was empty apart from a ribbon of bandage. The window was open as if she had flown away. On the way down the stairs—and I took my time—some part of me didn't expect to find either of them. They would be laughing in the back of his taxi somewhere. I would be the loser in a game I had never understood. Opening the door, stepping into the square of the living room, what I did find was Caitlin leaning over Bernard with a pair of scissors.

Get him out. Get this whinger out of my house or I won't be responsible for what I do. Then she did this thing with the scissors, cutting around her own outline, like she was a picture in a book.

By the morning, the situation hadn't changed much. Every light on in the house and the windows bravely holding back the rain. Neither of them was speaking to me. I felt they were waiting on me now to make a decision. Caitlin floated in the bath. Bernard's tongue hung out of his mouth. I could see he was in a bad way but was I supposed to drag him out the door by the ankles and leave him on the street? Or call a doctor? I didn't want to land him in trouble. After everything we had done, him and Caitlin, me and him, him and me, the three of us, I knew nothing about his life outside of our place, other than his taxi-driving stories, that he wasn't from Dublin and his opinions on the merits of Chinese versus Eastern European escorts.

Caitlin spent the day on our bed, in her boots and coat, writing in her book and running baths.

I rang work and that was it, the heave-ho.

Then it was dark again. Rain came down the chimney. The main thought was I would have to stay awake all night to keep them apart. The other thoughts were about what they wanted me to do. They were waiting on me. Expecting me to come up with something big and they would obey. It was my turn to roll the dice.

Caitlin was disgusted by the delay.

She said, It's always fear with you, isn't it? You can't tell the difference between fear and desire like every other excuse for a man.

I went through it, kept the watch. On them. On me. On the house. So it hit me as being completely impossible when I went up to the bedroom to tell her Bernard was a bit better and saw she was gone. She couldn't have got out of the house without me hearing her. I searched the house, under the beds, even opening drawers and cupboards, the back yard. After that I rang her phone in every room like I would catch her. Maybe because there was someone in the house behaving crazier than he was now, Bernard somehow managed to pull himself together again, made us a pot of tea and sat me down.

The man talked and talked for the rest of the day. I got his full life story. He steered away from what had happened in the front room and instead, the big issue was his fiancée. Yes, Bernard was meant to be getting married, only for the past few months, apart from what he was doing in Blessington Row with us, he was paying for sex with three or four women a day. He couldn't stop. The man had spent a fortune, run up some major debt. He was sinking and kept on shagging, eight women in one day he claimed. Eight hundred euro including petrol. And when the bills went unpaid, and the fiancée finally confronted him, he let her have it, the truth. And that's what brought him to our door. And his wife-to-be had a couple of brothers who were not amused.

At least now it's out in the open, he said, waiting for me to agree.

I had to find Caitlin. She would give herself away to anybody the first chance she got. I saw her flushed frowning face under a pile of men's bodies. The jealousy was worse than ever. Bernard wanted to lend a hand but I was glad to be rid of him when the taxi arrived to pick him up.

Don't be too hard on her, he said. Look how much that girl has done for you. She's a sweetheart.

I hit the streets, the city centre. When you are searching for somebody in the crowds, or running in and out of places, appearing in all that CCTV footage, you realise everybody you see is hiding, disguised, timid, they look at you as if it's them you're after, for a split second it's written on their faces,

Me? Oh no, is it me you want, are you the one I dread? And when they read in your face that they are not the one, not today anyway, the relief melts into a sneer and you become one of the lunatics they laugh at and ignore. I was ready to hit one of them when I remembered Caitlin's book. Had she brought it with her? She wouldn't go far without it, no way. So I crossed the river again for about the tenth time that night and headed back.

She was home with another guy, some student with a fringe. One smile from me and he legged it down the street. That was the night I told her, revenge is the only word for it, to show her how much she didn't know about me no matter how many questions she asked or how many pages she wrote in her mad greedy book, that it wasn't drugs I had done time for. I had beaten up some asshole from Inchicore who I thought had slept with my girlfriend. Then I went and found her and kept her hostage for four days.

I threw it into the river anyway, Caitlin said. My book.

The endings never stop and the beginnings are scarce. The endings are obvious and exhausting between two people but the beginnings flicker and die easily. Over the next few weeks we rarely left the house. We spoke in low voices and lost confidence in how to touch each other. She was talking about going back to college. I went out hunting for another job and read some of the books she was always lecturing me about. One day, I was in a barber's on Capel Street, under a black bib, and the face in the mirror was nobody I wanted to know—and the idea came to me.

Why London? Caitlin scoffed but anywhere else I suggested the next day or the next didn't catch her fancy either. London was cheap to get to and had the same language, that's all. Somewhere nobody knew me or gave a damn. Somewhere my body would feel different and my voice sound unfamiliar to me. There it was, the new start, the key, the magic leap, but she couldn't see it. In fact it had the opposite effect. She was eaten up by suspicion. I wanted rid of her was the accusation, I wanted to go by myself really and was just too much of a sap to pack a bag and clear off. She banged about the house acting as hurt as if I had already left. I may as well have been a shirt in the wardrobe, a ring on the sink, a painful reminder. She was going to see her father one day—ice-skating this time— and I opted out at the last minute mainly because I didn't want to keep falling on my arse in front of him. I listened to the commotions of the bracelets on her wrists while she fixed her hair in the hall mirror. She was taking a long time about it. Then a long stunning silence before she appeared in the living room and threw my new passport at me, cut along the spine, one piece at a time.

Within the hour she was back with her father and a bottle of wine. She made a sign to me she was desperate for a smoke and disappeared upstairs, leaving me alone with him. It was a set-up and we both knew it. If he was under orders from Caitlin to say something in particular to me while she was getting stoned above us, he didn't manage it. Or maybe he was just playing along with his daughter's whims without really knowing what she expected of him, hoping he wouldn't say the wrong thing if I asked his opinion or advice. Whatever he was really thinking, Mr Bennet picked up a John Lennon CD and told me a pretty decent yarn about how he was only two blocks away from the man's building in New York on the night Lennon was shot.

He's full of shit, Caitlin said later on but she had her head over the toilet, vomiting, until there was nothing left in her. She had a bad spell after her smoke, a full-blown whitener. What was funny though was that Bernard turned up the next evening, in an '07 Yaris in the same grey and invited us to his wedding. Yes, he had been forgiven. He was back in the saddle, the hair cut short, pumped up from the gym, refreshed, calm. Caitlin kept her nose in a book, ignoring him and shrugging like she didn't care when he asked me down the road for a pint. I told him about the London idea and his advice was get over there, get set up, and send her the address. She doesn't know how to believe in it yet. Tomorrow never comes for some people, he said.

What was funny was that his fiancée wanted a Lennon song, 'Imagine', on the speakers as she walked up the aisle.

The day of the actual wedding, the eczema was rife again and so bad on her ears and around her eyes Caitlin wouldn't get out bed. I had a few goes at changing her mind until I began to think she was enjoying the anger rising in me, the way she lay there staring at the ceiling. She wanted me to lose the rag, wanted to see it. You're doing it on fucken purpose—she was dying to hear me say those words and feel them wash over her sores. So the voice in my head was trying to convince me. I ironed my shirt and polished my shoes. I wrapped my hands in cellotape to lift the fluff off my jacket. I brought her up a cup of tea to tell her I was going.

You'd look good in London like that I bet, she said, and sat up in the bed, brighter, trying to be enthusiastic. The lust in her eyes was real. Whatever it was, had lifted from her. And the mention of London I took as a sign she was at least thinking about it now as an option, being away together, and I couldn't ask for more. If I played it right, didn't push her, didn't crowd her, let her find her own way to a decision, then there was a good chance it would happen. She cried for a bit, which was rare for Caitlin, a big cry which soaked through my shirt, but there was a good feeling afterwards, another shift, a new space.

There's one thing missing, she said. She gave me a major blow job and sent me out of the door with a fancy smile on my face.

Even so, I stopped at the end of the street, and thought about going back. It was cold and dusty in the wind, sunlight bouncing off the windows and cars. And I was keeping an eye for a gap in the traffic to cross the road, buy some fags in the shop and wave down a taxi. Just as I was about to make a run for it, a guard on a motorbike flew by, pointing at me with his black glove, ordering me back on the pavement. Then another one, identical, and four more after that, a formation. Then a black Volvo S80 and right behind, a government Merc, spotless, sleek, silent, but they had forgotten to roll up the window and the back seat was empty.

I was late, missed the bride's arrival and Lennon singing her up to the altar. The Chapelizod pews were stuffed with colourful hats and shaved scalps. Bernard—so the priest called him—had a lot more friends than I would have given him credit for. His wife had short hair the colour of cranberry and wore an ivory silk dress and had a laugh which came down the nave further than the choir. I was near the glass doors at the back, underneath the organ balcony, sending texts to Caitlin each step of the ceremony.

I got to shake Bernard's hand after it, the confetti blowing over the wall into the river. Him and the best man sported pink ties and cufflinks.

Go easy on her, slick, he said, his big arm around my shoulder, the hand patting my chest. God knows why, but she would go to the ends of the earth for you, that one.

I decided to skip the afters and do the long walk back to her in Blessington Row. I was feeling down. Sick. A fraud. I needed to tell her I was sorry if I had been punishing her, but I was afraid how I would feel if she believed me. And then if that became the truth what I would have to do to make myself believe it too and not forget, ever. I didn't believe in anything—that was the only fucken truth. I was sham underneath. I wanted to be empty like the back seat of that limo. And that she was right about London too—it was a stupid idea.

I heard her voice as I opened the front door, recognised the tone of it and thought she was reading out loud to herself.

I wanted to tell her about the cops guiding the empty Merc around the city—she would like that, I thought. She was at the table, reading from the book she said she had thrown away. Her father sitting at the far end by the back door

Caitlin, I said.

The kitchen knife was rammed deep in her father's eye. His good eye.

She licked her time-dark fingers and turned a page, getting it all out.

Downstream

Dropped out of the sky into Dublin for the day. Press some flesh in Georgian rooms because I'm here on business don't you know. Admire a skirted rump or two just long enough for them to see. This is Capel Street now, the sun on my face. And that strange coolness at the back of my neck because I've just had the rug trimmed. Halt at a junction waiting for their new tram to pass. She's a pretty machine. With bells on. Infinite are the ways it could have happened but who comes borne by behind glass, a private smile, seated like royalty, only the Redzer. We lock eyes. There's the gurrier's wink from her and this numbskull in a new suit forgets years of everything.

Now I'm not spoofing or making noises about being a stud but I could rise to any occasion for that chick. Indoors or out, down in the dumps or in bits after midnight. Sure remember the time in Huddleston Road and the gas leak, the entire street was supposed to be evacuated and where were we?

    She had our Hughie on tap. Those little fingertips at my throat. The lightness of her nudity on my back. I need cock mister every kiss said. The tits, the beefy freckled balubas she loved to lick herself. Right from the first time ever on a mattress on the floor of the Stamford Hill squat to the final sayonara in a power shower in Ally Pally, me pretending

I couldn't hear her crying, I never let the girl down. That's a distance of twenty odd years we're talking. Though the Redzer was never one for looking back.

Do you mind the time we hit Cornwall for the weekend? I'd say or something. You got all hot and bothered by the young dudes in the wetsuits. Remember? Phase two, this was, about two weeks in. We were living in—

Hughie, can we not just watch this film without you competing with it? And haven't I told you this phases talk of yours ruins my mood. This phase. That phase. It depresses me. Life put in boxes like that. Stacked and labelled in one of your smelly boss's misery-brown removal vans.

Remember the peacock feathers back at the hotel? You nicked them out of a fat bronze vase and did the seven veils. You were up on the window sill in your yellow knickers. Remember the day we bought those knickers together in that creepy wee shop near Paddington?

Neither of us knew it then but there would only be three phases. The first was six and a half weeks long, then we did a line for five months, and lastly, the big one coming in at just under two years. Three stints together ended by three ladylike disappearing acts. That girl could do one out of your life quicker than it takes to boil the kettle.

Where you going?

I told you.

Tell me again.

Stop sniffing my bra, Hugh. Give it to me now.

You have magic powers so you do. I wasn't in the mood there, right, and then I realised you were standing behind me, close up behind me, dead still, silent and I pretended I didn't know you were there, and I could hear you concentrating and your breathing getting deeper, and I started to feel it going into my back from you, waves of it and—

Baloney. Why do we always have to talk about it afterwards? Now give me my bra this minute or you'll never see these again, she said, with a priceless shoulder shake.

Or take that vintage scene of rattling through the tunnels under north London. There'd been a few days of full-on battles about the move back to Ireland. Throats raw, we went down into the tube at Angel, the deepest one. Normally, you don't catch me underground but this Sunday morning I followed her down, probably because I thought she was punishing me. And I was getting a taste for it. The escalator was out of order. So was the next one. We seemed to have the tiled rabbit holes to ourselves. Deeper and deeper ahead of me she sank. Left me alone with the fear. The characters in those posters for musicals and plays and the Tower and Kew all stopped having fun and stared out at me, licking their lips. On the third escalator a thick banshee fog of ventilated air set the stage for my comeuppance. Then down the last few steps on my arse, holding my nose. The way the train just about made the fit between the platform and the concave cliff, squeezing in slower, slower, then stuck.

There was Viv, her hair down now, stepping bravely on board. She took a seat by the door, her back to me. The carriage was empty. Of course it was. Because it was doomed. People knew not to get on. Good people had an instinct. And had I really seen a driver? There was no driver. It was Tony Blair's fault. The blood on his hands. Innocence can get you killed anytime. Yes, they were trying out a new type of time-bomb called Innocence. We had stumbled into some kind of classified trial run. We shouldn't be there. The cliff-sized ads rippled as the train doors hissed and banged against Viv who had put her body in the way. The look she gave me meant act normal Hughie or they'll eradicate us and she hoisted her blouse and bra and stepped back into the carriage.

Those anti-authoritarian tits did what the meds or the counsellor couldn't fix. She sat me down, knelt between my legs. Ripped off the belt like a shackle. The zip like a gag. Lights blinking. Grey roots in the red furze. That nose of hers had definitely been straightened. No don't look at me mister. She had you emptied by Moorgate.

The Wee Red liked a drink and a joke and a vigorous tête-a-dick when piqued but she never enjoyed hearing me tell the story of how we met. And met again eleven years later. And met again two years hence. Everybody else saw the funny side of it. And the scary side of how your life can take a surprise turn while you're crab-walking towards a Camden kebab shop or wolf-whistling a bird in south London. Infinite are the ways we might not be ourselves. One small decision, a detour or an extra few minutes in the sack and you might be somebody else. And somebody else might be you instead. The Redzer didn't dig the message. As a matter of fact, I was giving one of my better renditions of it, our story, the last time I saw her miffed freckly bake, when she walked out of a tapas bar on Green Lanes where our mates had gathered to wish us the best of luck on our move back to Ireland. They were mainly my crowd as it turned out, all except one, Sally, a Bollywoodish lab-technician who Viv had been messing about with, not quite behind my back. Only Sally and me, mid-flow, noticed her leave. That was our Viv for you, always slipping away before the punch line.

I said to her, Sally, I feel your pain, girl. She's walked out on me not once but twice and there wasn't a whore small or cruel enough in London to take my mind off her. Back in the 80s, right, during our first phase, you know what she said to me, and right, she was holding her asshole open with both hands at the time, no fancy nail polish then either, no, seventeen she was, a runaway, and she says, Do me Hughie like I'm

Thatcher. Maggie Thatcher. I'd never heard the like, Sally.

Sally, down unlocking her bike, said, Somewhere in your moronic heart I think you know Genevieve doesn't want you to go with her. You try so hard to embarrass her because you know this. She wants to be free.

You're being a sore loser, Sally girl. She was scot-free twice and she still came back. And why's that do you think? Because of my skill in the kitchen?

Don't you get it? She thinks she has damaged you.

You know your problem, Sally. You take her too seriously. This is where you went wrong. Irish women like to say whatever the fuck they want and then expect you to forget it ever happened. You're way too heavy. You're too—remember that night the three of us did our bit for love together? Me at the top and you at the bottom? Who was the one who got all upset and weepy afterwards? Who was the one who comforted you? Me. Not Viv. You need to lighten up.

Pussy to the saddle, she said, I would hurry home if I was you.

Viv and me had been in another fight before coming out. I'd pushed her. She was right in my face. I pushed her away and she hit her head off the door frame. It was the excuse she needed. How dare you hit me? I didn't hit you. How dare you hit me? I walked the plank of shuttered Green Lanes. The key turned without the usual resistance. In the hall, a recent blast of Givenchy corrupting the damp air. Light on in the bathroom and the living room. Her green coat should be over the back of the chair, her bag on the table. Kitchen dark. She should be in bed, a little drumlin under the duvet. You don't even have to check for the suitcase she keeps in the spare room. No note either of course. Never any attempt to explain. There never was. The Redzer had some strange notions about what should be obvious. You found the ring under your pillow.

Stop lying, Hughie. You don't want to go.

I do want to. I'm ready for a change.

I know you don't want to go. I know okay. It's obvious. So can you just stop lying about it? Just tell me.

All because I've had a few?

You're coked up. And you're never here anymore. You're out boozing all the time. Just face it will you. You haven't even found the balls to tell Tobias yet, have you?

It's called having mates. I'm saying goodbye to my mates. Just say you've changed your mind. I can take it.

Maybe you're the one who's changed their mind. Maybe you want to do another runner. How many fresh fucking starts does one woman need?

We all think about it at some stage, moving back home for good. The jolt of the touch-down on the Dublin tarmac that will finally realign the bones and exorcise those phantom pains. For some it's the death of kin with a plot of land or your own kid giving you lip in a squaddie's tongue, and some run out of excuses one fine day and pack their bags in a hurry. A voice inside which you normally treat as a crank suddenly makes sense while you're doing the shopping. Or after one last attempt to wreak havoc in your life, the voice falls silent. If you can survive that, London, or wherever it is, becomes your home and castle. I'd say it should be a recognised condition. And the nearest I came to it was with Genevieve Querney from the cramped streets of Fairview by the Liffey swells.

So why didn't I kill her that night on the bus back from Brixton? Why didn't I smash every tooth in her two-timing head and plop her juvenile's butt in the Thames. For weeks, months, she'd been filling my shell-like with her arguments for calling it a day in London. What a heartless city it was, so indifferent and rude, so many hours wasted on transport, where the pound is king and the pollution hides the taste of violence, the racism and the rent, the multicultural myth and meanwhile she's munching on Home Counties' best Bollywood promise. On the way back from that flop of a Morrissey gig was the moment she chose to fess up. All her guff about Ireland maybe, or the rain sealing us in on the top deck by the front window, had me telling her about the day I left Dublin on the ferry, and how I fell in with this German couple. Rainbow warriors roasted by decades of bonfires who took a shine to young Hughie on his big break for freedom. Who incited him with drink and kindness and bloody tales of the battle of the Beanfield in 1984 when the pigs had given the New Agers a lesson in authority at the solstice gathering in Stonehenge. Who took him below to the hold and laid him out in the back of the camper van and said they would cleanse him for his journey and they put their hands on him and pinned him down with whispers and Poor Hughie began to freak. He pulled his new flick-knife and pierced the husband's thigh. He got out the driver's door, ran for the stairwell and spent the rest of the trip like a stowaway on the misty deck.

I'm sleeping with somebody else, said the Redzer.

You bet you are, I agreed. I'm a different person now. And it's all your doing actually. Mind that shy wee bloke you made take off his clothes? You had to do everything. I couldn't even get my desert boots off. You know I never knew it existed, not for real, not for the likes of me. Beauty, I mean.

I'm having sex with another woman, Hugh.

That one Genevieve's tastes were always changing. Any hint of a routine in the bedroom and you'd notice she was talking more about other countries again, about the places she had never seen. Phase three, Ally Pally, she had less of the multiple Os but they were deeper, and more serious, and paralysing, and lasted for minutes on end. I used to have to check she wasn't deceased. A far cry from the days of phase one when she couldn't keep her hand out of her Yellow-Pack knickers. Or the woman of phase two who had discovered silk and white gloves and liked to stand on my head.

Tell me you never stopped looking for me.

Never. Every day.

And you couldn't get it up for anyone or I'll crack your skull.

Nobody gives me the horn like you. My meat was broke. Girls and boys too—I tried everything.

Baloney.

I knew I'd track down your gee again. Didn't I find you?

The boys and me in the van, coming down by Ruskin Park in Camberwell, winter, 2003, after a job. The traffic slow because of road works so we cut over to Denmark Hill. Tall houses behind wet bare trees on a steep slope. Spotting a bit of skirt skidding on the mowldy leaves, I stick my head out the window and shout, Get your tits out Ginger, show my gob for the reaction, and catch a face smile and wink back at me. We drive on for a few minutes before it sinks in and I tell them to pull over.

Put me down you big yob, she says in a shower of greasy drops from the high boughs.

We repaired to the nearest pub, right by the overground station there. Hair shortened to bob length again, a black cashmere turtle neck, no make-up. Two years since she absconded from Tufnell Park. She had got herself a new passport and cleared off to Estonia to teach English again. And now she was back living south of the river for the first time. I couldn't help wondering who it was she might have left killing a vodka in Tallinn after he'd gone for a dump and came back to find her gone.

What do we do? she asked after a long silence. She seemed shaken, awestruck by us meeting again.

LEVITATION

Did I really believe it when I said, We're not trapped in a lift or something, Genevieve. We don't have to do anything. We can walk away if we want. Was it not already decided, eye meeting eye on Denmark Hill? Wasn't I already imagining one of her specialities, the pitter-patter of her tiny fingers up and down my shaft, the muscly international tongue?

She took my hand across the table, and said, Hugh, I'm sorry, and I'm just not at all.

A few massive days later, Tobias invited me for a frame or two in the club in Soho. When he wanted a serious word, it happened over a game, an elder spider crawling over the walnut edges of the table on a nest raid, jabbing, retreating, the white horseshoe moustache twitching under the upholstered Stanfast shade. He plays like he's against the clock, fast, instinctual. Safety is not in his style. I've seen him do the one-four-seven in eight minutes ten seconds with his extra-heavy black and gold ash cue. If the old man had got wind already that the Redzer and me were rubbing shoulders again, he might find another use for it.

By the time the reds were down, he was still talking business. Around then Tobias was pondering the expansion into the specialist art stuff, transporting gear between galleries, museum pieces, exhibitions. I fluffed an easy take of the yellow.

You're not even here, he said. No concentration. No focus.

Late night, boss.

The reason you got out of the van, what, this claustrophobia of yours again?

He was on to us. I looked around and saw that the other eight green slabs were empty. I could have sworn there were games underway when we arrived. You don't lie to Tobias. I've seen where that can lead a man. Anyway, I owed him. He'd put me back together so many times the man could write the instructions.

It's a small world, I said.

Don't try to be smart son. That Irish dick of yours is happy only when it's dipped in trouble, he said, straightening his monographed cuffs. Dip it somewhere else. The Chinese. The blacks. Try the Brazilians. Those women could teach her a thing or two about her issues with authority.

She's all of those in one.

He uttered some Yiddish oath and said, Correct me if I'm wrong here, son, but didn't I hear lately that you had been discovering, what shall we call it, a new predilection for the more epicene arts of Greek Street?

Dumbly, I watched him smoothing the moustache, a sign he was aggravated.

Third time lucky maybe, I said.

Time you say? Time is our element. Each of us moving through time. At high speed. What have I taught you?

Rivers to the sea. I know. Rivers to the sea.

Well, stop behaving like an effing salmon then.

Not so long after that, Viv came home and said she had bumped into Tobias on the street near her work. Typically, she refused to believe there could be any other explanation for him being in the area than stalking her. No, he hadn't said anything directly but he had insinuated plenty, she claimed. All his melancholy pleasantries added up to a threat. He's only your boss, Hughie. He employs you to organise moving boxes around in an ugly van. I let the jibe pass. I even promised to think about finding a different job. I wanted to keep the peace because this was the day before the anti-war protest in 2003. Viv was going on it while I had made sure to be as far away as I could, out at Heathrow dealing with some missing cargo. We seemed to have agreed to avoid any mention of it this time around but the flat was tense. No calls or texts from her during the march either. The news on the airport screens showed it was colossal. In the evening, on the way to join

Tobias and some of the lads at our usual spot, a Chinese on Brewer Street, there were towers of placards in Soho Square and skeleton costumes were doing victory dances from the lamp posts over the hyped-up crowds.

The biggest in history, Viv said with a drum-roll on the table when she appeared in the restaurant. Tobias plucked his moustache, probably thinking I had tricked him. The others had gone on, thankfully. Viv treated the two of us to a noisy kiss on the mouth and then she slid in beside Tobias. After a while, he ordered her the Peking duck because she was too busy with the day's highlights to read the menu. Then she scoffed the whole lot of it without noticing, the steam from the pancakes melting the face paint. Hoarse, euphoric Genevieve didn't give a monkey's. She didn't miss a beat either when Tobias, after dipping the corner of his napkin in a water jug, began to gently wipe the smears of paint and hoisin sauce from the corner of her mouth.

From all reports the turn out in Dublin and Paris and Berlin and everywhere else had been huge also. Every generation discovers the secret anew, Viv needed us to understand, the secret the establishment works to blind us to with hourly blizzards of fear and hatred and envy and self-disgust and the massive trap of the unending present. And that secret is our power together in numbers, she said, looking hard at each of us in turn, her voice so tired now she was almost gasping. Yes, the grinning tyrant Blair was finished. The pseudo-battle between left and right was over. This is the new dawn, you two dopes, don't you see?

Infinite are the ways this could run, I was thinking, ready to jump in if there was a barney. To give him his due though, Tobias, who's the kind of Tory who believes people would eat their own children if you let them, encouraged her to keep talking, tempted perhaps to bask in the rays of hope from her.

I suppose he'd never seen this side of The Redzer. Or she his solemn way of listening and questioning that gradually made you realise there was even more to what you were trying to say than you thought. That man could scare the bloody life out of you with your own opinions on the cost of petrol or a condom or a chocolate éclair.

A few hours in and the two of them had more or less forgotten my presence across the manky purple table cloth. That was a sweet feeling. A wee quiet harbour in the corner of a Soho restaurant. Soppy as it sounds, I was able to kick back with my Courvoisier and behold the two people who meant the most to me in the world bobbing together briefly on the current that pushes all things towards the sea of tranquillity.

Is he Brahms and Liszt, sweetheart?

Crocodiles, Tobias, that man there is the type who cries his way into your life. And then your knickers.

I was her lover and her best friend's husband and her Butlin's doctor and her hunger striker and shy stranger and Brendan Behan and ghost and sad bull and pimp and virgin cowboy and Dave Allen on his stool and her child and a magic talking-tree man and the invisible man and pagan chieftain and three window-cleaner brothers one stormy afternoon, but she never let me be her bitch. It was the same night after the restaurant, a new request this, I asked her to use our one deep-frozen glass dildo on me and out she jumps from the bed like I was trying to oppress her. A week went by and she still couldn't look at me. I'm not going to apologise for it, she said, I can't do it, I just can't. I like my man to be a man. That's very deep, I said. Yes it is, profound actually, and you'll have to lump it. Shall I tell you a story about this man of yours you don't want to hear? Please don't, Hugh. It's time, I said. The time is right. Your man was just out of his teens, living in London in a squat, not long over from Ireland. I know all this,

LEVITATION

she said. And all about how one day this terrible bitch upped and left poor Hughie, deserted him, and lo and behold he ended up sleeping on the streets. Poor Hughie in the rough. I know your adventures on the streets till I could act in them. Yeah well here's a new role, I said. One night I met this man in Victoria Station, a man in a suit, with a leather briefcase and he asked me if I was hungry. He had missed his train, he said, and had time to fill. He had a faint Yorkshire accent. He offered to buy me some food in a café at the corner, on Vauxhall Bridge Road. An Italian place. Gone now. You bet, I said. He asked me a lot of questions and god knows what I said because I was too busy stuffing my face on the food, bread and ham and then meatballs, I'd never had meatballs before. And then he said he was tired and had a hotel room nearby if I wanted to sleep on a proper bed, a real bed. Sheets. The smoothness. A soft mattress. A pillow. Yes please, I said. Did you really, Hughie? Yes, I literally begged him. He laughed too. And I begged some more. Stop there, that's fine, she said. I don't need to hear the rest. Yes, you do. You see, Genevieve, I was a young girl in his arms. And he petted me. And stroked me. And cooed over me. And he was gentle. And he stopped when I told him to stop. And he kissed me on the back of the head and turned away from me and left me to enjoy the comfort and warmth which were even better than I imagined. Bliss. I fell asleep in bliss. A cheap hotel in Victoria? They probably weren't even fresh, she said. And I fell asleep, I said, and when I woke there was an animal on my back. I couldn't see him because I was pinned down. The power and the voice had to be a monster's. A demon. It was growling and gargling words, the violent stuff about how I had to be given to the beast. Please stop, Hughie. That happened to your man, Genevieve.

*

So the dame missed her chance on that front. The subject was never broached again and the freezer door stayed shut. The Irish question took over her thoughts soon enough. The first airing was after a strange incident in the grounds of Alexander Palace. We were out for a walk on a decent evening like many another law-abiding couple, enjoying the open space and the glimpses of the yellow palace through the old trees which had found the energy to bud again. A black woman came running awkwardly across the grass towards us and stopped to ask us if we had seen her daughter. The woman was obviously at her wits' end. I tried to calm her, asked what the girl looked like, offered to help, the stuff you're supposed to do. During this, Viv was shaking her head at me as if I shouldn't get involved. Then she pulled me aside and told me to stop encouraging the woman. She grabbed my phone. By the time I got it back, the woman had run off again.

We were arguing about it at home later. Viv saying she knew straight away the woman was a crazy and there was no missing child. I didn't agree. I thought Viv was being cruel. Cruel? she said and happened to knock her glass off the table. It smashed. Viv didn't move. Are you waiting for me to? I said. No answer. I got the brush and pan from under the sink, swept it away, wiped the floor. Viv still hadn't moved. Viv? I said.

That's never happened to me before, she said. Some new tone in her voice made me study her face. She was scared.

What? Breaking a glass? No big deal, Viv.

She shook her head, unconvinced.

I take back the word cruel, okay? I said.

It's not like me, she said.

What isn't like you?

She went to the bedroom. Hours later, I go to check on her, sit on the edge of the bed, and that's when she says it, Do you ever think about going home, Hughie?

Travel was always the answer for that one. Way back when, it had been Latin America, then Berlin, Eastern Europe. And now Dublin. The grass was always greener on San Lazaro or Prenzlauer Allee or the Clontarf Road. I began to curse the airplanes sallying hither and thither about in the London skies. The cops stopped me one night when I was pissing against the window of the local travel agent's. Sure didn't I burn her lousy passport right in front of her. When she slipped out of the tapas bar on Green Lanes, noticed by only glossy Bollywood and me, that's about where I had got to in the story, the passport burning.

Phase two this was, the Huddleston Road flat in Tufnell Park. Stucco ceilings, picture rails, an Edwardian hunting frieze around the living room. A massive wrought iron bed we didn't have sheets broad enough to fit.

You stole my passport, you control-freak?

Yes. I admit it. I damn well stole your passport. And I hid it in my porn stash.

We're around May Day here, 2001. Another protest rally planned for the centre of London. Reclaim the shagging streets. Smash the G8. I hadn't turned Tory or anything but the idea of being trapped in a big crowd had me waking up at night in a sweat. Viv said she understood but I knew deep down she was disappointed in me. I fucked her in a corner of the bed and harder again behind the front door before she left and then I stayed home and watched on the news how the cops corralled thousands of people for hours and the shit kicked off. Two full days later she arrives home. The only thing that kept me sane was that I had her passport.

The attack of the gay mutant stuff or the plain old bukkake cheerleader?

There's this new stuff from India, really sick stuff with singing and dancing.

You wouldn't dare. Give it to me.

Watch me.

Why Hugh? Because I don't have a panic attack at the mention of a plane or a boat? Because I think there might be more to life than London? Don't I talk about us travelling together? Doing something else than the 9 to 5?

I like having a job. It's what us ordinary folk do. We go out the door and come back in the door. But you? That front door closes and I'm left wondering if you're ever going to darken it again.

Give it to me now. Right now.

Crap. It won't fucken catch. Who decided to make passports inflammable?

Where are you going? We have to sort this out once and for all.

To find some fucking petrol.

She didn't stick around for long after. Five months we shifted our way through in Tufnell Park, the jungle wings of summer sunsets at her back as she straddled me on that sinister bed. Her purple hardside suitcase growing a pearl on top of the maple armoire. She had a job teaching English to foreign academics but she was bored. Behind the new long veil of fine red hair, she sat on the very edge of the antique chairs, reading books on the Crusades, smoking, hooked on the cheapest gin from the high street. It was eleven years since I'd seen her. How dare a dope like me even dream of making her tarry?

Stop staring at me, Hugh. I'm not going anywhere.

I wasn't thinking that. I was remembering one night in a certain gay bar.

Baloney. No you weren't.

Is your nose different?

People should stay in their homes, lock the doors and chain

themselves to the bed. If they have to venture out they should cover their faces and speak to nobody. Infinite is the variety of what could happen to you al fresco. A decent day's work done, you've had a few pints and instead of going straight home you might fancy a kebab from your favourite spot in Camden. The pavement is a sad old rainbow and ends suddenly with you riding a tiger-skinned stool in a bar mirror, a high stage of multi-limbed heresies on behind you. This geezer next to you, white vest and a muscle throbbing in his waxed skull, could shout in your ear, There's no more fun to be had in London, which might tempt you to shout back, I wouldn't know mate, I'm a tourist myself over from Ireland. And you might buy him a drink and play the star-struck yokel but your new friend turns suspicious, thinks you're fibbing about being a paddy and waves another guy over, the small dapper type, who has personal experience of the emerald isle due to his auntie or sister in ancient Clonmacnoise, and these two might decide for reasons mystifying and probably perverse to expose the truth about you and your ethnicity, and the questions become sharp and spiteful and the dancers get stuck tighter together on the stage, until, perhaps, the dapper one has an idea and vanishes and returns unwrinkled with a girl in tow, a small busty chick with damp red hair, and this chick might stare at you in disbelief and you at her, and she could wink at you and say, I know how, and pull you off your stool and stick her hand between your legs under your ball bags. Oh this one's Irish to be sure, a thoroughbred northerner if I'm not mistaken. Oh infinite are the ways.

Didn't this whole damn yarn of ours begin with a wink from her? Isn't that where I always start the story she despised me telling people? A squat in Stamford Hill. The nightly gathering of the time-travelling rabble in the upstairs room with the bits of stained glass in the bay windows. Cider and hash rollies and guitars. Winter 1990. Thatcher and the poll tax. Troops Out. Black Flag. Spot a new face on the floor in the corner, a small thing, short red hair with a fringe, a walkman, oxblood DMs. Even with her knees up inside a baggy jumper you could still see the weight of the tits on her. A dent in her nose. And then she bloody winks at you. I thought there was something wrong with her.

Next morning in the kitchen, she's there at the table poking through a book. There's always people passing through the house so she could be somebody's sister, somebody's girlfriend. I nick a few slices of bread, stick them under the grill. Out the window, the long February streets run down to the canal and the marshes. Fumes of mixed fats fog the glass as Morrissey gripes in her walkman, England is mine and it owes me a living. Her very first words to me while I'm scraping out a margarine tub, You have an arse like a girl's.

Now I was only a runt and easily pained. I hadn't much of a sense of humour then either. So I showed her what's what by pretending she didn't exist. Which worked fine until one Sunday morning arriving back from another squat somewhere, there she was sitting on the front stoop, shivering in her big jumper, blocking my way. I'm sorry, she said, I like your arse, I do, I just can't stand the noise of toast being buttered. Don't sit around the fucken kitchen then, I told her. Why are the IRA bombing Leicester? she said. How the fuck should I know? But you're from the north, she said. And you're not, I said. But I heard you were in a concentration camp, she said. I lost the rag, informed her it wasn't a fucken concentration camp, it was a big open camp you went to over the border if you had to leave your home in a hurry. And no it wasn't a fucken internment camp either. It was like a refugee camp. The Free State Red Cross ran it. So watch out with questions or you might get your hooter broke again.

Years later, Genevieve would laugh it all away like it never happened. The politics, the arrests, the pub collections, the dole offices, she was happy enough to hear me reminisce about, but not the astonishment of her breasts in my hands or her clit-bean between my teeth the first time or her eyes when she was ready to let rip or my two fingers up her ass or her total nakedness or what she could do with a condom or the bruises from her little heels pounding the back of this nervous young militant. And not the way, neither, how she deserted me after six and a half weeks.

I can date it exactly. The poll tax riot, March 31st, 1990. I lost her in the crowd at Trafalgar Square when the cops ambushed us from behind on their silky steeds, a cavalry charge from an old history book, batons instead of swords. Blood leapt like flames from skulls around me. The roar that went up from the crowd, the rage, they must have heard it in Birmingham. A girl dropped at my feet, caught by a Metropolitan hoof. We had nowhere to run. People on their knees howling. Then the snatch squads in the black overalls. Blue helmets. I managed to climb some scaffolding, searching for Genevieve below. All creeds and colours dragged away by the ankles. Screams going off like mines around Trafalgar Square. And when the first shock had passed and the fight back began, I threw myself in. We smashed through the windows up to Leicester Square, gutting everything in our path. I was covered in blood now. A transit van clipped me and I got right back up again. Two bobbies nailed a black guy next to me. Another two dragging this new ager woman by the arms and one of them won't forget me. Sometimes I stopped, just stood there and took in the chaos, staggered but admiring it somehow, the pigeons flying around in it. Then the blunt digit of a baton in the ribs near the Tube. Up again and two grabbed me. And another two. They ripped the clothes off me in the struggle to get me into the back of the van. The bastards threw me naked into a cell.

You're doing what? Tobias said.

I'm moving to Dublin with Genevieve.

You're mouth is saying the words, son, but I don't see it.

We're moving to Dublin.

Keep trying.

After the cops charged me and let me out in charity shop clothes, I went back to the squat. The Redzer and her rucksack were long gone. I wandered the streets for a few weeks. A man called Tobias, a bailiff, found me when he was clearing out a squat in Stamford Hill. A youngster in the basement, bricked up in a room, filthy, bonkers, who wouldn't even give his name.

You are throwing everything away for a whiff of the blarney cunt.

Go easy, Tobias.

What have I taught you? Most men amount to nothing more than a—

I know. Fear begets truth. But this is what I want.

Wake up sunshine.

Being the gentleman he is, Tobias was big enough to offer to move our belongings across the water in a private container at his own expense. I remember what was supposed to be our last game of snooker together, and how, on a fast break of eighty-two, he was speculating whether I might be useful to him in Dublin. I told him it was all off. Genevieve was gone again. For good this time. He was under the lamp, stretched for the white in the centre of the table. He looked up at me, sucking the moustache. You're telling me you're staying now, he said. I nodded, shrugged or something. He destroyed the pink and came down the table in the shadows towards me. Stood in close, resting his weight on the cue between us. His smell of egg and rubber. The watery eyes tried to make mortal sense of me. You know something? he said. I bloody well hate snooker, always have, and he laughed so hard he had to sit down.

Long and shiny as the years, the tram slides by me now on Capel Street with The Redzer on its back. Now do I give chase. Where might this Iosta na Rinne be when it's at home. Infinite are the ways and means. In the barber shop up the street, the same one I used the day before I took the ferry to London, this tall fella on the scissors with a ponytail and a London accent. Archway his manor. Turns out there's a good chance he got on the same boat after I got off, going the other way to find his Irish roots. We took each other's place we decided. Kept the equilibrium. The kilter. And is it my other duty now to clatter through Dublin in pursuit of one sedentary Genevieve Querney with the light limbs and the sailor's wink. Blimey, there's my phone.

Bjorn. Perfect timing.

How was the flight? The pill was a help, yes?

Not a bother, Bjorn. How do you always know when I need you?

I am missing you terrible already. I can hear the gulls. So romantic.

You know what, Bjorn. I'm a survivor. I'm fucken alive. Alive alive oh, Bjorn.

Show me later. Which time you home tonight?

hallion #2

... and aye that there yellow trigger up out in the sky is the moon Neil / a new moon / my ma your granny won't leave the house when it's a big full moon / she sits with the poker on her lap inside the front door / that's why once a month your granny has black hands and isn't allowed to hold you or your clothes will be spoiled / she doesn't mean to be ignoring you / but it's good she's out of the hospital now and here we are together the two of us in her kitchen / can you smell that bad reek a bit like in the lane that time in the fog / that's tripe and your granny will eat bowls of it until she can't stop laughing and she sees a horde of you

   there's been a quare lot happening lately you may have noticed yourself but I didn't have a single chance to fill you in/ since we were stuck waiting in the dark to hear Mulhern's crabbed wee bell jingles / your mother wouldn't let me see you after the whole furore but we knew that was on the cards didn't we / don't darken this door again you piece of balderdash she called me / some father you are / there'll be a united Éire before I let you anywhere near that wee boy again / nearly a month she went around claiming she'd never heard of me until only this afternoon when she banged on the front window while I was watering your granny's cactuses / you can't blame her though / did you ever see her eyes blacker they plastered her all over the teatime news / marking that journalist's card for him

you see Neil I had a big idea a good one a total zinger which I thought would save everybody's bacon and it nearly worked too only for the scumbag squaddies wanting to stir up trouble / I didn't know it would bloody happen I said to your mother and she goes back to me people think not knowing something is an excuse and I said why should I believe you and she lost the rag again and another book flaps toward your da a graph of unemployment numbers in slow motion just before it hits

I finally saw Mulhern the other day in the People's shop and out of the corner of his mouth he goes he won't be doing any more knees like it's a regret and what a severe loss for the community / I didn't believe a word of it / he was bluffing and he can't do that properly either / he had a roll of carpet under his arm and a neck brace and a plaster on his ear and he opened the buttons on his shirt to show off the bandage around his ribs and one of his front teeth is missing / the scumbag squaddies did all that / but he was in good form / sober too / good luck or bad luck then I had to ask him nudging him with my crutch/ what do you mean he said bending down to read the messages on these two of casts of mine / people can't pass you on the street without wanting to write their names on them / there's you know who himself and Harry from the bookies and ▓▓▓▓ and there's Iris look and see that one there from Camel out out damn machine / he was there too over by the wall where they keep the free butter / you know right well what I mean I said to Mulhern / how do you mean he said / it's obvious what I mean I said but he keeps up the dumb act and I say pointing out the door what we saw across the road by the Celtic cross Mulhern you're as bad at lying as you are at capping / and he taps the side of his head and says he must have got too many scumbag boots to the brain and he doesn't remember what day of the week it is he's useless at it / nobody's going to believe him / dring dring / dring dring when he turned up in the lane forty-five minutes late that last night and he didn't even have the bazooka with him / a black eye and no bazooka and slugging on a quarter bottle / your watch is wrong he tried saying to me / no it's not I said this is a Seconda and I checked it with the clock in the Big Time Barbershop and that's never wrong / snap he said and showed me his and it wasn't a bloody Seconda at all and he puts on a confused face like he had always thought it was / it's a fake I said and then wished I hadn't because the thought flew through my mind that it was Ladders who might have bought it for him / for a present maybe / he was having a look in at you under the hood making cat noises / kittens to make you smile / it's not his fault Ladders is the way she is / they say she's a bit touched because her first husband died on her while they were lying in bed together on a Saturday morning / hey presto he has a heart attack right on top of her supposedly / he was a boxer this man a heavyweight / unbeaten / Mulhern always liked Ladders from when they were only small my ma your granny told me / his dreams came true she said that's what's ails Mulhern

so where's this gun then I said to cheer him up / it's hard to understand but I wouldn't have minded touching it before it did the damage / it's like you want to say sorry

then I have to listen to the story of his day and what a disaster it has been and how this isn't a lane we're standing in in the fog it's more like a bad dream / and how there's no gun either / he hides the gun in a hole in a wall in this couple's place in the high flats you see these cousins of his / only when he went there earlier to collect it and knocks on the door a big dog starts attacking the door on the other side a German Shepherd he said it had to have been / this couple don't have a dog right / so he's wondering about that until

LEVITATION

a neighbour informs him they've moved they packed up and left a few days ago / they can't have moved said Mulhern / you calling me a liar says the neighbour and the two of them get into a scrap on the landing which was where he got the black eye from / I nearly believed him but I still wasn't sure / so where's the bullets I said where's the bloody bullets then / you must have them he said / oh no I don't I said / he thought Oodles McKinney would have been along before him he said / Oodles McKinney / Oodles was the man meant to bring the bullets / maybe you should ask your wife where Oodles is I said and felt bad about it straight away / what do you mean by that you slabber he said / nothing I say back / keep it that way he says people should just quit egging her on / is that right now I said / anyway he said you can talk / what do you mean by that I said squaring up to him / what do you mean I can talk / I can mean whatever I want he said / no you can't I said go on spit it out / I was about to deck him / and you were the one that lied about the last time I reminded him and pulled down my trousers instead / remember these I said / remember these / and do you know what Margot will do to me when she finds out I am up this back lane with the good pram

maybe it was the sight of my legs again but he starts apologising and saying he'll take you back to the house with him and wait for Margot to show up and everything will work out and I have to say but you've no gun and there's no bullets and I'm not coming back here same time next week and he's going oh I've had it I'm a dead loss they'll demote me I'll be washing the floors in the People's shop or tidying the barricades or sent up to lie on the roof for the night with a bit of a stick pretending to be a sniper / and that's when it hit me Neil / the big idea / like the sun coming out / I could see what we could do like it had already happened like it was an old story / and when I told him it he saw it too without any

hallion #2

persuading and the two of us pushed you and your pram out of that foggy back lane as though the stuff was after us

you were probably wondering why I threw the blanket over you / you listening right / this is the good bit I've been dying to tell you about for ages / why did I throw the blanket over you / well there was a good reason / imagine the three of us were scooting along the Lecky Road just where you get to the wee Celtic cross memorial and what do we see in the road what do we see Neil / know what it was / we were stopped in our tracks and I threw the blanket over you like an instinct / it has the sheep's curly hide but the fat shape of a badger low to the ground / and the long tail was there and a horn only a small slim effort but it had a horn / staring at us with the lizard eyes / not one bit scared of us / do you see that I said to Mulhern and he agreed / is it good luck or bad I said / what does it want / is it sick or something maybe / I started clapping my hands to shoo it away but it decided to come towards us / maybe it was angry you know about us disturbing its nest / Mulhern wasn't doing anything just standing there and staring / don't let it near Neil in the pram I said / nearer and near it was coming / I picked up a halfer to make it see I was serious / we've nothing to give you I said get lost or else / the big eyes had lots of colours in them / then I look at Mulhern and he's vanished well I thought he had for a moment but he was only down on his hunkers / he was stretching out his hand to it / what the hell are you doing don't touch it you don't know what it has I said / you could catch anything / the thing was sniffing his hand now with its black muzzle / the black snout / it had blood in the nostrils / maybe it had an accident I don't know / Mulhern I'm telling you it could take the hand off you I was saying but he wasn't listening to me and before I could stop him he was petting the thing just above the horn and it was letting him too it didn't seem to mind not Mulhern anyway what about that then Neil / whatever else they say about your da you can say he saw the lonely thing on the Lecky Road / and Mulhern can back me up / he couldn't believe it either / it was like he was drunker than he had ever been on the way over to the high flats stumbling around and tripping over himself / I wouldn't let him near the pram with his hand / the way he was was like he was singing an opera but no sound was coming out and then we got over to the bottom of the steps and he leaned back against the wall and fainted / dring went his bell as he hit the ground

Mulhern bloody fainted on me / so that was the next problem / how to get you and Mulhern up the steps to the fourth-floor landing / I couldn't leave him there / or you either / or the pram or your mother would have my life / I tried pulling him with one hand and the pram with the other and going up backwards step by step but it would have been a week tomorrow before I made it up to the plaster of Paris man / if I got the cast on my legs then we could say Mulhern had done the job and I had been to the hospital and we could all go back to our beds / that was my big idea and it should have worked too / but I had to get up there to see if he was even in and whether he had perfected the mixture

nobody was about /deserted just / some nights are very quiet / don't let bully-boy time order you about Camel must have done on the wall / I should have called it a day and taken you back home and hoped none of it had happened but the idea still seemed possible and I didn't want to give up on it / I would have felt dogged / it wouldn't have been fair / so I made a split-second decision and tied Mulhern's shoe laces to your pram jammed on the brake and ran up there

if I got the casts on your mother couldn't exactly throw me out on the street either now could she

Smullen I told you his name was from the Wells / he was sitting on the floor in a ring with the three wains holding his

hallion #2

hands / in the mummy factory / arms and legs lying about like hair in a barbershop / I'll pay you anything you want when I get the money I said but I need you to do my two legs pronto and come down and help me with the pram / and it's not Smullen but the wains who want to know the price / how much they say / and no that's not enough / and no that's not enough either / until eventually we're up to a tenner / no pity in them / and so they eventually agreed and we shook hands on the deal and I ran down to the ground floor and hey presto no you no pram no Mulhern

sorry isn't a word for you any more your mother keeps saying / sorry is banned / sorry is balderdash / but was I to know the scumbag squaddies would come along and lift Mulhern and you as well / bloody lift a wain in a pram / take you off in the back of a sixer / it had never happened before / a new low they're calling it / even on the TV / you were all over the TV son / you're famous now / wee Neil Quinn the youngest person to be arrested so far / your mother secretly blames me no matter what she said to the cameras about the British imperialist state / my wee boy manhandled by those animals / where's the justice / where's the rights for this community / an infant stolen in the night by the queen's henchmen / the protectors of her coffers / jumped up bank guards / she gave a good speech your mother / nearly a month she wouldn't let me see you though

hear that helicopter son / that's them up there too

so I hadn't a clue what happened to you and Mulhern / maybe the lonely thing had come back and Mulhern had fallen in love with it I was wondering and followed it somewhere dragging you along with him in the pram / how was I to know / then Iris shouts down from her window way above the pigs have taken your son and that other dunce you big dunce / why do you keep me calling me a dunce what did I ever do on you I shouted back up at her / I thought you were getting your knees done she said / it's true I said / tell that to your Margot she said and I said did you see anything else and Iris said what the hell are you on about you just better get him back / she was being honest / talk about a bad moment though / a bad day / the worst one yet / my son swiped by the scumbag squaddies and the cops / Smullen and his mummies were shaking their heads too / nobody could believe it / my big idea had backfired / then Iris appeared with her coat on and said any idiots in the vicinity should tag along with me / and that's how we got to the police station / and we banged on the gate and shouted to the sentry that we wanted the baby back me Iris and Smullen and his wains and the invisible man and other ones we met on the way / give us the baby back we were chanting / what do we want / the baby back when do we want it / all of us banging on the metal gates making the barbed wire shake rattle and roll / when do we want it / now and we would all bang harder

Faze your godfather was lifted once but never me / they kept him for three days in a room with no window / they need to make you believe them that they're the ones telling the truth / they aim for your weak spots things you like things you're proud of / like with Faze it was his dancing / that they'd heard how good a dancer he was / and that word had got round even into the barracks / how about showing us a few of your snazzy steps / your weak spots son / keep them out of sight / never let them see what you feel good about

and by the way I brought it up with your mother about hearing her say Faze's name in her dream

she took a bit of a reddener and goes I must have heard her wrong because why would she say that article's name / it was the same night he left I said funny that / can't a woman say whatever she wants in her sleep without being tortured about it she goes

maybe you knew I said

she lost the head / who gave me the right to stand on her doorstep on a pair of crutches with my legs in casts after letting the enemy pigs touch her son infiltrating her sleeping privacy

our doorstep I said it's my doorstep too

and then who starts screaming from their cot inside but you wee man and she gives me her look which means the entire state of the world civil rights poverty the problem of fraternisation fleadhs sectarianism the shyness of the Free State and the whole lack of trust between heaven and earth is my doing and shuts the door in my face / one day son you'll know how it feels / to be in the bad books with some girl / it'll be like she's waiting for you to come up with the magic word to make it all disappear / a magic word / and you have no notion and will end up making it worse / which is what your da did when he shouted through the letterbox / a fire in a bin you called him and you wouldn't even dance more than once with me at our wedding / I'll spare you the rest of it / shouting through the letterbox / she stopped answering the door to me after that and I had to sit across the street in the wheelchair they brought my ma your granny home from the hospital in waiting for her to take you out for the messages or somewhere

Detective Hawkins from out near the Glenshane Pass / that's the man who questioned me / a red face with an edge to it like a rusty hatchet / no eyes / no mouth / trousers and jacket from two different suits / he brings me down a corridor with more doors in it than the high flats into this room with four school chairs in it and stains and writing on the walls / and he's trying to be mister nice with me considerate and that there's been a huge error of judgement and as a father too he can understand my outrage and he starts showing me the pictures of his wains in his wallet / it's entirely natural he keeps saying / they go for your weak spots you see what I

LEVITATION

mean son / the things you're proud of / and he's showing me sadly the photos and they don't look anything like him / and I want to say that they're bloody lucky to be spared a bake like their so-called da's and as if he knows when to speak over the top of me to stop me he says a father just has to put the evil thoughts to the back of his mind and put the food on the table and leave the gossiping to the women don't you think and I'm wondering if that sounds like Protestantism and again he speaks over it like he's blanking it out and mentions your mother at the sit-in and how Faze is getting on in London and that he stole a car and dumped it and hey presto I have this memory I had forgotten about / from before the time we got into bother with the magazines / your mother went out and you and me stayed in because it started lashing / remember / we were standing by the window talking about the rain and what it is and where it goes / down the drains and out to the sea / and this car pulls up and the engine goes off and someone runs over and gets into the side seat / a woman you can tell by the sound of the shoes / remember / and I pulled the curtains

you're better off not knowing / if something is about to kick off a shooting say maybe or the boys scouting a dump you need to turn your eyes away / try not to believe it's happening / do something else / and when your ma came back in a while later she was hardly wet at all but wasn't she in a great mood and she gave me one of her special kisses right there in front of you and you were bouncing up and down and laughing away too and she said how we were her two favourite boys and who wants ice cream and then I realise Detective Hawkins is nodding along with me like I've been talking to him out loud and he's dying to hear the rest of it and I haven't been / I wasn't talking / I was silent the way you're supposed to be / and on the wall behind him I can read they put love in the water here and I jump up and

hallion #2

grab my chair and tell him I want my son back and he calls me a hair-brained ball lick and I call him ten times worse and he takes off his jacket like we're going to have it out there and then only the door opens and it's a soldier with a feather in his beret wheeling you in the pram and further up the corridor what do I see / what do I see Neil / a man getting the living shit kicked out of him and who is it / my da your granda / Da I shout and he sees me and he says

I told your mother what he said and she said not to worry about it / she thinks it was a set up that they staged it / she'll have a word with you know who about it she said / they'll believe your mother more likely

outside the barracks there was riot already happening in the fog / Iris and a gang of women grabbed you and the pram off me and took you away and I didn't see you again / ███ ███ ███ ███ ███ ███ ███ ███ ███ ███ ███ ███ ███ ███ ███ ███ ███ ███ ███ and Smullen and his mummies were watching the riot and I went back to the high flats with them and fair play to them in the end they did my legs for nothing / you see I was worried about Mulhern still / the least I could do was make it seem like he had done his job / so that's why your da is in these casts covered in people's names and messages / nice messages / people are kind / you're famous you see / the youngest ever to be lifted / just you remember what your mother told me that time / don't be an idiot and don't do what they expect you to ███ ███ ███ ███ ███

so she came to the door today / your mother / with the new hairdo / it suits her doesn't it / short / I can't stand it any more she says I can't stand it / my mouth had about a thousand sorrys stuffed in it / I kept having to swallow them down / why are you deliberately acting the sap she said everybody knows you weren't knee-capped what are you trying to prove / you never liked my legs anyway I said / take them off and I'll let you see him she said meaning you / done I told her I'd have them off by tomorrow as soon as I found a hacksaw / why the change of heart though I was wondering / only yesterday up the town she had ignored me / then Camel was passing up the street with a spray can and he calls over Margot the man's a genius and she shouts back at him what would you know you dirty brute / she looked at me for a long time after that / just stared into my eyes / minutes maybe / it all stops here she said / she could probably see I didn't know what she meant because she rolled her eyes and sighed and said all the talk all the bloody coarse rumours it all stops right here and now / I didn't start them I said and nearly ruined it and she turned on her heel / it all stops here I said quick as I could and she believed my voice

and that's when she asked about my da and if it was true that I'd seen him and I gave her the message from him / tell the boys they have a mind-reading machine / he was shouting it to me from inside the violence being done on him the blood splattering the walls and him roaring tell the boys they have a mind-reading machine / your mother said she would pass it on / and then she went up on her tiptoes and gave me a kiss on the cheek and said she would drop you round later

who I said to her who will you drop round

she looked at the ground and then back up at me / Neil she said

my son Neil I said and got a wee smile from her and then who was going along the street the other way but Mulhern and Ladders / and they were pulling a trolley behind them covered in blankets and there was a big tail sticking out the back wagging away like a happy dog and a gang of wains were running along after it

what's that I shouted

hallion #2

what's what Mulhern said back

and your mother called over you're flying low you're flying low

and so that's about the height of it Neil / all my news / I saw Iris too in case you're wondering and she's in good form and seeing this new lad from over the border / between you and me I didn't mention I had a postcard from Faze / a picture on the front of people on a tiny narrow bridge with high sides / hello from the capital he wrote for the laugh / he's training to be a barber he said / cutting the hair of the Dublin ones / can you believe that / he'll be filling their heads with all sorts of stories about up here / hello from your godfather he said to tell you

don't you mind what ones say about him

I'm your da and that should be all that matters shouldn't it

and you see these two plaster casts and the two crutches they're going on the new barricade in the morning

The Three Twists

The seahorse lamps were coming on and the water foaming as Ellison, carrying a tartan suitcase, crossed the bridge behind a couple of punks with stiff, high mohicans. The girl's was bleached white and her boyfriend's a shade of scarlet and purple at the tip. Hand in hand and swinging their arms, the chains on their biker jackets rattled in counterpoint to the song they were singing at the top of their voices. The car horns were next to join the anthem when, at the end of the bridge, they walked right across the traffic on the quays. They stopped for a kiss at the corner of Capel Street. As Ellison stepped around them he happened to catch a glimpse of the side of the girl's face and her one open eye, cold and green and plastic like a badge, and her middle finger went up at him. Further north on the street, he came to a stop under the awning of Terrence Roddy's barber shop, switched the suitcase to the other hand, and, bending his neck, went inside.

Dáithí, the young apprentice, who had a pensioner in the chair nearest the window, pointed with a metal comb towards the back of the shop but shook his head at the same time. Ellison nodded and took a seat on the low sofa, positioning the suitcase between his legs. The barber and the pensioner were talking about the bank robbery in Wicklow that had gone wrong. Dáithí claimed the guard on life-support in the hospital had been shot point-blank in the face, but the old man had heard it was flying glass. With a little brush Dáithí began to dust the hair off the pensioner's neck and face and then showed him the view from the back with an oval hand mirror. Once he got the nod, he untied the green bib. The pensioner stepped down from the chair and approached the till where Dáithí was waiting with his hands cupped together. Ellison watched the old man counting out the coins from a little cloth purse while Dáithí gazed out the window at the darkening street. Suddenly, the lights flickered in the shop. Dáithí said it had been doing that all day. The pensioner thought it had to do with radiation from Sellafield and the Provos should gather every man and woman they had and take the place over.

Ellison took a packet of fags from his pocket and found the matches in the other pocket. The first match was dead, and the next few were the same. Dáithí had walked the pensioner to the door where they were now talking with another man. Sliding the drawer out of the matchbox, Ellison was picking through the sticks for a pink one when he heard another door slam at the back of the shop and a voice saying, Over my dead body, Sandy. Get back up them stairs.

Terrence Roddy, the owner, appeared from the corridor, scratching at his chest chair under a red satin shirt and puffing on a slim cigar. He turned off the radio and crossed the green and black tiles in his sandals to the window. Yellow heels. A wad of notes in his back pocket. Sweat. The barber shop owner growled to himself, broke wind, and the fluorescent tubes flickered again. Ellison put his fag behind his ear and rose from the sofa, but Dáithí burst through the door asking who wanted to hear the best blue joke of all time. Roddy pretended not to hear. The young man then began to sweep the trimmings of white hair into the accursed pile in the corner.

Terry, Ellison said, do you have that money?

What fucken money now?

You said Wednesday. For the party gig that weekend.

Roddy said to his apprentice, I hear tell the chapel in Inchicore needs a new fucken roof. And the priest a new car. Will we make a donation, Dáithí?

Perplexed, the young barber looked at the faces of the two men, rolled his eyes, and said, All I know is, when he has that bodhrán in his hands, he's a different man. His fingers were bleeding. It was like a shield he was playing.

Right then, the telephone rang. Roddy dropped the cigar, stood on it, and crossed the tiles again. Ellison turned away from the trace of himself in the mirror and took a seat on the arm of the sofa. Dáithí turned the brush pole into a microphone stand and began to mime a song, pointing at the girls passing the shop window until a couple of them saw him and stopped on the pavement and put their hands to their hearts. With the brush pole now between his legs, Dáithí trotted towards the door, slapping his thigh.

A priest in the parlour and blood on the goat skin, Roddy said, over by the till now, this fucken country would drive you spare.

Three more time times the barber had to hit the button before the money drawer would open. Then, holding up a tenner towards the light, he said, What kind of cretin are you anyway?

Ellison reached for the suitcase, set it on his knees. I got the new one, he said, tapping the locks.

It's a new brain you need, son. Roddy was coming towards him. You're a fucken oddball, we all know that, but what the fuck possessed you?

I don't know, said Ellison. He sat the suitcase on the sofa, took the fag from behind his ear and put it in his mouth, patting his pockets for a light. Roddy was watching him. It was a stupid misunderstanding, Terry, he said and flinched back on the sofa because Roddy suddenly raised his arms over his head and made a big ghost noise. Sweat stains on the satin. The clump of notes fell to the tiles with a sound like a kiss. Roddy pressed his sandal down on it.

Only I had to talk him round, he said to Ellison, there was a certain four-eyed rustler who was very eager to make his own wee bongo drum out of your incense-flavoured hide. Do you catch my drift, drummer boy?

Thanks, Ellison said. Outside, Dáithí was feeling the ends of one of the girls' hair.

Thanks? And you still come in here looking for money? You should be on your bended bloody knees bearing gifts.

The others need paying, Ellison said. I promised them today.

The two men looked at each other until something made the ceiling creak. Roddy took his foot off the money and kicked it towards Ellison.

Youse did a good job, I'll give you that. But I'll tell you this for nothing, son. Keep your nose out of other people's business. And your eyes off what you can't have. Keep away from her. Dtuigeann tú?

Later that night he walked up the Inchicore Road and crossed the junction onto Sarsfield Road. He took a left. A banger of a Hillman up on beer kegs. An empty house, gutted. Further along, one bang with the lion's paw knocker was enough to bring a shout from inside the house to hold on. It was nearly half nine by his watch. Ellison stepped back from the door, put down the suitcase and then picked it up again. A new letterbox and a week's worth of rinsed milk bottles. The door was opened and Lana froze at the sight of him.

Just me, he said, after she had checked both ways along the street.

You're not allowed to be here, Felix, she said, shaking her head. Dungarees and a black jumper with the sleeves rolled up. Wiping her hands on a rag.

I thought I would call in person to apologise, he said. To the both of you. I was playing in a session down in Dolphin's Barn and the Special Branch raided it. So I thought I would walk up and clear the air.

That Sandy's not in, she said.

Bad timing then, Ellison said and made a move to go. She took a step towards him, the rag in her hands.

I've been trying to fix that bucken bike of mine. Any bright ideas on how to lift rust off the chain?

It's the handlebars, he told her. They're from a different machine altogether. The balance is off. You'll do yourself harm on that thing, I'm telling you.

She touched the back of her hand to her hair line and looked at him and sighed. I'm going off my head, she said, and then she came closer and asked, quietly, Have you seen him, Felix, have you?

Ellison shook his head. Her eyes left his face for something high over his shoulder and for a moment a sneer came alive on her lips. Then her chin dropped and she inhaled the night air of Inchicore deep into her lungs. He looked at the parting in her hair and then down the street where there seemed to be a figure made of fine glistening rain dancing under every streetlight.

Felix, you big dope, come on inside, Lana said from the doorstep.

Staircase to the right and a door on the left. The suitcase in his arms, he squeezed by the bicycle upside down in the hall and found her in the kitchen at the sink, rubbing butter into her hands. The bicycle chain and hammer on the draining board with the oil-stained butter dish. The radio on low on top of the fridge. Somebody had drawn glasses on the Dalek poster tacked to the door that probably concealed the bathroom. Lana, meanwhile, was giving out about the man across the street who had the nearest working telephone. Three punts she'd already wasted that day on the space cadet.

Standing over you with his wee egg timer, she was saying. The man's not right in the head, I swear to God. It can't be good for you, don't you think?

Ellison settled the suitcase on a chair and said, Robbing people, you mean?

Naw. Aye, Lana said. Naw, I mean knowing too much. Knowing everybody's business. It would give you the creeps. And take off your coat when you're in my house.

He did what he was told and hung it over the back of a chair. One after another, Lana sluiced her arms under the hot water as far as the elbow, her shadow doing the same on the blind over the window. Then she began to pat them dry with a tea towel.

You really landed me in it you know, Felix, she said, quietly. I didn't want to be a stool-pigeon, but Sandy of course thought I had gone behind his back and invited a priest into the house. And he is not one bit fond of the clergy. So what was I to do?

She looked for his face. I shouldn't have got involved, he said and sat down at the table. A basin of suddy water beside a stack of books and a soft case for glasses.

Sure you know what's he like, she said. A Trot to his core. And then you go and tell a priest to just drop in and bless the house on him without a by your leave… I've seen him lose the head for a lot less. He would have probably gone for you if he had answered the door to you there.

The volume on the radio rose by itself. Lana, while she rubbed some type of lotion into her skin, said that the thing had a life of its own. As soon as Ellison made a move out of the chair towards it, the volume went down again.

You see what I mean, she said, laughing, this whole house has a want.

He asked if it was almonds he smelled and she nodded, but her mind was still on the priest and how sorry she'd felt for the poor old man being chased out of the house by her husband. Ellison leaned across the table and lifted the suitcase by the handle.

Guess what, he said.

Acting shocked, a moist hand covered her mouth. Then she gave up the pretence and said, It would be just bloody typical wouldn't it if it was *This Is Your Life* and they catch me in the kitchen with oil all over me.

You're way too young, Ellison said and placing his foot on a chair, he balanced the suitcase on his thigh and clicked open the locks. Lana told him to wait while she removed the basin from the table and put it in the sink. Then he lifted out the new bodhrán. He asked if she fancied a song but she declined, saying she was in the wrong mood for singing. What she needed was a drink instead, she said and squatted down to open a cupboard under the sink. Ellison returned the bodhrán to the suitcase and put that on the floor. Then he sat down again. He had one cigarette left in the box he took from his pocket. Lana, straightening up from the cupboard, knocked her hip against the table and her rings spilled out of a saucer onto the polka-dot oilcloth.

There's your ghostie for you, Felix, she said. Just my big fat arse. The bottle sounded low when she banged it on the table. Two proper heavy glasses. Ice cubes in a cup. Her hair tied back showing her temples. And for the next while, she pressed him for news about what he had been doing since she saw him, and he told her the cream of the stories about the two bands he was in, and one about the folk group he played with some Sundays at the Oblates Church around the corner.

That's how I know Father Bassinger, he explained. I was talking to him after mass and he was getting himself ready for a house blessing and I thought maybe that would give Lana a lift. And, well, you know the rest. A bad idea. A dud. I thought you were serious on the beach though. I really did, Lana.

Don't be daft, she said. I had too much on my mind. Each time she took a sip of whiskey, the dungaree strap slid off her shoulder.

You said you couldn't sleep. You had to move downstairs to the sofa. There's something not right in that house, you said. My nerves are frayed. My hair is falling out. And the part about the door slamming in your face. You did a good impression of being scared out of your wits, Lana.

She laughed. I don't know what I'm saying half the time, she said. I'll tell you this but—if that priest had've been a few years younger, the place would definitely have been haunted. You know I was halfway up the stairs with him when that Sandy came in. Halfway up the stairs with a priest, Felix. It's not funny.

You're the one who's laughing, Ellison said and he picked a long match out of the household box and lit his last cigarette. Anyway you sang your heart out at the party. You've good articulation. And don't try telling me you haven't had any training.

That's just my party piece, she said, waving away the compliment. I had too much drink is all. You see me and his specky teetotal lordship there had a row beforehand and so I went by myself on the bicycle. And then sure the chain came off and it was raining and I was just totally browned off by the time I got there. Tell me the truth, though, did I make a holy show of myself in front of them lot? A drop of drink and I don't know who I am sometimes.

Ellison hit the table with his fist and declared, I'm not a bloody refugee, this is my own country. Don't you be calling me a refugee you free-state toilet-brush.

Oh mother of Christ, Lana said, her face in her hands.

Ellison said, It was nice down on the beach though.

When she showed her face again, her eyes were glowing. It was me who forced him to move down here, she said. Sandy, I mean. Away from his precious Bogside. First of all we were in this dump of a flat on Dorset Street and all I did was complain. So it's my own damn fault he went to that slime-ball Terry Roddy and got us this place. God knows what he had to do to get it. You see that Sandy, I'm telling you, underneath it all, the hard line, he's easily led. It keeps me awake at night what he might get sucked into.

Well you look great for someone who doesn't ever sleep, Ellison said.

I'm a wile worrier, Felix. You've no idea. How he puts up with me, I'll never know. My poor mammy was the same. When she was in one of her states she used to call me out to the scullery and wash my hair. It used to bring her peace. But that's why my hair is the way it is. All the body washed out of it. I'd be bent over the sink way past my bedtime and she'd be singing her wee airs and drowning me with pans of water.

Yes, he said. Peace.

She frowned. I'm wile sorry for what I said to you. I was upset just. And you did nothing wrong but only believe me. Look, she said, turning a ring easily on her finger. I'm fading away.

Ellison slid his hand towards her across the table. It lay

there knuckle down on the oil-cloth. There seemed to be a small smile on her mouth as she blinked and blinked her eyes at his open palm. The parting in her hair again. The loose dungaree strap. The round cheeks. Then the slamming shut of a door above their heads. Lana O'Hara looked up and right into him for a moment.

It's just a draught, she said, as she followed him out into the hall.

He had taken the hammer from the draining board. The light switch at the bottom of the stairs wasn't working. He heard her say she was out of a fortune on bulbs. A wall of darkness waited at the top. He asked if she had a candle, and when she refused, he bent down and unhooked the light from between the handlebars of the upturned bicycle. The beam showed him the blue carpet, a new naked banister, a book on the stairs. Half way up Lana called his name and he turned the beam on her. White faced, pointing with her thumb, and behind her the bicycle wheel very slowly turning.

If you have to, she said, it's the one on the right. Not the other one. That's my bedroom. Well, supposed to be. Are you sure, Felix?

The door was white gloss with a long gold handle and no keyhole. He tried to find a way to hold the hammer and the torch in one hand to leave the other free. Because that didn't work he hung the hammer by the claw from the lintel. He changed the position of his feet and took a deep breath, his hand just above the handle. In one move, he grabbed hold, pushed down and kicked at the door, which flew open without resistance, and at the same time made a snatch for the hammer. The torch, however, slipped from his grasp and hit the floor with a bang that made Lana shout his name. The beam stayed on at least, aimed across loose nails on the underlay to a carboard box from a butcher's in Derry. He picked the thing up and waved it around. One wall papered, the others scraped. A pink bed sheet over the window, rippling. A car battery. A broken knitting needle. A belt. A tin box of foreign coins on the window ledge when he lifted the sheet, wetting his fingers to feel for a draught along the join. Below in the street, at the door of the house opposite, a man with a long beard was flicking through the pages of a telephone book and talking to an elderly woman in a housecoat who had control of a white pup at the end of a piece of twine, the pup yapping up at Ellison.

He told Lana he had wedged some newspaper under the door to stop it banging. She was wringing out a green bra from the basin in the sink, sleeves rolled up again. The radio seemed to be louder now, more punk music from the pirate stations. He put the hammer and torch on the table, and said, It's beyond me.

Is it now? she said.

He waited a second before he said, I mean there's not much of a breeze from the window that I could find. Not enough to slam a door in my opinion.

Is that right?

You annoyed with me? he asked her. The punk racket grew loud enough to stop any conversation and then seemed to cut out altogether. Lana emptied the basin water down the sink and said, That policeman has died in the hospital. Then she took the basin full of wet underwear through to the bathroom. Ellison leaned against the Dalek, watching her as she pegged the clothes on a line over the bath.

You should just head on, Felix, now, she said as she brushed by him and returned to the kitchen where she removed the tumblers and the ashtray from the table and began to rinse them. When that was done, she wetted the dishcloth and wiped the table down. By his watch it was nearly quarter to twelve.

The Three Twists

And leave you alone in this place, he said.

Lana made a scoffing sound. And she said, gently, I'm never ever able to believe in that word. Not even the devil's all by himself. She folded the dishcloth and hung it over the tap. She was completely still now for a long time, her hands on the edge of the sink, dark thin hair to her shoulder blades. One bare reddened elbow. Then, she turned, stepped in close to him quick as a shadow, and jabbing him in the chest with her finger, she said, You stick to your music, do you hear me?

He shrugged and said, I doubt I'm good enough.

And don't pretend to be thick either, she told him with a final fiercer strike. And now I'm going to bed. My sofa awaits. You can do what you want. There's coffee in the press. And if a certain person happens to come back, well you can explain it to him yourself.

At exactly half one Ellison came out of the bathroom, passed through the kitchen and put his ear to the door of the downstairs room. For a few minutes, he listened. The hinges squeaked as he opened the door and leaned his head and shoulders in. A fire set in the grate. Her dungarees over the fireguard. Her zip up boots. Jumper in a knot on the pouffe. A wall light showed her outline to him on the sofa under a hand-made quilt, her neck stretched into a strange curve on the pillow, her arm twisted behind her back. A white T-shirt. When he spoke to ask if she had called him it was almost a whisper. A long breath left her body through her nose as he sat into an armchair, his shadow crossing her body. One of her feet was visible, the big toe inches only from an illustrated Irish primer stuck down the side of the cushion.

Down on his knees beside the sofa, he stroked her foot with the shadow of his hand. She had ebony gaps between her toes the fingers began to play. Whisking across the range of quilted squares, the shadow strummed its way up her arm. He plucked chords from the long flyaway strings around her face. Her ear was a little harp at the end of the bout of her plump jaw. Against the parted lips, the crooked cipín of his thumb struck and struck. Magically, the quilt began to rise to let him under. Her shins sawing, her knees clashing together. When he saw her eyes open, he smiled and when she screamed and her hand came out from under the pillow with a hammer and swung at him, Ellison fell back on the floor.

He was calling to her now through the letterbox. In between the apologies, he was asking for his suitcase. After a barrage of kicks, she had ushered him out of the house, taking swipes with the hammer. One had caught him on the shoulder. The new letterbox flap was stiff and he had to press hard to see into the hall. She was coming. When the door opened he was in the middle of the street. The dungarees down around her hips, she threw his things at him, his coat, his case, saying, Just you wait till I tell Sandy. And don't think I won't either. I hope he cuts the bucken hands off you. The door slammed and a milk bottle tipped off the step and rolled into the gutter.

A gust of wind blew up the street and right through him like he wasn't there. He could barely get his arm into his coat. He sat on the curb, the case across his knees. The Hillman and the beer kegs were gone and so were the rain dancers from under the lights. A few minutes passed before he noticed a figure at the window of the house opposite. Gathering his stuff, he crossed the street, knocked with his good hand. A bearded man in pyjamas showed him into the hall. Ellison was directed to a stool beside a small glass table on which there was a telephone and a new directory and an egg timer. The bearded man, a dog-end behind his ear, wanted to know if he needed help with a number. Left alone, Felix watched the trickle of sparkling red sand fall faster and faster and become a deluge. He lifted the receiver, did the three long twists.

Guards, he said.

Scissors

Your mother called over to our house one evening looking for you. Her and my ma were talking at the door under my window and it didn't sound friendly. Then I was called down. Nobody had seen you in two days, your mother said, watching for my reaction. She didn't look her usual elegant self. The worry made her seem even whiter and thinner. I told her I hadn't seen you and didn't know where you were and all of a sudden she started shouting at me and calling me a lying wee tramp. My ma stepped in front of me, a day overdue but she wasn't letting your mother away with it. The boys on their bikes out in the green by the bonfire spot could hear the screaming match. When I told her I broke up with you more than a week ago, it just seemed to make it worse, and your mother made a grab for my hair. I had always thought she was so regal and calm. Luckily, your little sister Therese appeared at the gate and begged your mother to come back to the house. And keep going, my ma said, she has a bad mouth on her sometimes, keep going, she said, all the way back up the north where you belong. Your mother stopped at the gate like she had been turned to stone. Poor Therese didn't know what to do. And then your mother turned around very slowly, dramatically, and her arm came up and she pointed at me and said, If me or my husband find out you know where my son is, you've no conception of how sorry you'll be. Mark my words. I had to hold my ma back from waddling after her with the house brush.

On a school morning, she takes the bus all the way into the city centre. In the toilets of Wynn's Hotel, she changes from her uniform into jeans, a Grace Jones T-shirt, puts on some black lipstick and lets her hair down. Normally, she is only ever in the centre at the weekends, and the streets today seem strange to her, empty, peaceful, and some of them are even beautiful in the sunshine, and the buildings are taller too, and prettier. She stands outside at least four of God's houses on the north side, watching the people pass in and out, old women mainly, a man or two, trying to discern if there is any difference in them after a prayer, or lighting a candle, or whatever they do, before she crosses the river, stopping for a moment on Mellows Bridge at the very spot where she had kissed him the first time, the cold stone against her back, the shock on his face sore with acne. You're not ugly, okay, she had said. She is certain she will know the right spot when she sees it, the pillars maybe, tall pale pillars, a heavy door chained open, the tiled porch, and the glimpse of the darkness inside, the single red eyes of the votive lights, and the silence where all the secrets of the city dissolve.

Under his nails were black because he never took his hands out of his pockets. He kept his face hidden under his hair. Under his clothes, his cold skin, always a cold boy. Under the table in the backroom of the barbershop, he said they stored the hair sweepings for an artist woman who made things out of it. A tree. A stool. Rings and bracelets. Every Saturday, under the canopy outside Scully's, she met him on his break. The men knocked out the window at them, trying to embarrass him. All he could talk about was the men and their yarns. He loved it in there behind the steamed-up window, in the smoke and the mirrors, the razors and newspapers, the smell of wet hair under that creepy sallow light. You would believe anything, she used to tease him. The beautiful Teresa Scully, his mother, would only allow him to work there on Saturday. She wanted him to get his education and be something else other than a lousy barber. Robert blamed her for making the family pack up and move down to Dublin, underneath to the Republic. She had forced his father into it, like she had put a spell on him, the witch, he called her when he was drunk. And he loved Clyde more than the rest of them, the man who was only an employee but acted as if he was one of the family, the big brother. Sleazeball, that's what she thought every time she saw him with his black hair and his murky skin and his stories and his clothes and his English accent and his big reggae eyes.

Robert don't-you-ever-call-me-Robbie Scully.

How am I supposed to know what to do? You turn up outside the house in a stolen car and want me to run away with you. You're drunk. Or it might be the hash. And the state of your clothes. It's a good job my parents are out with the boys at the match. Up in my bedroom you're talking gibberish, one minute you're high and shaking the car keys like Jim Morrison doing a rain dance and the next I'm worried you're going to wreck the place in a rage and get me into trouble. And when I say your mother was here looking for you what happens—you try snogging me and groping me. Next you grab a pair of my tights from the radiator and pull them over your head. You put on the Grace Jones album, turn it up loud and sing out the window like you want them to catch you. You weren't even my boyfriend any more. Is that what you wanted, somebody to stop you? I only kept on at you to tell me what the hell was the matter to calm you down.

Ulster. Unicorn. Unification. Uterus. Union. Unadulterated. UK. Uniformity. Unisex. Unit. Unspoken. Uncompleted. Us. Umbrella. Unfaithful. United Ireland.

Shauna, this girl in a school uniform who was kneeling on her bedroom floor, surrounded by pages from the newspapers she'd been snipping the headlines from with the big red kitchen scissors, she said to anybody who might be there, Why did you have to go and tell me for, why, and with a groan she folded over at the waist like it was a sudden cramp and the ends of her hair gave a lash to the paper. Beside her bare knee a photograph of a coffin wrapped in a tricolour, on some kind of bier on a street like her own outside, but on that street they have three men in balaclavas and army jackets with their guns raised, a salute, a volley, and behind them stand an audience of people, women and men, in their ordinary clothes, T-shirts and jeans, arms folded, a thing they see every other day. Again, suddenly, she straightened up, sitting back on her heels and said, Yes and you were wrong about Bobby Sands too because they did let him die, they did. Like it's a proof, held at each end between a finger and thumb painted black, she showed a strip of newspaper headline around the room, displayed it for anything there to see, from the ceiling to the open window and around the walls sagging with

Scissors

posters and back up to the pink tassels of the lampshade, and it read, Bobby Sands. They've forgotten all about your funeral now too because of his, she said, smoothing the strip of paper in her lap, Which I wasn't allowed to go to anyway. Yours, I mean. Not his, obviously. Nobody lit a bonfire on the green when the news went round what happened to you, did they? It's me they blamed for you, not the British. With the scissors she clipped the capital B off the strip, dabbed the nozzle of the glue bottle on the back of it and pressed the letter onto a separate sheet of art paper supported on an album cover on her bedspread, and that now read:

YOUR HUSB

Anonymous.

Not for the first or even the second time that day your mother points to the list of instructions on the fridge door for all eventualities she calls them while she is in the hospital what to do if the electricity goes off or the sink gets blocked or one of the boys goes over the handlebars or there's any strange callers and beside it is the list of things you should already know anyway madam she can't help herself saying stuff like make sure the boys clean their teeth and don't let them curse in this house or spit and warm the teapot before you make tea for your father and let him watch what he wants on the TV and don't tell him where the whiskey is and the boys have to do their homework and give the floor a mop before you go to bed and below the lists is the menu for the day's breakfast lunch dinner and supper when did it begin being called supper so posh now she is planning on calling the new baby Kimberly after a woman who helped her one time in a shopping centre when she got lost as a child but don't tell your father he wants to call her Deborah after his mother's sister he says the one who married the bigamist in Manchester but I think it's more to do with one of those page three girls Kim something or other men are just led around by their

Do you want me to hear your confession or not, young lady?
I told you I don't have a confession.
What is this secret then, this awful secret you've been talking about now for the last quarter of an hour?
It's not my secret.
Is it this barber you mentioned?
I didn't say he was a barber.
Yes, you did.
I didn't mean to.
I haven't got all day, young lady.
Neither do I. I didn't want to go to my local priest because he might guess who I was talking about. So I came in here. What's this chapel called?
Yes, you've said that already. The Church of our Lady of Mount Carmel.
So what if I have? I wish I wasn't here more than you do. I wish I didn't know. I wish I could go back time and not know it. Or just forget like some old person. I only know it anyway because somebody else went and told me. It was his secret. He saw something and it didn't see him. He didn't want to see it either. It just happened to him the way a disaster does to people, like he had been hit by lightening. Like something in the bible. And then he told it to me. Nobody else in the world knows but me.
What did this person see?
What?

What did this boy see?

He's not a boy. He's nearly sixteen. He would have been sixteen next month. He was so shy, Father.

Induce.

Shauna has been in the shop talking to her friend Dolores. Mrs Scully has come in. She has asked for her cigarettes and painkillers. Shauna has tried to hide behind the curtain in to the storeroom but slimeball Joe behind the counter in his greasy blue overalls must have been hoping for some gossip because he has leaned over the tray of stale bakery buns and whispered something and Mrs Scully has turned round in her dramatic way. Dolores has vanished. The woman has walked towards the teenager, gliding, floating, draped in blacks, perfume, and stopped and has held out her beautiful long hands, the palms white as the cameo on her lapel. The teenager now has folded her arms. I'm sorry pet, it wasn't your fault, Teresa Scully has said. God knows what was eating him but it wasn't you that put him behind the wheel of that car. Clyde's car, Shauna has said and the bereaved mother has said, I didn't even know he could drive pet and Shauna has the thought how it's obvious the woman still doesn't suspect.

Aungier Street. There he was when I came out of the chapel into the daylight again. I thought I was hallucinating. Right there on the street, talking to some woman, and looking over her shoulder at me like he knew exactly what I had been in doing, with that grin of his he probably practises in front of the mirror all day in the shop. He gave me a wave to come over. I waved back at him like I hadn't understood. He called my name. I wanted to be sick. The woman he was with who had an umbrella up even though it was a lovely day in May, a parasol, looked at me too but when I went over wasn't it a man in a wig, a canary and mauve silk dress, these gorgeous white sandals, and a lovely smile, you could only tell because of the square jaw and the big feet. Clyde introduced him or her but I didn't really listen to the name and then he made some joke about not taking me for one of the god squad. I said something about a school project, it just came to me. I couldn't look at Clyde, only the other one who complimented me on my Grace Jones T-shirt and wanted to know where I had bought it. I thought it had to be a trick, and even that dopey priest was involved, that everybody already knew. It was awful. Then the other one put their arm around me and told me it was okay, just to have a good cry. Clyde knew, I swear. He knew the minute he clapped eyes on me between the two gold saints at the door.

H eat from the bonfire on the green that night Bobby Sands died nearly melted the posters on her wall. And the spark burns on the carpet and the smoke smell in her pillow. I told you to shut those windows didn't I bloody tell you to shut every window in the house. Yes daddy.

O

Maybe she did drive him to it. Maybe if she hadn't finished with him he would be alive today. Maybe she should have let him take off her knickers that night, maybe that would have calmed him down. Maybe she shouldn't have listened. Maybe believing him right away was stupid, maybe it was all a lie, a nightmare in his mind, a hallucination, maybe she's not as brainy as she likes to think. Maybe she shouldn't have let him drive away again in Clyde's car. Maybe when she realised that his little sister Therese had seen them she shouldn't have begged her not to tell her parents or threatened to make her brothers chase her on their bikes. Maybe she should be making an anonymous message for Mr Scully instead. *I no WE know what you do in back room in shop. WANT £100 no £500 or ELSE. Leave money in ladies wynns hotel.*

Only with you, written on the back of the Grace Jones album brought back from a trip to London with Mr Scully and the other one Clyde and a T-shirt also from a Carnaby Street shop. Up full blast the last night in her bedroom, strolling around her bed with a pair of her tights over his head, Trip the light fantastic Shauna, walking, just walking in the rain. His favourite song. He wanted to call his own band The Dark Horses. You in a band? Dream on. The Shy Boys you should call yourselves.

And can you explain something else to me, Shauna? asked Clyde, lying across the steering wheel, his chin on his hands, bringing to an end a long silence during which they both seemed to be watching a gang of the boys striving to bring the bonfire back to life in the middle of the green, some of them smashing up wooden crates and some of them on their hunkers in the ring of grey ash blowing through their fists on the embers. She didn't answer him. His electric blue shirt was stretched tight across his back and there was a sweat stain under his arm. I keep wondering, in fact, it's annoying the proverbial out of me, how and where young Robert got his hands on my keys before he went for his wild child's ride in my motor. How should I know? she said before she could stop herself; she had promised herself not to say a word to him when the car slowed down on the street as she was walking to the shop, and followed along beside her until she agreed to get in; not a single word would she say. And she was right too because immediately she spoke he sat back in the seat and turned his puffy grinning face towards her like he had won something. Exactly, he said, and she could taste the breath from his mouth, a banana flavour to it. How should you know? That he would have had to have lifted them from the shop, from the shelf behind the counter where I keep them, where they always are. How would you know that? He reached for his box of cigarettes on the dashboard and offered her one. She shook her head. He used a brass lighter with a black star on it. Do you like the new wheels? he asked. It's only second hand, she said and he laughed and said, I miss the old banger. Gave Robert a few lessons in her on the q.t. His father would never have the patience for it. Now don't tell go telling anybody that. Especially not his mother. Teresa. Not right now anyway. The woman is twisting in her skin with grief. Some people are too fragile for this world. Too highly strung. Not like us hard cases, eh, born to survive. Shauna shrugged. Clyde blew some cigarette smoke out the sunroof and said, You see, and this is the crux of the dilemma for me, there's no other explanation for how Robert could have taken my keys unless he was in the shop that evening. Out in the green, a man had appeared and seemed to be arguing with the boys, chasing them away from the fire. Her two brothers were on their bikes doing circles and giving the man the fingers. Was he in the shop do you know, Shauna? Clyde was asking. She could smell aftershave suddenly. His eyes may as well have been made out of the same stuff as the steering wheel, shiny and sticky and cold. If you don't answer me Shauna, he said, I'll have to take it as a yes. Did he tell you he was in the shop that evening? He must have called in without warning to see his father, did he? A surprise visit. Was that what happened do you think? With a black fingernail Shauna picked at the bits of hard glue on the knuckle of her thumb. Clyde blew some more smoke out the sunroof and said, So I'm thinking then, Robert turned up in the shop this particular evening and the door must have been left open and something pretty bad must have happened inside to make him take my keys wouldn't you say, isn't that a fair enough guess, something pretty far out that made him angry enough to steal my car?

Shush of the street past midnight. Scurry like a shadow thing. Mister dream all you want. Cause you can't stop the postman coming. Not him. Not her. You can't stop the postman. Shush tutti-frutti. Shush tutti-frutti. Shush tutti-frutti

Kimberly was born with a hair lip. She was lying in a plastic cot on wheels at the side of your mother's bed, her little fists each side of her head, like she was falling, so peacefully falling. Lots of little spots on her red cheeks and a hairline which starts at her eyebrows. Your mother says your father's mother had one too, the cleft palate, your granny that nobody talks about, another secret. The doctors can fix it easily these days, she says, reading her congratulations cards. The boys are delighted their new little sister is a monster. Out of the blue, your father grabs you in a bear hug and says, Robert was a decent lad. I should have gone easier on the pair of you.

Crafty callous lying sneaking stinking pig of a creep he saw you in there the two of you in the back room yes Robert saw it the two of you he told me his own father and you and what you were doing and Mrs Scully's going to find out she is no matter what you

Love bites. Who could give the best one. Who could leave the biggest, darkest mark. She had them on her belly and up her back, eighteen she counted in front of the mirror one night, unable to see all of them herself. He was mad for them. Sucking away and scratching with his teeth but the trick was to stop before the blood seeped through the skin. The last of them on the inside of her thigh is now like a small blue island in a creamy ocean seen from miles and miles above.

Your mother calls you into her bedroom to sit beside her on the quilt as she gives Kimberly Yasmin Quinn a feed. Who was Shauna? you ask. Shauna it turns out is absolutely nobody. You were nearly called Bernadette until your mother heard the name in the hospital just after you were born and changed her mind.

Dew falling at dawn on a black-lipped girl and hissing— listen—very quietly on the ashes of a bonfire in the green at the heart of a housing estate.

End of fucken story, that's what your father said to me on the path. You're off the hook so away home with you. And he said it gently like he wasn't even an iota surprised to see me there on your path in the middle of the night. He had a suitcase with him, a big beige coloured one. I had the white envelope in my hand. The boot of the car wouldn't open so he put the suitcase in the back seat. His movements were sad. Every sound was sad, even the birds who seemed to be waking up together and singing as he looked at your house, at the windows, and then at me. You beat me to it, I said and regretted it. I don't know what I mean half the time. He found it funny though. He laughed and that sounded sad also on the empty street. Then do you know what he said? Or maybe you already do, you lot, the spirits or ghosts or whatever you call yourselves? Or maybe you are reincarnated already and you're an eagle somewhere in Donegal like you wanted. Or a flea on a camel in Egypt. Or a starving baby in a hut in Africa. Remember the argument we had about it and you wouldn't talk to me for a week because I thought I was becoming an atheist. The shock on your face was the same when I finished with you outside the chippie. You had too many shocks. And that's what your father said to me, he laughed about him beating me to it and then he went, I was planning to tell him in London there when we were over. But he was having too good a time. He spat on the road. I didn't believe him for a second and I told him. We'll never know, he said and then he asked me to keep an eye on Therese for him, she's nearly as mad about you as he was, he said, and got into the car and drove away, laughing or crying, who knows. I stood there for another while wondering whether to knock to check your mother was okay and little Therese but I eventually wised up, sometimes I'm too full of my own self-importance as my ma would say. I went back towards our house. It was getting light fast. Out on the green where the bonfire had been, I saw a curl of smoke rising like a ribbon, a long silky white ribbon slowly turning and twisting, like it was a dance to the slowest possible music. As I walked across the grass towards it I realised I was soaked with dew. The lovely elegant ribbon of smoke was coming out of this one red spot in the ash so what I did Robert was tear up the envelope there and then and watched the paper catch.

Ceremony

Dress it up whatever you want, go all Eastern or Muslim, go fucken quantum or dance around with the pagans in the forest, but it's still bloody terrible what can befall people who don't deserve it, I was saying to Siofra one evening back in ours after work. This guy Ringo had rung me during the day and given me some perverse news.

There's no point worrying about the future, Siofra said, throwing me a quick scolding look over her shoulder. She was chopping vegetables for another of her high-fibre soups. When she moved in a few months back, the first thing she unpacked was her soup pot; it was a magical pot blackened by a thousand fires and cured hangovers and colds and soothed all sorts of modern anxieties. These soups, and fruit and seeds and gallons of water had kept this girl alive in the city until the early morning on Capel Street when our paths had crossed. She was young and vegetarian and unemployed.

I poured us some more of the wine, said, I'm actually in a state of shock. It's just fucked up. You try to live the best way you can, you try to make a life for yourself, pay the bills, don't ask for too much and your fucken reward is what? There's no fucken justice. There's none fucken left. The cupboard is empty. We're like junkies after our stash is gone.

Is your stomach any better, babe?

My bowels were clogged up again; it was obviously connected to the painkillers for my shoulder; I was popping my way through a pack and more a day. The nausea had lifted since I got that call at work, I told her.

Poor Ringo, she said, and then shrieked and started hopping around on the kitchen tiles because a stray bit of carrot peel had landed on her silvered toes; she was trying to shake it off like it was a slug or something disgusting. Siofra liked to exist barefoot when indoors.

I waited for the drama to pass, said, Poor Ringo, why? Poor bloody Danielle more like. She's the one suffering here.

But I've never met Danielle.

What the hell had that got to do with it? One time only we had run into Ringo together on the street, the big junction at Fenian Street; a brief minute or two nodding along to his pompous crap from the bar of his new bicycle, and now these two were on sympathetic terms and humanity was saved. Ringo was involved with Danielle, who was an old ex of mine.

Anyway, I said, I'll have to show my face at this thing. I can't get fucken out of it, can I really?

Siofra put the spark gun to the gas. The coven of thin blue flames, tipped with orange, roared in our small kitchen. The darkness was earlier every evening now. She scraped the vegetable shavings from the chopping board into the bin, left a trail behind her on the floor. I was hit again by flashes of the first night she came home with me; only twenty-three candles to her name, a low heavy fringe the same moist brown as her wide-set eyes, the washed-out underwear and the jolt when my hand touched a hairless pussy.

I'll have to put in an appearance, I said.

She stopped, tilted her face, squinting: You're actually thinking of going?

They bloody asked me, Siofra.

After what happened? I mean, after how much they hurt you?

Choking on the wine, I said, that's years ago. Ancient history now, sure. You have to let things go or they'll kill you. You move on and grow. The past can become a cage if you let it, Siofra. One day you'll see what I mean. She looked at me sceptically, like I was exaggerating. What was I supposed to say to him then? No, thanks, I don't want to take part in your ridiculous love-in healing session for Danielle. And now there's this new baby. Listen: you don't have to come if that's what you're worried about.

She choose not to react, went back to her soup. I began to tell her more about Ringo's surprise call, how his parting shot was that he hoped I was mature enough to appreciate how important this event was for Danielle. Like, what the fuck was he insinuating?

Of course you are, babe. I'm sure he knows that deep down.

Too bloody right I can appreciate it. And so what did I say back to him? Ringo, I've no hatchet to bury, as you well know. I'm an unarmed man.

I'm coming with you, Siofra announced.

I won't have seen many of these people in years, you know. I'm not going to paint a pretty picture for you. It could be tricky.

You always think the worst of people, she said, then added, dreamily, I've never been to a christening.

It's not a bloody christening. It's a naming ceremony. They're going all non-denominational and secular with it. And that's Ringo's doing. They look down their noses at centuries and centuries of faith. Casting out the demon isn't necessary any more. It isn't fucken trendy any more. Ringo is having his way here.

I totally agree with him, she said.

Do you now? But her phone kicked off, and, as usual with

Siofra, the thing had nearly rung out before she found it, under a tea towel this time. Hearing her speak in Irish meant her mother was on the other end. Her parents weren't happy to hear that she had moved in with the likes of me. I went out to the back garden with my drink to let them at it.

Danielle and myself lived the suburban life for nearly eight years in a house in Raheny. Her parents and two brothers had houses nearby, and every evening one or more of them would come tapping at the front window. I used to wonder if they were secretly disappointed Danielle had shacked up with a man with no family to his name, nobody to bring to the party. They are a tight-knit crowd, the Nixons. The lot of us went to mass together every Sunday on the Howth Road. Even if Danielle wimped out, I'd join the rest of them in the pews. We all went on holiday together one time, to a big campsite in the south of France. I used to get on well with the youngest brother, a quiet, gentle guy called Philip; he often dropped in to my work on a Saturday afternoon, read the papers and sat around listening to the punters' stories in the one and only Atlas Barber Shop. I'd say it hit the Nixons as bad as it did me when Danielle and myself broke up. I took it hard, they say; even God must have heard about the state of me and had a peep down at the antics.

Sometimes you are given the chance to save the world, to carry the message to the king, to kill the monster. Then you wake up and try to go to work, and you realise the dream isn't over yet; it is spreading out across the city from the bell ringing in your soul. Some people hear it. They follow you, gather outside your place of work, peering in, waiting to hear your plan. The people you really need to explain it to, the dangerous bells, pass you by like you never existed, and the faces you'd be happy never to see again come frothing and spewing and all stuck together around every corner—that's what Dublin became in the aftermath. Not once did I run into

Danielle in the years after we split. Ringo, however, seemed to be enjoying the sound of his own voice in the centre of every room I passed through, both his paws reaching out for an extra-long firm shake of mine. A man a few years older than me, near the fifty mark anyway, who, despite the belly, still stuffed himself into his old punk T-shirts, a greying brush cut with a receding hairline, divorced from an old work colleague of Danielle's, some kind of engineer and a self-appointed atheist intellectual from near the castle at Rathfarnham. And before he released his overeager double grip, the man would already be expounding to me about the perfection of Danielle Nixon, what she was doing and thinking, how she'd quit another job, had a new hairdo, bought a new bed, the Nixon family update, then, eventually, that she was pregnant, a lot of stuff I didn't need to hear, and he shouldn't have been telling me.

When I heard news she had a baby girl, I sent a text to Danielle to say congratulations, heard nothing back, and thought no more about it. I wondered if it would have her mother's wild corkscrew hair, the big feet and problems with her thyroid gland. Maybe, one day, walking along a Dublin street, I'd spot Danielle coming straight towards me, pushing the pram, and maybe we'd be able to talk civilly together, and let what happened drop away into the past like a penny down a well. So, it was a shock to hear from Ringo on the phone that she was suffering with post-natal depression. Even so, he told me, they were forging ahead with the naming ceremony for the child, the idea being that Danielle might benefit from a day surrounded by all the people who loved her.

We were out in the back garden, Siofra and myself, after she was done arguing with her mother. The soup had been abandoned. It didn't matter to me; I had no appetite for anything other than the white wine and the chance to sit outside on maybe one of the last decent evenings of the year, enjoying our little terraced house in Kilmainham, with its strip of neglected garden about the length of a bowling lane, my old Vespa rusting in the ivy, and the prospect of bed later with my soft, enthusiastic, young girlfriend. I was pretty happy to stay in these days, just Siofra with her joints and me with a drink, but felt I had to hide that fact from her in case it led to secret thoughts on her part that I was becoming lazy and vague.

She was wound up so tight after the row with her mother there were tears in her eyes. She was too young to be in a relationship with someone my age, the mother and father, two Irish teachers who had met in the Connemara Gaeltacht, had always advised her, and yet they were proud of how they had managed to tolerate the relationship, giving her space to find herself, hoping and praying meanwhile that it would fizzle out quickly. I told Siofra at the time that there was no need to tell them anything had changed, but she couldn't be stopped; she couldn't bear to lie to them, she said. Now they were worried sick by the knowledge that their daughter was a full-time captive in my filthy lair. The phone battle went on every day with the same intensity and the same outcome, which was Siofra ranting about the boredom of her youth on the outskirts of Monaghan.

This night, it was a yarn about a family day trip to Dublin when Siofra was fifteen or so—if they had trooped down Capel Street together she might have seen me at work through the window of Atlas Barber's. The reason for this expedition was the fat furry mole on her mother's cheek and the appointment she had that day to have the thing removed after years of gentle persuasion and saving. The Ó Fiaich family had lunch somewhere, probably the safe bet of the old Bewley's on Westmoreland Street. Towards the end of the meal, the mother went off to the toilet. The minutes passed, the coals burned in the Victorian fireplace, someone famous went by, and Mrs Ó

Fiaich had still not returned. Siofra went to find her. No sign. The woman had done a runner. She couldn't go through with the operation. They wandered the crude smeared streets of Dublin, searching for their mam. It got dark. They went back to the car; silently, the windows steaming over, they waited.

It's not funny, Siofra said, holding out her glass for more wine. My father just sat there. He didn't know what to do. It was like he had already given up. It was disgusting. So, I jumped out of the car, and there was, like, a guard, who happened to be right there; I almost knocked him over. She switched her glass to the other hand and dabbed at her lips with her fingertips cold from the wine. Guess where they found her... No, don't. That big cathedral in town, Christ Church?

As the sound of an ambulance siren came closer, she stared upwards at the sky, and I took the opportunity to gloat over her profile, the strong jaw and stretched throat, the lily and the rose at war in her pigment. The siren stopped suddenly, probably at the gates of the hospital. Maybe, Siofra said softly, musing, maybe they are only trying to be nice, Ringo I mean, and they're expecting you to offer a polite excuse. You know, for not attending? A white lie? She said there was a great phrase in Irish for it, wanted me to repeat it after her.

I wouldn't; instead, and maybe I was annoyed because the thought had already crossed my mind, I said, now who's the paranoid one?

I have a past too, you know, she snapped back at me. I've been hurt too, you know.

I wasn't sure what was bugging her. This isn't about you, I said. This is about Danielle, the woman I spent most of my thirties with. The woman who now has post-natal depression. Can you imagine for a minute what that must be like? She can't even be in the same room as her own baby.

I know it must be horrible, but it's not your concern any

more. Aren't you always saying you wish Ringo wouldn't try to be so friendly all the time with you? She seemed to freeze for a moment, her breath caught, like she had been pricked by an insect, then said, crossly, when Simon nearly died in London I didn't go rushing over to him, did I? I couldn't even talk about it to you because you got so angry.

That's totally fucken different, I said.

He was my first love. And stop shouting at me.

You want to hear me shouting?

It's the truth.

You wanted to borrow the money from me, that's the real truth, isn't it? You wanted to ask me for the money to go to London, but you didn't have the guts.

Her face emptied of blood and seemed to pull me along with it. I was right on the brink of telling her a few more home truths to have done with it entirely, with myself, with trying to keep included day after day, with the bluff of survival, with the clear sight of seeing the two of us sitting way down below on that scratch of turf. I did the control routine, the breathing, brought myself down to ground level again, focused on the grass blade by blade, my moped, the soft wooden table between us and the seasons it had endured, tried to remember the good times. The threat got squashed. I'm sorry, I said, with no idea how long I'd been in a struggle with myself. Maybe you're right. I should avoid the whole fucken thing. Fuck them. What do they need me for anyway?

Siofra sprang out of her chair and dropped to her knees beside me, took my hand, always the dramatic gesture with her. No, you should go, I'm being… I don't know what's wrong with me.

I don't want to feel like a coward or something. I'm not running away from any bastard on earth.

You're not a coward, she said, her wild eyes offered up to me completely. We'll both go. Together.

Only if you buy the present for the kid, I said for a joke. She nodded, but she probably didn't hear a word: she had gone very serious, intense. Let me make it up to you, she said, and her eyes moved down my face and down my body to my belt. She even tried to lick her lips. She was getting better and better at that.

For the next week, hunting the perfect gift, Siofra ran all over town. She would ring me at work with, I'm in Blanchardstown, I'm on Clanbrassil Street, I'm out in Dundrum, wanting my opinion on some toy or little hat or whatever. Every day she came back empty-handed, defeated, hating herself; she couldn't make up her mind, she said, she was useless, so immature. I lost patience with her a few times, told her neither of us were going anywhere, it was too much hassle. I meant it too. But pretty soon, I'd start to worry I was hiding from something, that people would be thinking I hadn't really got over what had happened, and I couldn't handle that idea. I was trying to cut back on the painkillers as well. Years of stooping over punters' necks, years of scissors and combs and buzzing electric razors was the probable cause. It must be my brain is wrecked too after the years of listening to the opinions and bizarre lies of the men of Dublin.

We have this saying at work: other than behind the curtain of the voting booth, a man is at his most conservative up on the stirrups of the barber's chair. Danielle's brother, Philip, came in with his shyness this one morning just after I had opened up. He took the middle throne. We did our spiel about Danielle, of course, how bad it must be for her, and who else might be attending the ceremony in Wicklow the next day, but I had the sense he was agitated and had more on his mind than his sister and babies. Taking a few inches off his wiry Nixon hair, I tried to draw him out of himself with a story about a regular customer, a married man, five kids reared, who on the first day he was making use of his free travel pass had fallen head over heels in love with a young gay lad on the train to Galway. Philip's response was to blush right down to his large Adam's apple and confess that he was bored to death of his civil-service job; he had reached a decision to pack it in and start his own landscape-gardening business before it was too late. He got a hold of my eyes in the mirror as if my advice was desperately important to him; he was letting me in on the dream that had taken shape inside him, which was now hungry for a bigger field of play—he had found his dream that would destroy him whether he made it happen or not. Clumsy, weak, painfully shy, Philip, the landscape gardener; a wheelbarrow and a spirit level, a skivvy for the decadent— it was so preposterous it had be true. The road less travelled is empty for a reason, was the best I could do, and it seemed to hit the spot, because he smiled with his eyes shut the way his big sister did. It was a nice moment between us, which the clatter of the cowbell above the shop door brought to an end. I turned to see who had come in, and there was this tall, middle-aged woman with a badly cut bob stepping onto the green and black tiles. Good day, she said in Irish, and then in English, I'm looking for Nathaniel McWilliamson.

He's not working today, I replied, before the ugly sound of my full name had stopped bouncing around the mirrors and walls. The woman muttered to herself, perhaps repeating what I had said. The mole was on her left cheek, near the crease of the nostril. No, he's not on today, I went on, the way you might do to the infirm. These little pouches at each corner of her mouth swelled and deflated like gills. From her neck to her ankles, she was concealed inside a puffy mustard-coloured overcoat, and the laces on her trainers didn't match. He mightn't be working tomorrow either, I continued. The lucky bastard won the Lotto. Maybe you'll catch him at the airport, love. Do you want to leave a message for him in case he drops in to rub our noses in it? Her mouth puckered, and

I may have noticed a slight tightening of the eyes before she announced in Irish, I shall return, or something like that. She paused in the doorway, thought better of it maybe, stepped onto the pavement and turned left towards the river. Philip, whose presence I had forgotten, lowered his eyes when I turned back to our reflections in the mirror.

    After work, I went out for a few pints. I was belching gas from the compost heap in my guts. I didn't like what I had done, but that didn't stop me trying to justify it to myself. What the hell did Siofra's mother want with me anyway, coming into my place of work, in her Dalek's puffa habit? To plead with me to take my grim arthritic hands off her meaty sweaty daughter? And then there was the prospect of seeing Danielle and the swarm of mild-mannered ghosts the next day. By the time I got home, after two on the clock, I had made up my mind they would have to do without me in their circle of love, they could bloody find somebody else to gape at. Also, I was all set to come clean with Siofra about her mother, deny I knew who the woman was at the time, say it was a joke that had got out of hand, tell her anything, get it out in the open, stop the rot—but only after I had plucked the clothes off her back and pressed and shaped her body under mine like it was my own imprint.

Far below, propelled by some mysterious urge, a single drop of blood moves silently along the crust of an endless, winding black scar. That was us, Siofra and me, down there trying to make up lost time as we drove across Wicklow the following day. The tarmac was the only human route through this high bogland of heather and stone and monster ferns. I had Siofra's purple shawl over my shoulders against the cold; even my hands on the wheel were aching. We didn't seem to have a word to say to each other. Neither of us were in the mood for music either. I accidentally let one off inside the car, a pure stinker, and Siofra pressed the window down, stuck her head out into the ballistic wind. Hours of work had gone into her hair and face, and now she didn't seem to care. I caught myself checking her skin for any new marks, scratches or bruises on her neck or upper arms. She sat back inside, blinking her eyes like a child after a rollercoaster ride. Maybe we should break up, she said, like it was one word. What are you even doing with me? I can't manage a simple thing like buying a little baby a present. I told her it didn't matter what you bought for them, that she was making too big a deal out of it, and she asked me why I hadn't bought the bloody present then.

To keep the peace, I agreed it should have been me. Arriving home the previous night, before I had my jacket off, a very distraught Siofra announced she had failed to get a gift for the kid, she had been to every shop in Dublin but just hadn't been able to make up her mind. It didn't matter; it shouldn't have mattered, but I still lost my temper anyway. Siofra fled the house, returned after a few minutes, and we did some talking, and calm was restored. She showed me what she was planning to wear, danced barefoot around the room for me in her short green dress with nothing else underneath. I grabbed her, forgot everything I had planned to say, and a lot more.

Under a sky of jammed-up cloud, the road took a dive down from the hills and miraculously straightened out across the bottom of a valley. Our little red blob of blood trickled along faster. I didn't like the idea of arriving late, attracting attention to ourselves. As if she was reading my thoughts, Siofra said, I tried to wake you. I tried to wake you three times. You couldn't wake up. I know how nervous you are and on edge about today and seeing all those people again, I really do, but don't take it out on me.

She had kept away at a safe distance, over by the bedroom door, while she called my name a few times early that morning, and I hadn't moved. I heard her voice each time, knew she was there, and couldn't find the will to lift my head from the pillow or show her any sign of life. I had a cruel hollow feeling in my chest, that sourness you can taste after a big row, after the tongue has nearly torn out its root and your eyes are sore with what you've seen. I knew it well enough by now to be sure it wasn't a hangover or the constipation. I'd stayed up after Siofra went to bed, doing nothing, drinking a bit more. She must have come down to me later on, maybe tried to get me to come to bed. I couldn't remember what had happened, but I could guess I had gone too far, crossed a sacred line. That morning, the three times she tried to wake me up, afraid to lay a hand on me, my name in her mouth was barely more than a hint, a little question to see if it was really me under the duvet.

The first drops to hit the window were thick and distinct enough to have their own names. Up ahead I saw there was room enough at the start of a hiking trail to pull the car in. Siofra said, rapidly, I had this terrible dream last night about my soup pot. It was so disgusting. What are dreams really? I had the impression she was only talking to keep me away from her, like she thought I was after a bit of dogging. Listen to me, I said. That's when I told her about the unbalanced phase after the split with Danielle, how she took a barring order out against me, how there was a voice in my head with a message from someone who knew the son of God, how I woke up during a bed bath in a state-of-the-art mental ward.

We were over an hour late by the time we found the right hotel and pulled into the car park. Siofra had jumped out of the car before I turned the engine off; I watched her staggering in heels across the gravel, the shawl over the head. I took a minute to clear the gas out of me. A tiny Brazilian girl showed us to the hotel's back entrance and pointed to a paved path running downhill towards a line of old sycamores. No one had bloody bothered to tell me the ceremony was taking place outside; we weren't dressed for the weather. A few metres down the path, we saw people coming towards us the other way, about thirty of them in small groups, children and adults in bright raincoats and wellies. At the front were Danielle's parents, the mother in a wheelchair and a baby in her lap wrapped in a white blanket, the eldest Nixon son sheltering them with an umbrella. I stepped onto the grass to let them pass, and Siofra did exactly the same, stood by my shoulder with her hands joined under her chin like she was at a tear jerker. I doled out the nods to every familiar face, and a few were returned, just about enough. Danielle, as she passed, seemed to be in a world of her own inside the hood of her coat, surrounded by a chorus of ecstatic women. More people trooped by us. Finally, at the very back of the procession, there was Ringo in a pair of red brothel creepers and a fisherman's waterproof cape. He approached us, took both our hands wordlessly, too full of emotion to speak supposedly, and, after he had looked up and felt the succour of the rain on his face for far too long, asked Siofra, did he manage to get you both lost? Shame about the weather, I said. Nothing, absolutely nothing, could spoil this day, he said, and put his arm around Siofra and guided her ahead of me back up the path into the hotel.

I followed them, slowly, through an empty bar into a reception room. The next act was already under way; at the long white-draped tables, the different family units were feasting en masse in a steamy incense of gravy and stuffing. I spotted Danielle at the main table; she was staring into space, her back as straight as ever, but her hair was shorter and a harsh red colour. I felt stranded, wrong, an extra thumb; I went to find a toilet, sat in a cubicle for a longish time without any success. I came back to the reception room. The feeding had eased. Kids flew deliberately against the windows. Siofra waved at me to join her table, but it was made up of lads I'd probably known before they were legal. Danielle was staring in my direction. I waved; the stare didn't change. She looked ten years older than her thirty-seven winters. Ringo was showing off the baby. I'd never liked him, right from the first time I met him, when he was going through that divorce from Danielle's friend. You did the right thing, this guy Ray said to me, with a dessert in each hand. An Armagh man, he was married to another friend of Danielle's. We used to know each other well, head out for a few pints together without the women. Maybe, I said. Fair play to you, he said. We looked around the room. Philip received the baby from Ringo. Terrible about Danielle though, Ray said. I followed his gaze and saw her beside her mother now. I better get these back or there'll be murder, he said, waving the desserts. Good seeing you, I said. He came back and said, I never felt right about what happened, just so you know. You were in a bad way, and I should have stepped up. I shrugged it off. Siofra was coming toward us, tottering in her heels. He gave me a dirty wink on the sly. Catch you inside for a pint in a while, he said and returned to his family. Siofra threw her arms around me extravagantly, tried to kiss me, but I leaned my head back. She gave me the what's-wrong-now look. There were a lot of possible answers to that. I don't feel well, I said.

I got to sit alone with Danielle at the end of a table while the dishes were being cleared away. A gang of her protectors stood at the other end: Ringo, the elder Nixon brother who was in the army, other men I used to know. Siofra was probably outside smoking with her peers or arguing with her mother. Hello Danielle, it's good to see you, I said, not knowing what to do with my hands, and she replied with a sound blown from between her lips, which I took to mean, don't be fucken ridiculous, look at the state of me. I grabbed a seat. Up close, her hair, which I used to slag off as an Afro, was a weird metallic red, her lips were chapped, and her eyes almost black and sealed over, maybe to do with medication. Even so, her cleavage was on full display. Congratulations, it's what you always wanted, Ellie is a great name for her, I said. Danielle stroked the knot she had made in her napkin. Some kid must have taken a bad spill because there was inconsolable screaming for the next few minutes.

My eyes moved from stain to stain on the tablecloth, and every time I braved glancing at her, she was staring at me with those unholy blind eyes. Philip had joined the wise men at the top of the table, his tie loosened under the inflamed Adam's apple, avoiding my eye. Ringo rang me and asked me to come, I said, in the hope of a sign Danielle wanted me there. I really needed to know she hadn't been forced into it. I needed to know what I was doing there as well. There's no hard feelings here, Danielle, I said. I've moved on. If that's of any use. Forgive yourself.

Nothing happened on her face, and her voice was monotone as she said, are you for fucken real?

Maybe that came out wrong, I said.

You want to forgive me?

You're taking me up wrong.

Am I? Her eyes moved in close, and her hand touched mine under the table. I knew you'd come, she said. You were always a glutton for punishment.

I wasn't sure you'd be too happy to see me.

I couldn't tell you who's actually here or not, she said, removing her hand and gazing around the room and then up at the ceiling. I saw my granny earlier, and she died when I was three. You know how she died? A thing fell on her. What's the godforsaken word for it again? One of those things, she said, pointing at the ceiling. Yes, a roof. An ordinary roof fell on her and crushed her to death. There's not a mark on her though, which makes you wonder. Anyway, you could always have proved me wrong and not come.

Maybe I didn't.

Like the memory had come alive again, she gasped and said, You with your petrol can thingy. Threatening to set yourself on fire. Outside my house. There's a word for it, isn't there? You still reek of it. She leaned in closer, more of her breasts on show, and smiling, asked me, Would you have done it?

I wasn't too well, I said.

Would you have done it? Tell me.

She wasn't having me on either; she wanted an answer and the lewd glint in her eye told me it had to be the right one. In my head, I heard a voice saying, this isn't really Danielle, something else is here hungry for knowledge most foul.

Would you, Nathan?

I did, I confessed to her. Yes, sometimes I think I did it and—

Danielle sneered in my face, sat back, folded her arms and said, I heard you won the Lotto.

Nabbed, I hung my head. For some stupid reason, I suppose I'd been hoping Philip might have done me a favour and kept the sorry tale of the visitor to the shop to himself like he seemed to do with everything else. Danielle didn't like lies; even when she started fucking Ringo, she would come home and tell me. I reminded myself she was on meds, wasn't responsible for what she was saying. You must be exhausted, I said. You don't have to be here, you know.

Ringo, come here, she called to the other end. Come here quick.

I waited for whatever was going to happen like it had happened before, again and again, and asked myself why I was still no nearer learning what I had to grasp to make this the last time. Ringo stood behind her chair, put his hands on her shoulders. Nat is here to forgive me, she said. Isn't that nice of him?

He's a saint, said Ringo.

And you're a fat pompous bastard, I said, jumping out of the chair. She should be at home fucken resting or something, not here in the middle of this farce.

A saint with a temper, Ringo said.

I had landed a few on him years ago outside Danielle's, and he drove straight to the Guards to make a complaint. He had no witnesses, but they gave me a warning. Maybe that was it, where I had lost myself; I had missed my one big chance, my true moment, and I would have to pay for it for ever. I couldn't tell how many might be watching us this time in the reception room. A counsellor once told me I had a problem letting my anger out as if the mayhem would burn itself out fast like a scrap in a pub and everybody would go home to the safety of their beds. His arms open wide for me, Ringo was coming towards me like he was walking on the water. Let's not do anything to ruin this special day, he said. Danielle just stared up at me, cryptically; I didn't know what she wanted me to do, what she hoped would happen. Then I heard Siofra sing my name; it distracted me, this image of her running barefoot through the maze of tables across the reception room. Before I could stop him, Ringo took me into his arms like he was saving me from the deep, and a blast of fumes got expelled from my arse for all to hear.

A while later, most people were in the hotel bar. Things had calmed down. If something had needed to happen, it was over with now, and out of the way. People seemed more relaxed as if they were backstage after the show. Anybody who wasn't driving was enjoying the free tab. I stuck to the weak coffee. There was a game on the big screen so you could stand by yourself and act absorbed in the action if you needed a break from the banter. The bar area's French doors banged repeatedly in the wind and with the comings and goings of the kids with armfuls of flowers and twigs and feathers like they were building a wacky new creature in secret in another room.

Every now and again, there would be a song in the corner, and a round of applause. Siofra and another girl brought the baby for me to see and then rushed off to change its nappy, the lucky thing. Ray stood with me for a while, reminiscing about our nights on the pull in town, then Philip and his elderly father, who shook my hand; one by one, most of the old faces from Raheny found their way into my orbit and we exchanged a few good-natured words. When the soccer finished, I disappeared to the toilet, one far away from the children on the other side of the hotel, near the pool. It was another fruitless session. On the way back, through a deep circular window, I watched a man who was missing a hand bless himself with the stump and disappear into the brimming pool.

It was a very special moment, Ringo was telling my girlfriend at the table where I'd been sitting. You would have appreciated it I think, Siofra. You know, there's a pagan stone at the end of the path out there? Yes, well, that's where we all gathered. Now, I don't normally tend towards the superstitious—opium for the people, yes, of course, but this little island of ours is historically very prone to mass hallucination and groupthink for reasons we should leave for another time—but the place down there definitely has a power of its own. So, there we all are by this ancient stone, I have my speech memorised, and everybody is waiting, everybody who matters in my life, when what I can only describe as a kind of current of warm energy rises up through the ground into my feet and rushes up my body and wipes every word right out of mind, every single word. I was a blank slate, Siofra. A tabula rasa; you understand what I'm saying. Siofra gave him the Irish translation, which impressed him no end. So what else could I do but speak from the heart? And that's what I did. Simple, truthful, spontaneous words. Just let it flow. Have you read Walt Whitman? Of course you have. What a great man. A visionary. I don't know the words or the facility to describe what happened out there, but whatever it was that flowed up through me was as real to me as the love I feel for that beautiful new citizen of the world over there.

Thank fuck Ray appeared just then with Philip and two other men, barged in with, We are discussing the pros and cons of barbershops.

We get plenty of cons on Capel Street, I said. They come in for a trim before they head to the courts to hear their destiny.

Siofra put in with, Nathan is in constant pain in his elbows and his shoulder especially. It's repetitive strain injury, but he won't listen to me. He won't talk to a doctor.

I gave her a look to keep it to herself, but she didn't catch it.

Who's the most famous person that's been in? Ray went for the comedy as usual. Somebody interesting now. Give us an aul story there, Nats.

What's that actor's name you told me about? Siofra said, excitedly. Tell them that story about you and him. Was he Canadian? They went on a four-day bender. He was really famous.

He used to be an actor, I said. He gave it up. They pressured me for more, but I wasn't for telling. What happens on Capel Street stays on Capel Street, I said.

Tell them about the man who pretends he's a detective then, said Siofra.

Why is it so tempting to tell the biggest lies in a barbershop, Ringo couldn't resist wondering aloud. When I lived in London, I had my local barber convinced I was a chauffeur for The Clash. He was a big fan. He would swear on his mother's life he wouldn't tell anybody the stories I was spinning him about nights after the gigs. It got completely out of control. Eventually, I got so sick at myself I had to move out of the area.

I was about to tell him I didn't believe a word of that, only Siofra raised her voice again, her hands joined, to ask, Please? Just for me? It's so funny. Tell them about the man who wants to be a detective. She looked drunk; maybe she'd had a smoke as well. I wanted her to stop giving away stuff about my work I had told her in private.

He pretends he's a guard, not a detective, I said.

Whatever. She stretched out her legs and wriggled her toes.

Philip said, unexpectedly, it's all about men's grooming now. That's the way forward for your line of business. I'd say we're seeing the last of the traditional barbershop.

This man has his own illegal uniform and goes out every night on his bicycle, Siofra said. Stopping crime like Batman.

The man bloody lost his wife in a car accident, I reminded her.

Calm down, she told me.

Is he still feeling bunged up? Ringo leaned in to ask her.

I wanted him to repeat what he'd just said.

Siofra was telling me you're having some trouble with your stomach region, he replied. There was a spate of laughter of course and the usual riffs on constipation while I tried to catch my girlfriend's eye; she was too busy listening to Ray's mouth whispering in her ear, her hand over her mouth, playing all amazed and easily shocked.

I caught Philip's eye, said, I hear you're spreading rumours about me winning the Lotto.

He blushed, checked over his shoulder for the exit. I gave him the nod to encourage him to tell the story. I was in with himself on Capel Street the other day, he began tentatively. He took them through it in his own way; added some new details I hadn't spotted, like the woman's classy emerald ring and a man who had been staring in the window the whole time. Ringo tried to change the subject, but the others were gripped. I watched Siofra's face harden into a mask when finally Philip mentioned the mole on the woman's face. She peered at me, her pink mouth agape, horrified.

*

I found myself outside, took the path down towards the line of trees. Off to one side, down three steps into a boggy hollow, there was this thin worn pillar stuck in the ground. I fingered the Ogham marks down one side of it. The path carried on into the trees, turned into a track. An idea tempted me to keep onwards: to walk deep into the woods, never come back. Never be found. Become a wild man. Despite what had just happened, I think I was hanging on to see if Siofra would come out to look for me.

Instead, it was Danielle who materialised in the space next to me. I was beyond feeling surprised by this point. What's it like to hate your own child? I said.

The worst of it is she knows I do. She's already afraid of me. Danielle sounded as indifferent as I did.

She probably doesn't. Even if she does, she'll forget.

What, like you did, you mean?

My guess was she was talking about me being adopted. Danielle used to blame anything she didn't like about my character on how I'd been adopted, even the fact that I was happy enough being a barber. She pushed and pushed me to find out who my mother was. Then, one morning in Raheny, I open a letter from the agency informing me the woman didn't want to know. The entire Nixon clan had gathered in our house before lunchtime to commiserate.

I hope the day has done you some good, I said.

That's not even a real one is it? She meant the stone. I bet the hotel had it put there as a… what's the godforsaken word I'm looking for? Maybe it's these tablets, but I couldn't remember the word for toothpaste the other day.

I told her I thought the marker was real but Ringo was an asshole to call it pagan because the Ogham alphabet was early Christian. Danielle said, elbowing me, do you still say your prayers every night? and the stone seemed to darken suddenly and tremble like a barometer, and a shower of rain swept in over the trees. Neither of us had coats on, but I asked if she fancied a walk into the forest. She was knackered, she said, suggested we sit in the car out of the way of people.

She clicked on her seatbelt as if we were taking a drive. I launched into the story about selling our old car, a funny story to lighten the mood, but she cut me short to say, it was me told Ringo to invite you, okay? He was against it, so I made him do it right in front of me in the kitchen. He does anything I tell him. She held my gaze like she wanted me to witness the cruelty in her.

The man's only trying to look after you, I said. Why though? Invite me?

She seemed disappointed by the question, by me. She put her hand on the belt as if she was about to get out of the car, changed her mind: it's like this is all an act. It's like I'm pretending. But I've no choice. I have to. I can't stop, because, you see, if I do, if I don't behave like this, exactly like this, there's going to be a lot worse will happen. A lot worse, you know what I mean? I'm being watched day and night, and if I'm caught not playing along, not pretending, it's going to be worse than horrible what happens. You understand, don't you? she said, nodding her head so I had no choice but to agree. As long as I keep doing this, nothing can happen to anybody, we're all safe, that's just the way it is.

Well, keep doing it then. Until you're ready to do something else. Things only change very slowly.

Then the other day, she went on, reaching for my hand, I came downstairs to look for her, and I heard Ringo in the thingumajig feeding her. The kitchen. And for a moment I just stood there in the hall listening, Ringo was whistling to her as he fed her her bottle, and I forgot and put my hand to the door handle, and I just froze. I couldn't go in. I wasn't allowed in. So I went back upstairs. Other than that, all I think about is sex.

We laughed together. Just hang on, Danielle, was all I could say.

Says the man who pissed through my letterbox. And wanted to go up in flames. I always thought you were just pretending to be mad too, that's why I didn't take you seriously. I thought if I just ignored you then you'd get a grip and do one, Danielle said, and yawned. Please let's not get into whinging on about if only this and if only that. We couldn't have done it any differently, not a single day of it—that's the way I see it. We'd no choice. We played it out to the end. Five years ago though—can you believe it?

A gurgling racket started in my stomach that felt to me like a plug being pulled and the past five years of dead time glugging away down a hole. Through the windscreen, the afternoon was fading around the hotel, the trees bristling in unison and the sky busy with all sorts of birds. I had this other sensation of having been catapulted forward in time and that I had just landed and caught up with myself again, here in the car with her. There was a definite relief in just seeing her, actually seeing Danielle in the flesh, and a kind of shock too that she had aged, that her body was done with me. I used to console myself after we had finally split with the idea that nobody would ever fuck her like I did and nobody would ever make her laugh as much either. Sitting behind the wheel now in the car with her, I knew I was wrong, and suddenly I was relieved to be wrong. Turning to say some of this to her, she seemed to have dozed off; her face leaning towards me on the seat, her mouth open slightly, the skin on her breasts goose-pimpled. I turned on the heating. She would be okay; she would fight her way through this bad patch. We would both be okay. We could be friends now from this moment on. I started the car, as a joke really, switched on the lights. I wanted it to be funny. I thought Danielle would open her eyes and have a fit but enjoy the cheek of it all the same. She only mumbled something, licked her lips and sighed. Then I was reversing. I'd no idea where we were going. Where the hell was there for us to be headed for? Then I was taking the car towards the gate barrier when Ringo and her brothers and Siofra and even some of the children ran out in front of the car and made a brave line to block our way.

Back in Dublin, hours afterwards, Siofra cleared her throat to show she was behind me in the garden. We had run out of words by the time we came down from the dark hills into the streets, even Siofra's Irish curses on my head for abandoning her among strangers had died away. Of course, I tried everything to make her understand I wasn't sick or mad enough to kidnap my ex-girlfriend; that it was a bit of a joke and I was just taking us on a scenic spin around the roads. Then we would switch to the issue of her mother's visit to the shop and what type of person was I to keep it from her. Then back to Danielle, and the darker suspicion of what I was planning to do to her; she was too afraid to come right out and ask me, but it was on her mind I might want to hurt Danielle. Inside the walls of our little house in Kilmainham, I couldn't find a corner to hide myself, so I evacuated to the garden with the end of a bottle of vodka.

I need to go, Siofra said. She had changed her clothes, put on the baseball cap I hated, and there was a bag over her shoulder. I think you need some help, Nathan, she said. A few seconds later, the front door slammed behind her.

I knew a big thing had happened and wasn't over yet. The repercussions were only taking shape. I had crossed another line. Hunkering down, I ran my fingers through the grass and tasted the dew. A thunder rumbled in my guts. What I did next was a brand new one: straightening up, I started to dig out a hole in the ground with the toe of my shoe, then with the heel. Then I got to work with my fingers, gouging and scooping up the soil. It was hard work and took a while. When I was satisfied, I dropped my trousers and shorts, squatted down and out in a long roll without any effort whatsoever came the dump that had been living in me for nearly a fortnight and dropped into the hole. Even when I was emptied, I remained squatting over the hole, inhaling the stench, as I stared up into a corner of oblivion.

Eventually, after belting the trousers, I scraped the loose soil over the steaming pit, pressing down on the surface with my foot, covering my tracks.

It was a good experience out there. For as long as it lasted. One day every soul will be found.

Critical Mass II

(*Abandoned Work*)

Far out by the padlocked weather station the cliff birds slagging the dying stars, and nearer on the hills the sheep bells in the heather and reeds around the misty turlough, and quick long and short beams of new pink daylight streaking through the venetian blinds in the dormer window and the boy wide awake in bed when the first of them arrived outside the house, a woman and a man from the sound of their shoes on the tarmac that was still sticky. Right the way through the night the boy hadn't slept a wink, he was positive about it, from his father setting the glass of water on the floor by the bed, switching off the light and pulling the door behind him extra tight, he had kept his eyes open the entire time it took to get here, through the darkness to this dawn and the first woman outside who was probably Mrs Pearson in her silk scarf knotted under her chin, she read the palms on a Friday evening, and the man with her who said, We've got a front seat anyway, a voice the boy couldn't place. Soon, another set of feet was heard, a man with a stick. Two women came after that. Nobody needed to talk yet. There seemed to be no wind this morning, the trees quiet along the road, black cables threaded through the branches, new leaves. Vigorously, the boy rubbed the back of his head into the pillow; blonde hair shaved tight all over, a sharp pointed hairline. Now he thought he could smell seaweed too, tarmac and seaweed and pipe-smoke. Death-ray sunbeams shot at the robots on the wallpaper. Did you hear that, Mrs Pearson said under his window. The stranger with her, after a long time, during which another two pairs of feet took up position, a man's, stamping the tarmac into place, Lucas Hardy maybe, and a girl's, dragging her feet, Melanie he guessed, small bows on her socks but none in her greasy black hair, and a car came along the road, answered Mrs Pearson with, Why, what did you think it was? Mrs Pearson sighed and said, I'm not definite but it doesn't feel right. You always think the worst, the man told her and rubbed his hands together in short bursts. Two more arrived. Then someone by themselves. Then a group, a family maybe, hand in hand. Something went by the sun, massive, fast, too fast to read its shadow in the room. The kitchen clock was on the bedroom wall.* His mother had hung it there; the boy had watched her hammer in the nail herself. Then a bicycle came bumping over the cattle grid and whoever it was squeezed their horn and the people outside laughed; there was already more of them than he had thought, maybe twenty or so. A silence began, and lasted until a phone rang, and Mr Kilmartin, who the boy had not heard arrive, said, I'm where I told you I would be, Signorita, I'll keep you a spot if you get your skates on. Next was a sound the boy couldn't figure out, a puncture noise, gas, a blow-torch maybe. The sunlight now reached nearly as far as the bedroom door. A woman, Doreen Gordon, who could keep a ball up longer than any of the boys, announced to everybody, I think it'll be a great day for it, and the people seemed to agree. It couldn't be worse than last year, the stranger with Mrs Pearson said, too late again. People must be standing on the grass by now, the heart-shaped lawn. Before he heard the lorry on the coast road, his mother got up, those were her house slippers coming along the hall and then ceasing outside his bedroom door. He didn't know what should happen. He had to wait to find out; sometimes it was like nothing ever had really happened yet, nothing, and this might be the beginning. His mother on the other side of the door waited too. He wanted to call to her, show her he was awake, that he hadn't shut his eyes even once, only his mouth was dry as a bone and then Hoop Kiely shouted over the others, Look it's the first kite. Now the people would be lifting their faces to the sky out the front of his house, on the black lake of the new driveway. Icicles still on the gate under the elm tree. Concrete lions with a raised paw. Meantime, his mother must have left the other side of the door because now he could count her steps on the stairs, the wet slap of the sole against her heel, twelve times on ten stairs. The hinges of the kitchen door. The kettle spout against the tap. Log in stove. The brush through her coils of dark hair, ruby in the sunlight. At last, suddenly, he heard a high tricky whistle, which meant Manus was out there among them, fingers at the back of his throat, they used to practise that whistle in the weather station hut, climb over the gates and in through the broken window, only he could never get it right, the fingers in the right position between the teeth, and Manus would lose his temper and leave him in the hut alone among the charts and wires and the cats in the walls. Some girls were laughing now; the Knoxes it had to be, the whole gang of them, and double-jointed Donna. She had come to the front door last night but his mother wouldn't allow her up the stairs. As he said her name to himself, the boy heard his father cross the hall into the bathroom, turn the big key in the lock. The sides of the lorry were kicked down. A few people clapped. He couldn't keep track of the numbers any more. His mother would be out soon to offer them hot drinks. No photography, a man shouted. Have some respect, said a woman in agreement. The rumble of the new oars in the back of the lorry, smooth as butter. Car horns at Harrigan's crossroads. The people, pressed shoulder to shoulder. Fart face, the boy heard so close to his ear he went stiff under the blankets. Kneeling beside the bed now was a girl in a blue nightdress, hair in curlers, her arms covered with layers of shiny transfers and cat's whiskers drawn on her face in black eyeliner. She put a finger on her lips and they listened together to the heavy footsteps descending the ten stairs. There's Hugh, the girl whispered. Don't call him that, he's your da, the boy said. It's his name isn't it, she said, and why doesn't he have a nickname like all the other men anyway? When I grow up and have four beautiful daughters they're going to call me by my own name. The boy asked where she had come from and she pointed under the bed and he shook his head; it wasn't possible; he would have heard her come in because he had been wide awake all night. He said, How long were you under there then and she shrugged and said, Centuries, and said after, You look like an astronaut with your new haircut. His mother had done it the night before, moving around him in circles as he sat in a chair in the kitchen with a towel around his shoulders, head bent forward and his hair falling in different ways to the slate floor, or head resting back against her, blinded by the glare of the bulb. The crowd sounds humungous, his sister said, are you scared. He said, You'll have to wash those whiskers off or ma will murder you. The cat disappearing last month had upset his sister; it was the fourth cat to flee, none of them stayed around. She made up cat names for herself, a new one every day. Below them now, their father singing in the kitchen and the screech of the rusty ironing board legs being opened. No bloody photography, somebody else shouted. What do you want, he asked his sister and she said, You promised to tell me, touching his shoulder under the blanket, so many transfers on her skinny arms they looked like long fish, eels, like she had scales, a salmon in a night dress. The boy hadn't been to sleep so he had nothing to tell her. Water, he said. She lifted the glass from the floor and held it with both hands while he took a sip. Some spilled on the pillow. After she put the glass down, she took something from her sock and laid it on the bed between them, something wrapped in toilet roll. I'll make a fortune, she said, opening it to show him curls of his own hair. That would be all that was left of him. You promised you would tell me, the girl said, leaning in close to him. The boy's eyes began to feel heavy for the first time since his father had come into the room and went down on one knee with the glass and wiped his hands on his trousers, how you had asked for your pay, it's Friday you said, I always get my pay on a Friday, and your father had got the joke and laughed and said do you think I'm daft because he had given you two weeks last Friday, the gall of you. Please, the girl said to her brother and he told her, I didn't have a dream, I made myself stay awake and she said, Fiddlesticks, I heard you snoring like Hugh down there but she couldn't have, his eyes were open through the night and the rain showers and the big silence before daybreak. Outside the house, the sound of the crowd changed; some voices got louder and some people seemed to go quiet. The boy could guess who had arrived. You can't break your last ever promise, the girl said, and made one of her cat sounds.

Notes:

Use that dream from the time up the mountains in Rondane. The hut the colour of Buddhist robes. Summer by the big lake. Mosquito nets on the windows. Antlers over the door. Nightmare more like.

Horror. Wake up screaming and K bolting out of the cabin naked. Ten nights in a row. K used to drive up from Oslo in her father's Merc. She blamed the cabin. You can't stay here, she said. It's det er farlig. *Menacing, she meant. Her fear of trolls in the forest. That moist look in her eyes when she began to see I might not be what she thought I was—I loved to see it. The bad thrill of it. I am not what I am. Watching her swimming in the lake from the jetty. So deep they say the cold in the middle will paralyse. No matter how much I want to I can't follow her in. The lake is huge, the trees come right down to the water on the other side. Nothing beyond it but the mountains. The carnal redness of the peaks after midnight. Elk paths. Smell of hot sap. Sex in the ruin of the boathouse, names carved in the wood from a century ago. The giggling behind every tree.*

Daytime and I'm in the hut and hear my name being called. A female voice, sensual, distant, singing from outside, from the birches behind the barn. The sun on my face and the voice coaxing me. The lake is glittering, flashing, hard on the eyes. I enter the trees. She is always somewhere ahead of me, promising me all sorts of pleasure if I can find her. She wants to play. Deeper and deeper into the summer forest. Dragonflies the size of birds. Snakes. Butterflies like discarded lingerie. An old ladle hanging from a branch. Heat. Blue sky nearly a mirror. The voice sometimes very near then off in the distance. I have the horn bad.

I follow the singing voice far into the forest where the trees are closer together and I have to fight my way through. Glimpses of sky tell me that the day is over. Longer shadows. The voice sometimes stops for long enough for me to realise I have gone too far, that I'm lost but then she will call again just in time, very nearby, luring me on, making me forget. Soon I know it is night.

The forest seems to be coming alive. Every tree stepping out of its skin. Rustling. Grunting. Tingling like tiny bells. I know there are things watching me, things following me. I have gone too far. I long to sit down and rest. The only thought in my head is that I must not fall asleep. Everything around me is waiting for me to close my eyes. The voice has abandoned me.

Am staggering between the trees, fit to drop. Fighting to keep my eyes open. About to give up. They are watching me, waiting to pounce. I stumble into a clearing, such a perfect place to lie down and sleep. So welcoming. I hear water too. A little further and there it is, the lake. I wash my face, splash my face with ice cold water to wake myself up. It's good. Exhilarating. Ravishing. This is what she wanted me to feel. I give thanks to her. Far across the lake I see a cabin, my own cabin I realise. There is a man outside. This is when I wake up screaming because the man is me.

Fart face, the boy heard so close to his ear he went stiff in the bed. Kneeling beside him a girl in a blue nightdress, long striped socks, her hair in curlers, arms decorated with layers of shiny transfers. She is wearing the false face of a cat, her finger up to the red and white nose holes, and they listened together to the footsteps descending the ten stairs. Mammy was crying all night, she whispered to him. I didn't hear her, he said and his sister shrugged and looking at the blinds, said, It's going to be good weather. You're lucky. Last year for Peter Arden, it was lashing down. He could smell that she needed to clean her teeth. Behind her on the wardrobe door, wrapped in cellophane, hung a heavy green cloak with a tooth-button at the neck. He heard what he guessed were planks laid down across the cattle grid. They've all come to see my big brother, she said. But its only me he'll tell his dream to. When the boy said he was thirsty she reached for the glass of water and he seemed to know before it happened that she would knock it over. Oops said the girl but she didn't sound the slightest bit sorry. She licked the back of her hands; her tiny nails were painted black. The boy smiled at his sister, wondering what her name was today. I'm ready, she said. I won't forget a single word. From beyond the window now there was a different noise, a grumbling, a sighing, a tutting, like something bad had happened. Hold the line, they heard. Don't let that man through any further. That's Fresh Jules, the boy said and the girl said, I wish he would drop dead. They listened to their father's steps running along the hall, the front door opening. Da will sort him out, his sister said. The crowd went quiet immediately. Gently, his sister ran her hand along his forehead and across his scalp. Stop this barbarity, they heard Fresh Jules shouting again and again over the other voices. Tell me quick while there's time, the girl said so close to him now her plastic mask touched his cheek. I don't know, he said. Now this minute, the girl said. Then a woman screamed right under the window, maybe Mrs Pearson, a moment before everybody outside started shouting like they were trying to stop a fight. Quick, the girl said. The boy's lips so dry they were stuck together. Will you break your little sister's heart, the girl said into his ear, tell her now all that you saw. The room went dark and darker as a brick came through the window, smashed into the venetian blinds and fell on the bed.

*The day before, returning to his room, he saw his mother in there, wielding a hammer, a silver nail in her mouth, and another one between her fingers against the wall. At her feet the clock from the kitchen with the red rim, battery-side up. She looked at him, annoyed, as he crossed the floor and sat on the edge of the bed.

  Boy: Did you ask him if you could borrow it?
  Woman: Your father?
  Boy: That's his first hammer. He says he got it before he even knew you existed.
  Woman: (dropping the nail) You're putting me off.

Boy: Do you want to hear what happened to me earlier?
Woman: I'd have thought you'd have more on your mind.
Boy: It's funny but.
Woman: Think about tomorrow instead and let me finish this.
Boy: Is Fresh Jules coming?
Woman: Never you mind him. Some people don't believe in anything unless it's new. Did he speak to you?
Boy: I'm the last one, he told me.
Woman: Don't be daft. There'll be others follow you over to the island. So what was so funny?
Boy: Nothing. Me and Manus were watching Donna making funny shadows with her hands. She's double-jointed. DJ we call her.
Woman: She'll miss you for a while.
Boy: I was thinking about it and I don't care if I am. The last one. I don't mind if you all stop after this time. I might be enough.
Woman: You were always kind... There. That should hold it.
The boy watches her hang the clock on the nail.
Boy: Are you proud of me?
Woman: Just you stick to what you're shown. That's all I ask of you. Stick to what they showed you, especially when you're in the boat. Stay at the back of the boat.
Boy: It's easy, Ma. Don't worry.
Woman: It'll be a special day for everybody.
Boy: I'm going to stay awake all night.

Notes:

Money scattered on the floor. Coins and notes. Have this sense something else has happened. Someone—who is it—what have they done—slaughter, carnage, disfigurement—dreaming the dream with the boy in his bed. What will they do this morning to the boy? Why are the crowd gathering?

Crooked venetian blinds. Curtain. Clock. Doorknob. Small details changing with each re-run.

Cat/Girl's names: Shalimar. Miss Enid. Perssy. Rebel. Thanatella. Baez. Angel. Stickleback. Crumpet. Rococo. Red Foot.

Why all the Norwegian stuff in my mind around this? It's been years since I thought much about it. Then last night I had a dream I was in a hot-air balloon, high up, above the birds, above the clouds, in great form, and leaning over the edge of the basket, I realised I had this very same dream before in Norway. And when the gas cut out and I began to plummet I didn't panic this time, I knew I was coming down smack in the middle of the desert. The scorched dunes infinite. And I knew that along would come a handsome Arab sheik, all in his white robes, riding a camel and he would announce to me that my real name was Skibbo.

So this time I told the sheik all that had happened to me since I last met him in the desert. He seemed alarmed. He demanded to know who I had told my secret name to. Nobody, I said. If I went round telling people I had a new nickname that I was told in a dream by a sheik, it wouldn't go well for me. It's hard enough getting people to take me seriously as it is.

The Sheik stood up—we were squatting in the sand in the shadow of the camel. Again, he asked me who I had told. He was agitated, scared. Nobody, I answered again. What's the problem anyway?

The last one is the first, he said. And he said it in Norwegian.

Then we heard a rumbling far across the sands. A big cloud of dust coming towards us. The sheik looked at me as if all his dreams had collapsed. A cloud of dust coming towards us across the desert like a city on the move. (Caravan trail)

I woke up and felt depressed. Utterly empty. Thought I wouldn't write a word today until I heard some kids passing in the street and one of them, a girl, said, he doesn't even have a phone.

Then I remembered that I had used Skibbo as my first email address. The first one I wrote was to K after she had left me for that rich German asshole, advertising exec, way older than her. And it turned out he was under the control of another woman, an ex-girlfriend junkie who made all his decisions for him from a cottage in Devon. Big and small. Clothes, investments, romantic. Willingly. Gave up free will. Abdicated thought. Not to be yourself, the opposite of Peer Gynt. He confessed it all to K when they were away together in Brittany, said he didn't want to change it. Said this woman was a kind of seer, that's how he had made so much money. This was the sacrifice he had to make. Claimed the woman knew if he acted against her advice. Was he confessing this to K, I wonder, or telling her under orders? Anyway, K wrote to me from there. We tried again, didn't we, me and K? I think we did a few months more together, in London this time. I should get back in touch with her and see how life has treated her. Those long hands of hers. Never a hint of make-up. The jawline protruding from the hood of her parka, nose to the wind. Snow.

The wee sister or whoever it is behind the mask needs to know the dream the boy has had on his last night. Before he is taken off to this island. A cave?

And maybe I'm wrong but wasn't it during that last stint with K in London that my sister and her boyfriend came to visit. Took them to see The Cocteau Twins. Sister collapsed. My sister's secret abortion. K guessed before I did. I wouldn't believe her. I was dead set against abortion. Was that the final row for us? The nail in the coffin.

Look up what year it was you were first allowed to take the Eucharist in your hands. Those dark mornings going to the retreat mass before school. Men only on the streets. My da and me took separate routes to the cathedral. Never sat together like all the others. Monks from abroad giving the sermons. I enjoyed the accents. One morning, leaving the pew for communion, the man beside me dropped something. I thought it was a handkerchief and picked it up for him only it was a pair of girl's cotton white knickers. He took them off me with a wink. Coming back from the altar my da nodded to me, there was a space free beside him. I walked on. Sat back down beside the stranger. Holy wafer dissolving on my tongue. Paper. Cursive. Mrs whatshername who taught us writing. Blue perm. Coal. Wooden rulers. Road. Crocodile. Houri. Heavyweight. Mrs Higgins! That night by the river in Avignon you nearly went in. Punt. Courtroom. Sheila's brooch. Quantum. Knights. Double-dip in the Shelbourne Hotel. Parole. Dry cut. Lion.

Fart face, said a voice right into his ear, and a hand covered his mouth to keep in the yell. His sister was kneeling over him in her crinkled Puss in Boots mask, the finger of her other hand across the smiling sharp teeth; they listened together to the footsteps of their father descending the stairs, only six it took him, and two coughs. Your hands stink, the boy said pulling his face free. At least my hair doesn't look like it was painted on, she said. Hers was in a dozen purple curlers. A blue nightdress and so many transfers on her skinny arms she could have been half a lizard thing that changes colours. The elastic of the false face cut across her little ear like a tightrope. How did you get in anyway? he said and she answered, How I will get out is more to the point, which made him look at her, at the rip in the left eye hole, at the flaking paint, two Halloweens old it was, he was in Rooney's shop with her when she put it on and spoke her first word since the last cat had gone missing; they all took off, the gang of them that preferred to live wild around the weather station, eating frogs and gulls' eggs, sleeping in the walls, Manus said. And right on cue, Manus gave the whistle from outside in the crowd. Your friend must be proud of you, the girl said, even the sun is shining for you, it's your big day. Behind her on the wardrobe door, a yellow robe, the arms cut off. There was money spilled on the carpet by the door, coins and notes with blood stains on them. Give my hair to Donna, he said, don't be selling it, you can have all that money on the floor. His sister leaned in close and said, Do you want to hear a secret about Donna? The boy shook his head. Your breath stinks too, he said, after they had listened to the crowd for a few minutes. Clean your teeth, he said. His sister then started to mime brushing her teeth, like she was playing an instrument, using her finger that wasn't painted black any more, until he told her to stop. They heard the screech of the ironing board below in the kitchen, their father's voice, and their mother laughing. The crowd seemed to share the joke, everybody was laughing outside the house, on the new tarmac, the grass, along the hedge. Not many know such a day, the girl said. The crows lifted from the tree by the well, heading inland, their shadows hitting the bedroom door. The boy kept his hands under the blankets. Maybe I'm the final one, he said and she came in close again, very close, her bad hot breath in his face and said, All them beyond will rot in their narrow graves but you will be broken, torn apart and devoured, you will know joy. Now tell your sister what you saw. He asked for the water, heard the glass fall on its side. The kitchen clock was gone from the wall. Turning to his sister, the boy saw her hand was inside the mask, and he said, what are you doing now nutcase, his own eyes suddenly heavy, first the left, then the right, blurring, the two together, the right, the left, they were going to close, the muscles wouldn't work, the first time since his father was in the room, how he had knelt down on one knee to put the glass on the floor and then wiped his hands on his trousers, how the boy had asked for his pay, it's Friday I always get my pay on a Friday, he had said more as a joke than to be serious, and his father hadn't gotten it because he said like he hadn't even heard, I think they've chosen the wrong one, I don't think you're up to this, all those hours and hours ago until this second here, this dawn, this day of dying, his sister's breath near his ear and the touch of her finger now on his mouth, smearing his lips with her spittle, over and back, gently over and back with her tiny wee finger, until it is so wet you can barely tell if her finger is still there. There will be black kites above the treetops. There will be buckets of petals thrown on the waves. Drawings in the sand. Drums. Cars parked lopsided in the ditches all the way from Harrigan's crossroads. Minibuses. Manus and Donna and the children on the rocks. The shallow boat to the steps, deep and narrow, which rise out of the sea at the island. The weather station on the high cliff. The slow procession to the cave mouth.

Notes:

Expand this. Images of the sacrificial journey. King for the day. Comedy. The stake at the cave mouth.

Tell me now, the girl said, you've had your pleasure. Fresh Jules was shouting now outside, Stop this barbarity, and his father opening the front door and the crowd cheering for a scrap. I didn't sleep a wink, he told her and she leapt in an instant on top of him, on to his chest, her hands at his neck. Tell me immediately or you know what will happen if you break your promise. The boy looked at the green sparks in the eye holes of the mask. I know your name, he said. No you don't, she said, hissing. I know your name, he said again, her hard thumbs pressed to his throat. She leaned down, put the mask against his face, nose to nose, and what's my name little human boy, she said.

Notes:

When he guesses and tells her her name the creature vanishes. Puff! The father pushes open the bedroom door perhaps. Caught.
Think more about who is dreaming the dream of the boy? What has he done?
More images from the journey to the cave/stake/sacrifice/ritual. Solaris.

Found K on Facebook. No activity in years. Said hello anyway.

Levitation

PART ONE

If there was one thing Valentine Rice couldn't tolerate any more, it was Tintin's story about cutting the hair of some ordinary looking gent who turned out to be a killer, a serial killer perhaps. Valentine had been listening to it now for nearly twenty years above the noise of electric razors and cheap hairdryers and the traffic on Capel Street, which, as everybody knows, had got worse and worse. How one sweltering day, the story went, into the shop stepped a plain, tallish, lightly freckled gent, a broad chest under a loose white shirt with the sleeves rolled up, fortyish, no accent, humourless, and the only odd detail about him was how fussy he grew about his hair. It was a good story, it had to be said. People couldn't get enough of the picture of Gemmel in the middle chair under the apron, studying his reflection in the mirror, before he went off to kill another woman.

Valentine Rice had cut the hair of famous, dissolute actors and musicians, that poet who dug up his dead daughter, all grades of Provo, a reincarnated Hungarian king, two false imprisoners, a Formula 1 winner, umpteen amateur paedos, a man who claimed he was being followed by an ostrich—but he simply couldn't compete with an old-fashioned, homegrown rapist and strangler.

LEVITATION

How could you have not known? Valentine, unable to contain himself, shouted over his shoulder into the shop. He was standing in the doorway, smoking, and watching the people go by along the street. Tintin was telling his unbeatable story to a young lad in the chair, a student already gone grey who had never even heard of the killer Gemmel.

What am I, a mind reader? Agatha bleedin' Christie? Tintin said, hamming it up for the young lad. I'm a barber, your average toe-rag. And may it long continue that way. Sure, the guards didn't have a suspect yet.

I would have known, Valentine said and Tintin said, blowing a chewing-gum bubble, But sure you're a superior being to the rest of us.

Giving the finger to somebody across the street, and after putting out his cigarette in the New York Chelsea Hotel ashtray on the glass coffee table, Valentine said, I would have sensed it. His eyes. His mouth. His aura. And anyway, it should have been me who was working that day. Not the likes of you. Then, to the fascinated student, he added, I was the one meant to be on that day but I let him replace me because he was saving up to get married and needed the extra cash.

At least there's somebody would have me and my aura, Tintin said and the youth sniggered and Valentine sighed, and pleaded of the ceiling fan, Will this higgledy-piggledy torture ever end?

The shop went darker and the window and every little thing began to shake because of a lorry stalled in the traffic. Tintin scraped the back of the student's neck with an ivory-handled cutthroat. Valentine, facing into the long mirror, wetting his sideburns, decided he had more to say: I was a much happier person back then. The world at my feet. I actually used to like people. They didn't take themselves so seriously. I had friends and interesting, fateful lovers. But I'll tell you one thing, if it was my story, I'd tell it a damned lot better than he does. No sense of the moment. No panache.

With that, he lit another cigarette and sat down on the far end of the sofa from me. A drag or two later, he said, You're the damned writer. Or you were anyway. Doesn't he make a nun's fist of that story, doesn't he?

They always come back to the scene of the crime, the student said and would have registered the abrupt pressure from Tintin's hand tilting his head forward and the sweet puff of talc on his neck.

I was never meant to be a barber, Valentine said to me, continuing in his reflective mood. I may actually be living somebody else's life. Sometimes I think I must have rubbed shoulders with somebody out there on the street, any street, and they took my life and I got landed with theirs. I'm watching the TV and I'm thinking is that me there, is that the real me? I wasn't meant to spend my days listening to denim-clad, gum-chewing hypocrites. I should be above all this. I should be quoted. I should be respected. I should be held up as an example. I should be flying down the San Fernando Valley with the sunroof open and a personalised number plate.

Valentine Rice was forty-nine years old. The hair still intact, the same length all over, fairish but grey down the burns, fat cheeks and plump moist red lips. A silver cross in one ear and a green pearl stud in the other. A blacked-out name on the inside of his right bicep. Never jeans, always ironed black trousers with a slim belt. Boots with a heel. And he was proudly single, and without dependants. In fact, only recently, he had moved back in with his mother to save up for a car. It would be his first car. On the edge of his half-century, Valentine Rice had decided to do something about the embarrassing fact that he couldn't drive.

~

He had been through nine instructors already. One had an ugly laugh, one was too jumpy, one looked like him, one couldn't speak English properly...

Eventually he had found Mr Wells. Valentine liked Mr Wells from the moment they met, his merry blue eyes under the rim of his fisherman's cap, his flash mobile phone and the elegant way he stroked his precise grey goatee when he speculated on the future of humanity. That first lesson, early evening in Mountjoy Square, leaves falling on their heads, Mr Wells gave Valentine a short and entertaining lecture on the history of the hydraulic engine by the raised bonnet of a navy Daewoo Kalos. He wouldn't even allow Valentine to sit behind the wheel.

It was lesson four before he was given the nod of the cap to start the car. Of course, Valentine already knew the basics of how to drive. There had been good people in his past who had tried to teach him, friends, lovers, acquaintances, whatever the word was for them. And the instructor was very curious about each of them. How they had treated their cars, if they were kind and respectful or if their behaviour was demeaning to the vehicle. As the two men drove around together through the dark winter evenings, safe in the Daewoo's faux leather interior, Valentine slowly began to realise he should never have gotten into a car with any of those people, their behaviour had been appalling, and that the roads were crammed with neurotics and bullies who did not know the first thing about having a relationship.

Become one with the machine, Mr Wells liked to say. The vehicle is an extension of your body, not a mode of transport. Let it understand you. Tell it your secrets. It wants to serve you. Listen to you. Mother Nature is not your friend.

One evening, then, the two men were in the Phoenix Park for a lesson. The gas lamps were burning along Chesterfield Avenue, beacons of hope in a low, green and purple sky.

Valentine was telling Mr Wells about Tintin and his damned story, and that he had to come up with a better one.

Treason, Mr Wells exclaimed. I've always wanted to meet a man who has let his country down. The entire nation.

It sounds a bit lame to me, Mr Wells. Nobody cares. We need to aim higher, Valentine said. And I don't mean the so-called famous.

You know, I've never met anybody really famous. There must be something about me that doesn't appeal to them. Now take the next left. Follow the yellow Sierra.

It's brown, Mr Wells. We had a film star in the shop the other day. That actor who was in the big flop last year about vampires on a nuclear submarine. And you know what he told me? He said that famous people are crap drivers. They are in more crashes than any other sector of society.

Mr Wells stroked the hair on his face and said, Every road leads into the future where none of them exist. Light entertainment is good enough for me anyway. I think we'll always enjoy a good soap or a chat show.

We get plenty of criminals in also and they seem to be mad about their cars.

Lights up ahead. Take her handy.

What's the worst thing a man can do? Valentine wondered. I mean, what's the most terrible, outrageous thing you can imagine?

The Sierra beat the lights and Valentine brought the Daewoo to a halt. The two men sat in silence, thinking, while the flanks of other darkened vehicles moved across their line of vision.

Mr Wells waved his hand at them, the people in the cars, and said, If you ask me, there's enough going on right out there. Who needs to pay to sit in the cinema? There's entertainment to be had when you open the door in the morning.

Eventually, the green light swapped for the red. A horn sounded behind.

LEVITATION

Giddy up there, Mr Wells said.

Five minutes later the Daewoo was still waiting at the lights, the hazards on. Mr Wells was outside in the darkness directing traffic with sweeps of his cap while in the dark interior, a man could be seen staring straight ahead, his hands gripping the frightened wheel, incapable of any progress.

~

Crusoe's, across the street from Connolly Station; this was Valentine's usual spot for a pint after work. His favourite high stool was the last in a line along the bar, right at the back of the underground room. He could walk into Crusoe's by himself and find company and distraction easy enough among the many long-time regulars or he could turn his back and drink his pint in peace. He had fallen in and out of love in the place, taken a few punches, even a bottle over the head, he had come in depressed and left enlightened, laughing, furious, and hard on his arse. It was a home from home for Valentine. And that's where he went after the episode in the park. Mr Wells dropped him off, saying, There was a time I couldn't get out of the bed. Total immobilisation. A bit of rewiring is all you need. Keep the faith.

Don't make a big deal of it, Valentine said. He gave the instructor his money, watched him nudge back his cap to count it. Then he took the familiar four steps down from the street and went inside. People nodded to him, winked or raised their thumbs. His favourite seat seemed to be waiting for him. After the softness of the car seat, the stool had the right hard support and even the brass bar he put his elbows on seemed to take his weight without any fuss, and believed in him. The new kid who asked him what he would like was thin as a snake. With crooked dreads, a pierced eyebrow and those wooden rings that stretch big holes in your ears. Valentine ordered a pint, lager tonight. He was the kind of drinker who didn't know what he wanted until he looked at the glittering gold and silver taps.

Are you a boy or a girl? he asked the kid, a few pints later.

The kid said, What difference does it make?

And later again, Valentine said, I've been thinking about it and you're right, it doesn't make a difference. Can you drive?

The kid shrugged.

Valentine thought for a moment and asked, What's the worst crime you can think of? No judgements. Who's the worst person in the country?

Leave it with me, the kid said. But he never came back. Another kid took over that end of the bar. Valentine, unflustered, drank on, nice and slowly, nursing his thoughts, and bothering nobody.

~

The busted end of a three-man leatherette in Wylie's barbershop, that's where I was spending most of my time, the afternoons anyway. Upstairs I had a bed in a flat with an impressive Venetian window at one end, an enormous dirty semi-circle of glass held together by tape which, on a windy night, seemed to be learning how to breathe. It was a junk room really. Old sinks, hat stands. Boxes of tiles. Suitcases I didn't dare open. And one of the original upholstered chairs with wooden arm rests. Around lunchtime I would take the side stairs down, occupy a valuable spot on the sofa and try to keep out of trouble. Valentine would have been on his feet for a few hours already.

A dialogue in progress: Have I seen you in here before?

First time. Moved to Dublin about six months ago. Read about this place in a guide book and have been meaning to come in and soak up the atmosphere. I love Dublin.

Next.

What?

Next.

Or to a different customer: I'm surprised you would even show your face after what you did.

Sweet Jesus, who told you about that stuff? Was it Cormac, was it?

I'll be sure to ask him now anyway.

Or: Are you a sex tourist? You have that look. Isn't it a bit soulless? I like to get to know a person first.

What look? I've lived in Dublin all my life.

Or: I think you're only trying to sound liberal because that's the way you think people are supposed to sound. I can see it in your eyes though. Your heart's not in it. You're a Catholic.

I'm an atheist.

Next.

Or: There was a man came in the other day who said exactly the same thing, I mean told me exactly the same story. Same hospital. Same nurse.

That's not possible. I was there.

One of you is shitting me.

And as happened a lot: Let me guess. Short back and sides. Number two on the clipper. Straight along the back. No sideburns.

Spot on. So how's business? You must be worried about this smoking ban coming in. They loan us the money to build a few roads and then they start telling us what to do. It's the thin end of the wedge.

Next.

One afternoon, Valentine threw his scissors in the sink and ordered a customer out of the shop. You're a skank and a tosser and a substandard human, he informed the shocked little man, fuck off back to the MacGillycuddy Reeks. Wylie was present in the shop at the time. He was portly and hairy in his pink vest and straw hat. He had been giving his staff last-minute instructions before he went off on holiday.

Levitation

I mean it this time, he said, giving Valentine his last warning. You'll be out on your ear. I'll make sure as well there isn't a shop in this city will give you the time of day.

Valentine sat on the sofa and lit a cigarette. You don't care who it is or what they've done as long as they cough up their cash, he said to Wylie. Some fucker could come in and say he's chopped up his children and you would nod and say that's tough and crack open the till. And all so you can fuck off to a beach in South Africa and chase the salty young boys around a volleyball net. Wave your credit card like a dick in the sun. Don't pretend to me you care about the customers. You're too fucken old and ugly and wrinkly and there isn't a junkie kid in Dublin who would look twice at you. That's the truth of it.

The boss told him to get out and not come back. Valentine refused to move. He sat it out while the boss called the guards. There were four other people in the shop, Tintin working on a man in the middle chair who only spoke Irish, the electrician waiting to get paid, and old Ultan the Yogi cradling his cup-a-soup, and myself. Valentine finished his cigarette, put it out, and said to old Ultan:

I had this dream the other night, right? I'm in a car on the motorway. Me driving. Middle of the night. And we're flying along. There's some big hurry. But the delinquents coming the other way won't dip their headlights and I'm getting blinded. It's me behind the wheel, right? And next thing the windscreen shatters. The pieces fall into my lap. So the drag coefficient is terrible. And I wake up and you know what I'm thinking? Sunglasses. I need sunglasses. It was like a revelation. The point is always what happens when you wake up afterwards, isn't it? You see I've had this dream a few times, more or less. And I was thinking sunglasses. So, I predict we are going to have some very fine weather. Good news for you, out there on the street all day. But shitsville for me. I tell you, Ultan, there's nowhere worse in the world to be on a hot day than stuck listening to puerile double agents in a very passé siopa bearbóra.

Nobody said another word while we waited on the authorities. However, when the door opened again, it was the same customer who Valentine had rudely evicted, and the little man was glowing with anticipation.

Did he fall for it? he said, looking at our anxious faces.

Then Valentine began to laugh.

You shower of bastards, said the boss, and he stormed out the door of the shop.

~

One day when his mother was out Valentine took the spare key from behind the clock and borrowed her car, a two-door Fiesta.

He stuck to the terraced streets of Crumlin at first, Kildare Road, Clonard Road, Raphoe Road, all more or less the same. Growing in confidence, he came down Bangor Road to the crescent and the parade of shops, and onto Sundrive Road. He waited at the junction, turned left. Mount Argus. Harold's Cross. The R137 now. He hit another red at the canal, behind a silver '03 Mazda with two dogs in the back, big ones. He added up the numbers on the registration. The light turned green and he followed the Mazda across the canal bridge. Easy. He pressed the button on the door to bring the window down. It often didn't work but today it obeyed. Good sign, he hoped. Now he was moving downhill to the junction with the South Circular, R137 and R811. This was the one he was afraid of. Three lanes going each way, turns left and right, buses, lorries and the taxi drivers who never gave you a chance. The Mazda switched lanes. In front of him now, a Fiat, the same colour as the car he was in, a cinnamon red. Was that another good sign? The important thing was not to think about the other drivers, that's when he got stuck. Don't look at them. Count the number plates. Dream of the open road. The toot of a horn behind him. Green. Release the handbrake and he was away.

Clanbrassil Street welcomed him like a victorious king. He should give people a wave. Dublin city centre was what lay ahead, however, and he didn't want that, too hectic, so he went left into the Coombe. On Francis Street he saw a spot to park, and that too went smoothly. Sitting on the bonnet, he had a victory smoke. The world had secret rhythms. He got back inside the car and nearly surrendered to the temptation to call Mr Wells. No, first, he had to do it again, in reverse now. He poked the nose of the Fiesta out into the street, checked the mirror again and saw a good gap. He took his foot off the brake, turned the wheel, touched the accelerator and was almost clear when something hit him from behind.

It was an Audi, tinted windows, white as a new fridge. The driver, a blonde lady, accepted responsibility for the damage, a broken light and a dent. The cost didn't matter, she said, as long as nobody was hurt. She was a Dublin woman in her fifties, he guessed, heavy on the make-up and hair freshly blow-dried. He stood in the cloud of her perfume at the door of the Audi while she searched in the glove box for her details. The back seat was awash with folders and papers. A box of business cards had spilled out on the front seat. Lauren Musgrave, he read, some kind of PR work.

You know how it is, Valentine said, maybe we could avoid the paperwork some way? Sort it out between ourselves like?

The lady looked out at him with soft, shining eyes that seemed much younger than the rest of her.

Is it stolen?

Valentine took a chance, a big one, and said, Not quite.

No insurance?

No licence either, he confessed. Just the provisional.

The lady's long, tinted eyelashes fluttered hectically. The big face on you, she said. Like the dog ate your homework.

It was kind of her to agree. She gave him one of the business cards and he was to contact her with the bill. Valentine thanked her and then happened to ask who did her hair and it turned out that he not only knew the salon but the man who generally looked after her.

Tell him you ran into Valentine. Valentine King—I mean Rice.

The girlish flutter of eyelashes again. A strange man who has to think twice about his own name, she said disapprovingly, and smiled.

Rice. Valentine Rice. Maybe it's whiplash, he said and as he put his hand to the back of his neck to feign a discomfort, a very real pain shot up his arm, and he roared and sank to his knees on the tarmac.

It was his wrist. He must have damaged it against the steering wheel when the Audi struck. The lady seemed devastated by what she had done. She parked the Fiesta for him and insisted on taking him to A&E. Luckily, it wasn't far. They almost had another accident on the way up Thomas Street, rashly trying to overtake a bus. He was relieved to get out of the car.

Thanks again for your discretion, you know with the insurance stuff, he said, but the lady shook her stiff hair and said, You go on in and I'll park the offending beast.

Valentine had a last smoke, wondering how long she would stick around. Inside, a nurse asked him to wriggle his fingers, which he could just about manage. She told him to take a seat. There were all sorts of casualties to observe in the waiting area and some with nothing visible wrong with them. Wrapped in a kind of pink shawl, Lauren appeared with a bottle of water for each of them. He told her there was really no need for her to waste her day and again she shook her head in that way she had, slowly east and west and back again. For a while, then, they told each other hospital stories; she wasn't half bad either, he thought, she knew what was funny and what wasn't.

Maybe we're done with that subject now, he said.

You're some gas, Valentine, you really are. The ladies must be dying about you. And, by the way, I'm still wondering about that name of yours, whatever it is.

Coincidentally, his mother had done some research on the history of his surname so he took the opportunity to sound intelligent about it for a few minutes and prove he was one of them, the Rices of Munster. Lauren responded in kind with some odd facts about the Musgraves, not the least being that her mother and father shared the same name before they were married. Her eyes grew moist as she spoke about them and their love of the horses, Punchestown, Listowel, Cheltenham, and yes, they had taken her to the Grand National as a kid. Luckily, there was bit of a commotion in the waiting area. Somebody thought another human had died in a yellow plastic chair, but then they woke up. Next, Ms Musgrave's phone rang. Her nails were done professionally. Three expensive rings on her hands, but the significant finger was unsheathed.

Whoever it was on the other end, she was cutting strips off them by the lifts. She was a posh, confident lady with a soft centre, he thought. Divorced most likely. Children: doubtful. He also had time to wonder whether it would be possible to return to the front gate in Crumlin before his mother got home and claim total ignorance of the damage. In heels and shawl, the lady businesswoman hurried across the hospital tiles towards him, as if she were late for a meeting.

The pool cleaner? he enquired.

An utterly hideous man, she said. Ugly to the very core, I'm sorry but he is. You know when you get a chill? I don't like to talk ill of people but I sometimes think he might be missing some human DNA. Behind his back, they call him Doctor Gonzo.

Does he live in Dublin by any chance?

Lauren Musgrave thought he was being funny and laughed and smoothed her skirt as she resumed her seat beside him. So, anyhoo, where were we, Mister Valentine Rice? Oh yes, you were telling me about your parents.

He most certainly was not. Instead he told her a story from the shop. She was laughing by the end of it, but she was soon talking about parents again and how her own two doted on each other. Not wanting to appear rude he offered a few uncontentious glimpses of his mother, that she had once run over a hare in her '92 Fiesta and when she stopped the car and looked in the mirror she saw another hare in the road beside the body and the hare was glaring at her and she panicked and drove off, that she had arthritis in her left elbow and probably should be driving an automatic, she made lots of lists and never threw them away, she had an amazing sense of smell, spent most of her time these days on demonstrations against the war in Iraq, had a mild phobia about scarves, struggled to be a vegetarian, and that, recently, she seemed to have developed some moral objection to adoption.

Maybe we're done with this subject now, he said, and he launched into another story from the shop, one he thought she would appreciate, about a man who ferried the tourists around in a horse and carriage.

I think I would prefer a different one, Lauren Musgrave interrupted, gentle but resolute.

The horse saves the day, Valentine protested, but the moment was gone. Across the way, there was an elderly man with a bruise on his head and beside him a younger man in a suit and tie holding a bucket he might get sick into. Three doctors in their white coats came bursting out of the lifts.

Valentine turned to Lauren and said she was entitled to her opinions about show jumping, but when he was a kid he had seen a miracle on a Dublin street.

I was in town with the parents, he began. Embarrassed as hell. I needed to get a new pair of hiking boots. I'd deliberately mislaid my other pair in a hole in the grounds of Stanaway Park, but that's another story. So there we were, the three of us, crossing the hump of the Ha'penny. A smelly aul drunk pushes past us, knocking the father up against the railings. The mother is for getting stuck in but the father as per usual prefers to let it be. They start into an argument about it. I can see the aul drunk up ahead. He's pushing people out of his way, waving his fist at the sky. It was funny in that sad sort of way, you know. So we cross onto the northside. Liffey Street. And I see the drunk vanish around a corner. I'm curious to know where he's bound, who's going to bear the brunt of the anger. And then we reach where he vanished. Strand Street Great, it's called. And I see him there, with his fist raised. And right before my eyes he's lifting off the pavement. He's rising into the air. About two feet in the air. Like superman, yes, but just stuck there. Hovering. The fist up. This truly terrified look on his face. We're looking at each other. Thirty seconds, a minute max. Suspension. The parents see it too. Then, bang, he hits the ground. Ultan his name is. He comes into the shop. Likes a cup-a-soup. And he's been sitting on that same spot every day since.

Lauren's mobile phone rang again at this point. It wasn't the hideous man this time but she had to take it. The same as before, she paced up and down in front of the lifts. He liked this lady, he decided, she was good company but it was a shame she wasn't his type. He was only a two-bit barber and she seemed to have a taste for expensive things. And she was older than him. Maybe they could be friends though. Sex wasn't the only thing in the world. Yes, maybe they could be friends. It was then he heard his name called from the desk.

After they had fixed him up with a bandage and a sling, and he left the hospital building, and saw it was dark, and the traffic was clogged up, and he managed to get his fags out and light one with one hand, a text came in from Lauren. To be continued was all it said.

~

Valentine's luck was in. He had made up his mind to come clean with Muriel about the car. If she threw him out, so be it. He would move into a hotel; he knew a man who managed a place on Gardiner Street, a regular from the shop, and he owed Valentine a favour. He would tell his mother about what happened in the Phoenix Park and how he was determined not to allow it to beat him, that's why he borrowed her car; she would like that, she admired people who stood up for themselves. It was why Muriel had let him move back in. His mother had been hassling him for years to stop being dependent on other people and get himself a car. She had one condition; he had to open a savings account and show her the money going in each month. Other conditions, like no coming in drunk and singing at the top of your voice, and no overnight guests, male or female, began to accumulate, but nothing that had caused too much friction between them. And when he reached home after the hospital and saw the place was in darkness he lifted his good hand to heaven and praised the ruler of the night sky.

As soon as he was inside he had an idea. He called his brother-in-law, Graham, explained what had happened and waited for the man to solve the problem with the car. That was the type of Graham. He hated to see anybody stuck. The man had to quit the guards because he was too sensitive. In less than fifteen minutes, he had pulled up out front of the house, where Valentine was waiting with a taxi for him, and off he went to collect Muriel's car. Ten minutes later he was back with it. Not being able to shake his hand in gratitude, Valentine slapped him on the back a few times.

I would invite you in, Graham, he said on the front path, but I'm in a lot of pain here and just want to lie down. How's Skippy?

He's just great. Thanks for asking. You peek in on him in the cot at night and he's lying there with the huge black eyes wide open like he's thinking hard about the world.

A wise head on young shoulders. He'll be an important addition to the life of this country. You can tell him that from me.

Tell him yourself. Sabrina was saying only the other day that we haven't seen you in a while.

Valentine promised his brother-in-law he would be round soon and got the front door closed. No sooner had he sat down and found something to watch on the TV than Muriel arrived home with a take-away pizza.

You're the brightest star in an overcrowded sky, Muriel, he said, and holding up his arm like a wing, he told her a cyclist had collided with him in the Liberties. A young drug dealer on a bike.

You were always a terrible liar, Muriel said. You'd be sick for a week if you even as much told the slightest fib. A real goody two-shoes you were.

And the two watched television for the rest of the night, news for her, then a film for him, then the news again. War may have been spreading across the world but the Rices, mother and son, managed to have a quiet, pleasant evening together in their own home.

~

LEVITATION

Our Valentine went to work the next morning as usual. Tintin suspected it was a trick at first, the arm in the sling, the sunglasses, the yarn about a kid on a bike. He took the first customer and waited for Valentine to surrender to the inevitable day ahead. The baker dropped in the day's loaf. The postman lingered for a smoke. A cardboard box was carried in and set down on the table by a deliveryman and a standoff ensued between the two barbers; one insisting he was injured and couldn't sign for it, the other claiming that it would be easier to believe the moon was a poppadum. The deliveryman had time to drink a cup of tea before Tintin relented and the matter was resolved.

Don't be getting uppity now, said Valentine.

Uppity? Tintin, flummoxed, was stopped in his tracks. Uppity?

You just don't get it. You have to accept what you are, my friend, and that's a nobody. Some people are your betters. Don't shoot the messenger, is all I'm saying.

What's it like to be hated by everyone who knows you, tell me that?

A solace. I don't need to join your clubs and your teams. The denim-clad downtrodden. I am my own person. If you had stayed on at school you might realise that. How is the marriage counselling going by the way?

Watch your mouth, I'm warning you, said Tintin.

Seriously, how's it going? Let's try to have a conversation. What about it? I tell you something and you bore me with something else. So, what would you like to know?

When will you fuck off out that door, that's all I want to know.

You're being small-minded again, said Valentine. Marriage. Let's talk marriage. Why do people get married? I was nearly married once you know.

From what I hear, I doubt there's even a word invented for what you're into.

Small-minded and prudish. This is what I mean. You northsiders don't like to see people enjoying themselves. Anyway, what is wrong with liking to have your feet tickled?

Please use them to fuck off somewhere else, Tintin said. I've to ring round to see who can come in.

They are mighty big shoes to fill, Valentine said, as he went out the door. He turned left on Capel Street, skirted the road works for the new tram lines, and hugging the outside lane of the granite-edged pavement, he offered the occasional nod for someone inside one of the shops, the few older shops that had survived, selling things much more useful than sushi or Polish crisps or shirts made from hemp, until he reached the splendid roar of traffic along the quays, and soon found himself crossing the arches of Grattan Bridge towards the pillars of City Hall, a tricolour at half-mast. It was around eleven in the morning. The day stretched ahead of him, and high above him too. He could do whatever he wanted. Normally, out on the streets like this, doing his rounds, he was on the clock and had to be back at the shop before too long. Today, he was his own master. The hours were his own to fill. He waited at the lights to cross Dame Street.

Fuck, is that Rachel Holt over there in stripy tights at the corner? Not in the mood for that at all. Skip down this cobbled lane.

As every native knows, the charm of Dublin is all about who you might meet when you're out and about on its miserly handful of streets. It might be someone you haven't seen in a long time or a face from only the night before. It might be a lover you've never forgotten or your brother's handsome headmaster or an old landlord you still owe money to. The encounter could bring remarkable news or distressing information or more of the same old drama despite the years that have passed. Passion might be rekindled on Watling Street, barefaced lies told on Wicklow Street, a secret shared on Sráid na gCaorach Mhór. And, of course, this feeling that you never know who is round the next corner can lead to some strange behaviour among the natives. People on bicycles, for example, flying around so no one can stop them and demand to know what they're up to these days. Or the number of people in disguise. Or impregnable behind prams and pets and phones.

It can also mean you are regularly forced to abandon your destination altogether. You have to think on your feet in Dublin, stay alert, keep your options open. Pick any pub and study the expressions of those coming in the door; what you see is disbelief that they somehow, God knows how, have reached their port of call, or the equally famous resignation that this place would have to do. Some days there is so much avoiding to be done, so and so over there who made you take an unexpected turn down one street, only to be forced to veer off again to escape the approach of that other so and so, which leads you into the path of someone else, endlessly, inescapably. You can accidentally come face to face with your destiny because you thought it wise to avoid a tricky interaction with someone in stripy tights whose fortieth birthday party you ruined five years earlier.

And this is, more or less, what happened on this particular day when after Rachel, he saw Quinlan, and next Mad Emmet, and three more, and before he knew it Valentine was standing somewhere else and a voice said to him, Anything strange, Valentine?

On his wooden pallet, lotus-style under a fisherman's cape, his long gunslinger's moustache turning yellow, there was old Ultan. In his lap was positioned a sign stolen from a hotel which read Do Not Disturb, and squeezed in below, handwritten, the words, *please donate quietly*.

Valentine provided him with a smoke, put the lighter to it, and told him the story of how he had hurt his wrist.

Muriel should move those keys out of temptation's way, Ultan said.

What she doesn't know won't hurt her. But tell me, Valentine said, Maybe it's these sunglasses but are you unwell or fed up or is there some lack about you today?

Indeed there was too. Some young lads had run off with his collection box. Valentine's outrage was tempered by his admiration for the old man's dignity in the face of injustice. Then one man seemed to study the dangerous end of his cigarette while the other considered the unique vanishing point of his smoke plume. From a passing car, a voice called, Beam me up, Scottie.

That's a new one, said Valentine. Not bad either. I get it. The Caped Canaveral is still my favourite though. Even if I did mint it myself. You've more names than the big man above on the throne.

My confirmation name was Tomas, you know. If I had been called Tomas, my life might have taken a different turn, who knows, not me anyway, Ultan said, shy as ever when he spoke about what had befallen him.

You were chosen, Valentine reminded him. You can't back down now and prove those smug bastards right. My nephew is called Tomas, sure. The kid my sister adopted. He's a bit mad to be honest. The way he looks at you, you'd think he wants to eat you. Suck the bones out of you. Seriously. My nephew thinks I'm a big tit.

The two men had a good laugh at that until Ultan said, That dream of yours, I've been turning it over in my mind. Good deeds are what you need. For the driving I mean. No matter how harshly people treat you. If I feel out of sorts with the world, I like to do a good deed. Only a small thing now. Lend a hand. A kind word. Restores the harmony maybe.

I'll stay in bed an extra hour, Valentine said, but his old friend's advice was still on his mind a short time later when

LEVITATION

he burst through the door of the shop. However, the rare, round smile vanished in a heartbeat when he laid eyes on the other barber who was there in his stead, and he collapsed into the armchair by the brass urn for umbrellas and the eerie amount of forgotten walking sticks.

Tintin, having waited for the right moment, probed the mystery with, You not saying hello to young Jay then? I thought you two were the best of buddies.

Sculpted, tribal tattoos down his long arms, holes in his earlobes you could stick your thumb through, a headphones necklace and a lime green paisley bandana tied around his head, born and raised in Dublin 10, Jay King glanced in the mirror at the same moment as Valentine who said, Hello, good to see you, yeah.

Howdy, said the new boy.

There were two conversations to be heard in the big chairs: Tintin airing his views on Baghdad while Jay and his customer discussed the ill effects of making Irish a compulsory school subject. Two guys on the sofa with me, they had come in separately and recognised each other, they were catching up on friends in common. Tintin sparked up the hairdryer. Valentine was smoking, casting shy glances in the direction of Jay. People passed the big window. On the other side of the street, a camping shop, an acupuncture joint, a Korean restaurant…

Tintin gave the nod to the chair for the next customer and, quick as a flash, Valentine filled the vacated spot beside me.

I'm going to kill him, he confided, out of the corner of his wet mouth. I'm going to scalp him and kill him. That's what's going to happen to me. I know now. I'm going to murder Tintin and go to prison. Maybe that's what I should do. Cold-blooded murder. Do it right here. Tie him to the chair and scalp him first. The last face he sees.

I asked him what Tintin had done this time.

Jay there, that's what he's done. I tell you, there's no one more cunning and devious than Tintin. He's fucking with you and nobody else but you can see it. Twisting the knife like a fucken Rumpelstiltskin.

Obviously, it wasn't the right time to be quibbling over children's stories so, instead, I asked him about Jay, and how the youthful pagan coiffeur had offended his sensibilities.

And he leaned in and told me this story:

Jay started working here last year, right. Late last year. Only part time. He's good, trained in London as a stylist. Wanted to break into fashion. Something didn't go right for him anyway, and he came back. A home-bird maybe. He's good, though. Likes the new scissors with the long blades. Signature finishes. Everything has to be a statement. But he's good. The punters like him. He's only twenty-five, can you believe that? When I was twenty-five I was… What am I talking about again?

I don't know what happened. He started working here the odd day and I would get chatting with him, you know. He's very open, that's what I liked about him. No bullshit. Not the brightest, a bit of an airhead at times actually, but you know he's not defensive and hyper-insecure like a lot of them. He's not looking to impress you, that's what I mean.

And he's mad about cars. The different engines, the interiors, the spec or whatever it's called. Loves driving. He has this souped-up black Plymouth Fury. You can't miss it. Cars and going out at the weekend and how drunk you got, that's what it's all about. He'd tell you all about what he did at the weekend. But he knows when to shut up too. He's sound. And he's got a good sense of humour. So I didn't mind having to work with him. It was something new anyway. And he seemed to enjoy talking to me too. He did. He talked to me about himself.

We went for a pint in Crusoe's one evening after work. And that turned into a few. I'm not mad about those boreholes in his ears and the self-decoration business but he's got a good few stories about London. McQueen, Yves Saint Laurent, Versace, all that crowd.

To be honest, he was one of the reasons I started to learn to drive. He couldn't believe it that I didn't even have a car. Like I was some sad aul one.

Then we're in Crusoe's again another night. And it gets to closing time and we decide to head on somewhere else. It was a genuine summer's night, a real beaut. And we end up in this gay bar with some friends of his. And we did a bit of E. One of those nights. This transvestite starts talking to us anyway and she's obviously really into Jay. Or I thought she was anyway. I didn't know they were friends already. I thought she was all over him, you know? Ruining the buzz. And so I say something to her. I'm just trying to get her to ease off and let everybody enjoy themselves. You know, quit the heavy assault. He's too good for you—that's all I said to her. And I may as well have said… I don't know… like it was some big insult. She got so upset I may as well have set her wig on fire and they all turned on me then like I was the cruellest fucken monster they'd ever seen. He's too good for you, that's all I said.

And he hasn't spoken to me since.

And you know what else I didn't know, your man the tranny, he was the son of one of those women Gemmel is supposed to have buried up the mountains. How the fuck was I supposed to know like? Get fucken over it.

Yes, that's what Tintin is up to, the fucken rat with the quiff. Twisting the fucken knife and acting all innocent. Fucken Rumpelstiltskin. Do you fancy a pint?

~

The next morning, Muriel accosted her son on the landing outside the bathroom. It was a favourite spot of hers for speaking her mind. What was bothering her was she could smell the legacy of her son in her car. Standing opposite her in his bathrobe, wet, toilet paper on his upper lip, still wearing the rubber glove he used to protect the bandage in the shower, Valentine began to deny it and accuse her of being paranoid, but it was a waste of time. His mother placed more faith in the evidence of her nose than she did her eyes or any other of the senses, however many there really are. Next, he opted for a half-truth and when that was given short shrift also he reknotted the belt on his gown, had to stop because of a twinge in his wrist, and told her the entire story, or most of it anyway.

There's a war going on, the mother said, jabbing a finger into his moist, hairless chest. There are people dying while I have to stand here listening to you. And if you think I'm going to waste my time feeling guilty for your insignificant handicaps, you've another think coming.

Who said I was blaming you? the son said.

I can smell it off you. No. It smells like fuchsia just before it dies. What I want to know is what that cretin of a son-in-law was doing inside my private car?

Muriel didn't like Sabrina's husband one bit. She thought he was a born victim. Child-abuse, self-harm, pornography, gambling, depression, a failed cop and a wife who walked all over him—the man was never happy unless he had drained every ounce of pity out of you.

You're losing it, Mammy, Valentine said. What would Graham be doing in your car? You're stressed out by the war and all the death and destruction for a few barrels of oil. These are troubled times, Mammy, and the nose might be overcompensating. I can see it by your hair.

It's very dry looking, isn't it? Muriel said mournfully, touching the ends of her hair.

Valentine rested his gloved hand on his mother's shoulder

and gave her some advice: Just because we're letting the Yanks land their soldiers and whatever else at Shannon Airport, he said, it doesn't mean you should let yourself go.

Together, they went downstairs to the kitchen and had a cup of tea. Valentine, who occasionally would put a colour in for her, or straighten the ends of her bob, made an appointment for her at her favourite salon, insisting also that he'd pay for it as a treat.

After she had gone, he got dressed and looked out the window at the street for a while. It was windy. Then he turned on the television. His phone rang and it was Lauren Musgrave. She was in her car, between meetings, and she was wondering how the hand was and why she hadn't heard from him about the bill.

It's a long story, he said and, I love your stories, she said right back.

While he was entertaining the lady on the phone, making her laugh and worrying she might have another crash, Valentine remembered he had a driving lesson that evening.

But Mr Wells wouldn't hear of him cancelling. He had seen this type of behaviour before, he said. Self-inflicted incapacity. The body was our Achilles heel. No matter how many times Valentine described how a total stranger had rear-ended him, the instructor would not be dissuaded from his interpretation that it was another aspect of the same fear which took over him at traffic lights.

That evening, Mr Wells at the wheel, the two men travelled to the Red Cow roundabout and there they parked.

I've been putting some thought into your problem, Mr Wells said. This debilitating panic of yours at junctions. The lack of trust in your fellow road-user.

I see them every day in the shop, Valentine said. I know what they're like. And you expect a set of lights on a stick to keep them under control. Every one of them, you don't know what's been happening for them during the day. They could have just been sacked, dumped, heard they had cancer, realised that their life is shit.

Been caught in a latex orgy, Mr Wells said. You seemed to think that was an important possibility to keep in mind the other night.

I was joking.

You are blinded by empathy, Mr Wells said. Study the traffic. Notice how much of it there is. It's a big sample. Notice how they stay in line. See the order in it. We humans love order. We love systems. Order is what has liberated us from the prison of nature. The key. The key to the future. Study the traffic.

Valentine counted the cars while Mr Wells continued with his lecture. The law of large numbers was the name of it in logic. The more of a thing there is, the more it tends towards order. The more cars on the road at a given time, the less likelihood there is of a random event. On a lesser road you're more likely to meet a chancer than on the motorway. The more, the better, that's what you need to be thinking at every set of lights. Safety in numbers. You're safer driving in the city than anywhere else, Valentine, latex orgies or not.

Their next lesson was at an amusement arcade in Tallaght. Mr Wells stood behind Valentine's racing car seat while he competed for the best lap times in Monaco and Brazil. It seemed to be working too when, a few nights later, Valentine went the length of the Long Mile Road and back again to Crumlin. The two men met as many as four times a week, particularly once the date for the driving test came through the letterbox. Even after Valentine did what he did in the barbershop, Mr Wells was one of the few people to stick by him.

I met Mr Wells only the one time. Valentine and me on Aston Quay ran into Mr Wells and another man, both of them with cheap briefcases. Mr Wells was in a hurry to move on. He barely broke his stride. No sign of the fisherman's cap either. In Crusoe's later, I asked Valentine if he had seen evidence of Mr Wells's qualifications. He sighed and hung his head, exasperated. I think this might even have been the day before I was sent across the street into Coogan's Camping, and heard what I heard.

Listen to yourself, will you, Valentine said to me, a pill-popping failure under the doctor's care, squatting in a junk room above a barbershop, trying to look down your nose at other people. That man has picked himself up more times than anybody I know.

Whatever happened between them, in the end, Valentine wouldn't tell me. He was like that about some things, aggressive, locked tight, though never around the subjects you might expect.

But we're running ahead of ourselves here.

~

Nighttime and a car is speeding down the motorway in the wrong direction with a fat bald man at the wheel. The windscreen is smashed, the wind tearing at his face. Another car is coming straight at him. Then another. Each time, as they pass, the man shields his eyes against the glare of the beams. He turns the steering wheel wildly, ineffectually. There is a box of toffee apples in the passenger seat, sprinkled with glass. In the driver's mirror, he catches regular glimpses of a struggle in the back seat between a man with bolts in his head and a Sumo-child struggling to free himself from a booster seat. Shut him the fuck up, the fat bald driver shouts a moment before he goes completely blind.

The real Valentine was lying in his bed re-running the nightmare again when the phone rang.

Freaky or what? he said to his sister. Here I am dreaming of Skippy and then you call me.

His name is Tomas, she said. And why aren't you at work? Have you had a breakdown?

Don't sound so excited, he said. Not everybody needs to have a breakdown once a week.

Yes, some people like to draw it out for years, Sabrina said, fast off the draw.

I'm a perfectionist, he said. There's nothing worse than a boring breakdown. Where's the hope, the panache?

You wouldn't pick your nose unless you had an audience, she said, and she said it again, or something similar, in her kitchen a few hours later about how he had always craved attention as a kid. Tomas was babbling away in a language no one could understand, making hesitant stabs with one little brown finger at his uncle's damaged wing as though he could heal it. Valentine, meanwhile, was teaching the child how to wink.

I've had my second quarter of Xanax for the day so you can quit trying to get on my nerves, Sabrina said. Anyway, it's a filthy habit in a man. Daddy never winked.

And look at me, his only son, Valentine said, moving from two knees to one on the kitchen floor. If I had learned to wink earlier in life, I would be married now to a lady with her own stables and a Land Rover with four-wheel drive. Wouldn't I, Skippy?

Since when have you been interested in horses, never mind ladies? And stop calling him that.

It's either that or Kermit. Or maybe Zebedee. He hops around the place on his arse doesn't he?

We have to tie him down, Sabrina said.

Valentine looked at his sister and she nodded. You've no idea, she said. If you leave the room he starts bouncing around the place like a beach ball. You can hear him laughing his head off.

Only when you leave him alone?

When he thinks nobody's watching, Sabrina said, with a helpless shrug. But at least he sleeps. Ten hours like clockwork. The opposite of yourself, of course, who would charge money to watch you go to sleep. Remember your books of raffle tickets? Top prize a private audience with Valentine. Watch him do a handstand. Watch him look out the window.

Sabrina had caught him unawares earlier. Hearing he was off work, she had easily cornered him into agreeing to pay them an overdue visit. He'd caught a bus into town and headed for Connolly Station only to be tempted in the door of Crusoe's which was opening up for the day, and it was on his usual stool in the empty pub, lighting the first cigarette from a new box, that he was reminded that in less than fourteen hours it would be illegal to smoke indoors.

Typically, Sabrina had an ulterior motive for bringing him all the way out to Portmarnock. His sister never did anything unless she had a hidden reason; even as a child she would only ask you a question if she already knew the answer. Or in the back of the car, she would start crying and say it was because she felt happy and then she'd get her own way for the rest of the day. She had brought him out there on false pretences, making him feel bad on the phone for not visiting more often. But then again, had he not been looking for the opportunity for a good deed and here it was on a plate? Go see the sis and try to act normal around black-eyed Skippy. Make people chuffed, that was the plan for the day.

Tomas was a chubby Guatemalan kid. He was just over the year mark, still wasn't walking, and the colour of oxtail soup. Sabrina had adopted him, went over there with a laminated photo of him and a bag of money, received the child from the arms of his teenage mother and shipped him on a jet plane back to Dublin. Tomas Skippy Simmons. And he loved his Uncle Valentine. He babbled away to his uncle like they were the best of friends. He had a tantrum every time Valentine looked at the door.

Sabrina was under the impression that her brother's initial enthusiasm for his first nephew had simply waned, the shine had gone off it, the reality had set in, and Valentine was content for her to think that way. He wanted to protect his sister from the real reason, which was, well, it was hard to describe.

One day he was playing with Tomas, they had the cars out of the educational crate, presents from Valentine most of them. Sabrina was writing emails in the study. Uncle and nephew were alone. Valentine would push the car towards Tomas and wait for him to roll it back. It was going well. Peaceful. Relaxing. Valentine was glad to be there, sitting on the floor with this strange, small creature from the other side of the world. The kid, in his own mysterious tongue, dished out endless instructions. It was good to be an uncle. He would teach this kid everything he knew.

The little police car rolled on its squeaking wheels in Valentine's direction. It came to a stop between them. Then it began to move again, slowly, in short forward jolts and finally rested at the sole of his boot. The kid's hands were nowhere near it. Valentine looked at his nephew and his nephew smiled and clapped his hands and said, well, yes, he said his uncle's name.

Privately, Muriel and Valentine had hoped the arrival of Tomas would bring a healthy change to the Portmarnock house. At one of their family Sunday dinners, Sabrina asked for silence and announced she had been to see a man who was in contact with the dead. In the argument that developed, she went as far as to accuse her mother of having murdered her father. Muriel hadn't been back to Portmarnock since.

You know what day is coming up? Sabrina said, feeding spoonfuls of yoghurt to the kid in his baby seat screwed to the table.

It'll be like jaywalking, Valentine said. The cops won't enforce it. Sure most of them smoke themselves. Well, apart from Graham. He had to give them up, didn't he?

Sabrina scowled at him and said, It's Daddy's thirtieth anniversary. Am I the only one to remember him? Am I the only one who even gives a damn that nobody has ever been caught for running him down and leaving him lying on the street?

Skippy began to laugh at the yoghurt dripping off the spoon onto the table. The world was a magical place. Sabrina said she wanted Valentine's help to organise a memorial. She was as determined as their mother when she made up her mind about something.

You owe me this, she said.

Back on his favourite stool later in Crusoe's, he still wasn't sure how he owed it to her. But, to keep the peace, he had agreed to play intercessor, and broach the subject with Muriel at a good moment. He had a long history of playing the intermediary between the two of them. For years and years he had ferried messages from one room to another. Mammy says this… Sabrina says that. But who cared about any of that when you had a few quid in your pocket and the bar was packed all the way to the door, and everybody was in great form, like it was a party, a big party, somebody amazing was throwing a big party, somebody powerful, illustrious, outrageous.

The government… the namby-pamby government… the fascist namby-pamby government… we fought for our freedom, somebody or other was shouting into his ear, four cigarettes burning between his fingers.

There were only hours to go before it would be against the law to smoke in a pub. In a shop. In a taxi. At the cinema. The ballet. In a brothel. On an airplane. Down the mines. In a barbershop.

Just in case it was true, our Valentine and many like him

decided the only course of action was to make a glorious night of it. And for a few hours, like every other man and woman, he reached that dizzy height where he forgot everything.

~

If you need an answer to a question, no matter how difficult or embarrassing or downright dangerous, a good place to find it is in Crusoe's pub. There are people in Crusoe's who are always keen to help. These people know true wisdom yearns to be shared and Crusoe's is one of the last places to offer them a roof to do so. These stalwarts will put their heads together on your behalf and an answer will be found, one way or another. Take for example, the Couple as they are called: a man and a woman, late fifties, well wrapped up, slow spirit drinkers, and deathly quiet. It is a rare privilege to catch them exchange a word. Around two o'clock every afternoon, other than a Saturday, they enter the pub hand in hand as they have been doing for many years, back as far as the time they first crossed paths, two strangers stumbling in off the streets with the same question they could not keep to themselves the length of another lonely night. They have not been apart since, it is said, and now they wait every day for the next question but only until 10.30 when they put on their coats and leave as quietly as they arrived, hand in hand. People are mysterious. People want to help each other. And in Crusoe's these two human qualities come together and flourish.

Who among you dismal shower of gasbags and non-entities has any information on a businessman called Gonzo?

Such was Valentine's question. Crusoe's saw a lot of him the day after it became an offence to enjoy a cigarette with your pint without the risk of being mugged on the street. He might have stayed out all night, went to another party, or back to some other drunken soul's bed, anything is possible, mind your own business he would sometimes say to me, suck on your butt. Whatever he did or didn't do he was back in Crusoe's around lunchtime the next day and spent the afternoon there, going in and out for a smoke, and waiting for an answer.

As soon as he had it, he marched off to confront Lauren. He had gone some distance before it dawned on him that he didn't know where to find her. He wasn't sure either where exactly he was. Irishtown perhaps. Ringsend. Had he crossed the river or was it a lake? Leaning against a wall, he rang her phone again and again. He left many messages, each one different. A kid went by on a bicycle, arms folded, and returned to ask him for a cigarette.

If you tell me where I am, Valentine said.

The kid took a cigarette. He was no more than ten but he could blow perfect smoke rings. Valentine complimented him on this skill and reminded him of their bargain. The kid looked at the sky and he waved at something up there, somebody or something Valentine had the impression that was very far away. A moment later, he was surrounded by a gang of them, kids, and they took everything he had, his wallet, one of his earrings, his phone, his sunglasses, and they left him in the street.

But now Valentine was sober again. Yes, and as soon as he got his breath back, he dusted himself down and went in pursuit of them. He raced along cramped terraced streets quicker than a scandal, sharpening the edge of every corner until he got his hands on one of them, a kid slick with gel and sweat, dragged him out from under a parked car. The rest of them stood around jeering.

A man in a kaftan came out of the houses and told Valentine to let the kid go. The tough guy claimed he was picking on the wrong kids. Valentine, panting for air, magnificently sober, refused. The guards arrived. Valentine was sure he recognised one of them from the shop but it didn't do him any good and they took him away and put him in a cell with people he wouldn't be seen dead with and after a while, for everybody's sake, they switched him to a holding cell of his own.

~

The following afternoon, presumably, I had only begun to warm my corner of the sofa when the lonesome bell warned of a patron's entrance and Valentine Rice cleared the threshold, chose a spot on the tiles and declared he was ready to come back to work. Tintin paid him no heed; he was talking to the postman. Jay blew on his thinning scissors and leaned in extra close to the head of a man who, apparently, was on his way to the courts to have his divorce finalised.

Flexing his fingers for all to see, Valentine pleaded, It's a fucken nightmare out there. Even the sky is the colour of prison bog roll.

However, despite the poetry and some of his best pleading, it simply wasn't to be, this sudden resumption of the normal routine, not so quickly anyway. After the departure of the postman, and the man soon to know liberty again, Tintin reminded him that Jay had been promised a certain amount of hours. It wouldn't be fair on young Jay now, would it? he said, sorting through the post. Valentine looked from Tintin to Jay, then to me, a man keen to discover the truth of himself through work, a man stopped in his tracks, denied, flabbergasted, and sat himself down.

A picture of dawn over the Bloubergstrand on the front, Tintin read aloud from a postcard as follows: Greetings from paradise where you will never steal enough from me ever to be. Floor better be spotless and sinks too. Make sure Fiddler doesn't leave streaks on the window. Make him do them again. I have my spies remember. Might have bad news on my return.

He's planning to sell the place, Tintin said, as though it was an answer he had been expecting.

Get fucked, Valentine told him.

I have my spies too, said Tintin.

Valentine laughed and put a fag in his mouth. Then he took it back out again to say, Spies? You mean that greyhound-obsessed, sacked lollipop man with the rat's tail?

My uncle was taken by cancer six months ago, Tintin said. Don't get uppity.

Uppity? Change the fucken record.

I'll say it again. Uppity. Don't talk to me about funerals.

How is saying my uncle—ah, forget it, Tintin said and turned away. Then he turned back again and said in a kinder voice, I know you have, Valentine. Seen a few funerals. I know you have. It's what I remind myself about every bleedin' day.

I wear it lightly though, don't I?

Sure you do. Cool as a cucumber. That's Valentine Rice.

So don't get uppity, is all I'm saying.

Whatever you say, Valentine.

And the shop's not for sale either, that's more disloyal bollocks. The boss will be waked out of this joint. They'll have to take out the fucken window to get the coffin out, Valentine said, pointing to the wall of glass through which we all saw two people engaged in a kiss, an Asian guy and a redhead, a ferocious kiss, hungry, brutal, totally oblivious to the world around them.

Put that cancer stick out, Tintin said.

What felt like a long time after, three more customers into the day, a man came into the shop who, from what I could figure out, should have been bald. He was there to show off his implants and the barbers were utterly fascinated, tugging and twisting at them, petting them like children at the zoo, and for a while all the rancour was forgotten.

We have an audience, someone said. A woman was waving in from the street. A middle-aged woman with shy agitated eyes and golden bridal hair, South Sea pearls around her throat, in an open pink leather coat with a cluster of lacquered strawberries on the lapel, a substantial bosom, to say the least, and a phone at her ear. We all waved back.

~

In Valentine's absence, the shop began to fill steadily one by one with customers. Yes, it could happen like that; the empty mirrors, the sinister trio of pump-action chairs, the coruscating low-paid hours instantly annulled by the lonesome cowbell. And a man stands before you. He is followed by another. And another. And again the cowbell heralds the next to be bibbed and shorn, the next to be exonerated. Men arrive like they are heeding a call to the threshold and although they can see there are three or four others in front of them, they choose to wait, even if they have to stand, and it is so much more than the fact that they have decided to drop what they were doing and make their way across town to Capel Street and now they are here they might as well see it through, or if they are men who have been planning it for some time, a bit of shopping in town and a cut and tidy afterwards, and they have made the trip in on buses and in their own cars, or there's an important occasion looming in the calendar, or men with transformation on their minds, radical alteration, a bright new look—no, it is the lure of the big chairs which draws them in irresistibly, those twenty minutes or so in front of the mirror, face to face with all their deeds and hopes, mediated skilfully by the barber with his blades and powders and stories, or in mutual silence, and afterwards, after it is done and complete, after they have paid, each of them will linger for a moment, and check their reflection, and catch the hint of a rekindled light in their eye before they resume their hard-won roles in the insubstantial world.

Yes, Tintin was in his element, conducting at least five different conversations. Jay worked quietly, speaking only to seek the customer's assent. Hair of different shades and texture collected in the corners. Towels in the sinks. Bibs shaken out a third time. Then they ran out of change. Giving me two twenties and a ten which he counted into my hand one at a time, with another man as witness, a robotics engineer no less, Tintin told me to make myself useful for the first time in my life and run across the street to Coogan's Camping and Outdoor Life, with the three gold Medici balls still hanging over the door.

Sleeping bags and furry car seat covers pinned to a wall. Shelves of walking boots and socks for the intrepid family. Camouflage netting, a one-man polar tent, inflatable mattresses, portable heaters, knives. Overhead, hung like trophies, there were stools and lanterns, shovels, water bottles, torches, canoe paddles and the bald heads of mannequins in ski-goggles. Hearing a man's laughter from deeper inside the bazaar, I moved towards it, a ground-level light throwing my shadow across a large poster of the Titanic at anchor in Cobh harbour. The man was on the phone behind a half-wall of binoculars. And this is what I overheard:

What... You're having me on... the day after tomorrow... Who told you... There'll be murder. There'll be blue murder... sweet Jesus... time flies... What... me too... me too... they should give him the chair like he wants... the guillotine if you ask me... he wouldn't dare... he wouldn't... Gemmel is a... he won't... that's justice for you... are they telling the other families... he won't come back this way... it's a bad line, Raymond... a new bunk bed... it's a palace in there... how many in with you now... eight... twins... (a sneeze)... get lost... from Santry... was he... I thought Gemmel was from the midlands... why would he come here?... time flies... you know what though I would love to see the face on Tintin if he shows his face again, he'd wet himself, he'd literally piss himself... Rice... he would probably suck the cunt off... hold on, Ray...

Only looking for some change, I said, waving the notes as proof. Tintin sent me over.

He ended his call and returned, blowing his nose on a large chequered handkerchief. Busy beyond, is it?

Mental.

Wylie away on his jaunt?

I shrugged. Bog-cotton hair flattened like a crop circle. Another tuft under his lip. Hawaiian shirt with a pencil torch in the breast pocket. Wheezing, with manicured fingers, he did the business with the money, building the coins into stacks on a foldaway table. There was a book on the table also, open at a page showing a damaged photograph of old Capel Street, a penny farthing, men in hats on horseback, the Victorians.

You a friend of Rice?

Big time, I said, pretending not to hear the sarcasm.

An eyelid twitched. Has he learned how to… he said but another big sneeze cut the question short, bent him over, hands on his knees. Long twisting snake of spine.

You dumped a book in the river, I hear. Writer or something.

Or something.

As I was walking out of there, I took another glimpse at the doomed liner, the travellers crowded at the rails, tripped over a lead taped to the floor, and managed to spill some of the precious change. Tintin would have a field day if I was short, no doubt about that, but I wasn't about to get down on my hands and knees for a few euro, especially when Coogan, only a few steps behind, unable to contain himself a moment longer, launched into a recitation: We inhale the Atlantic vapours and they turn us into mystics, poets and politicians and unemployables with school-girl complexions. Oliver St John Gogarty. Now there was a real writer.

~

LEVITATION

Two days later, we were waiting, Valentine and me, the door to the shop wedged open—the April morning was so kind, and soft, and eager, the traffic fumes adding a new twist to the regular singed aroma of the barbershop. Tintin was there too, of course, and although we watched his movements as closely as we studied the faces traversing the window, there was no sign to betray that he had got wind of Gemmel's release also. Both barbers were kept busy enough, but nothing too demanding, and nobody too strange either, nobody who might be checking out the lay of the land, so to speak, a scout, an accomplice; these murderers always have their pen pals, Valentine had already decided.

Mid-morning we were outside for a smoke in the sunshine and so was Coogan across the street. The man had put on a new Hawaiian shirt for the occasion.

Great to be alive on old Capel Street, he shouted across to us.

Another day on the farm is all, he got in reply from Valentine, and then a line of three army trucks blocked the view.

And that was all. The three of us pretending we had nothing on our minds beyond nicotine and the sun on our faces. I gave Valentine that same quote from Gogarty about the Atlantic vapours, and as if he knew where I had got it, he made an appalled face and advised me to increase my meds.

Maybe you could do with some, for those panic attacks of yours, was my attempt at offering some resistance.

He scoffed, like I was well wide of the mark, and said, We have to get rid of Tintin.

But how was the question. We discussed a few absurd ideas and went back inside. You can imagine our shock a short time later at the peak of a young guard's cap leaning in the door to ask for Valentine by name. There was silence. Valentine chose a spot on the ceiling to ponder. Tintin quit chewing his gum, dropped his eyes to the floor. The guard said his quarry's name again. Valentine looked at me, cornered, a world of doubt in his eyes, or some rare form of comprehension. I just shrugged.

All it was, the guard had to explain first, was he had the man's phone. Some good citizen had found it on the street and handed it in. While we were still laughing about it, and Tintin, unable to work out what was going on, had gone to the back of the shop to use the toilet, we heard a brief wail of agony. It turned out he had cracked a tooth. He had it in his hand, stuck in a ball of gum. He may as well have been stabbed, the noise he was making, moving from seat to seat.

It is meant to be, Valentine said.

We had persuaded Tintin to go to the dentist by then.

It is meant to be, Valentine said again, humbled by the work of destiny.

I had to admit, at the very least, it looked likely. The stage was set. I asked him again to tell me more about this dream of his, bombing down the motorway with Gemmel and his nephew in the back.

It's a hunch is all. He smoothed his sideburns in the mirror, caught my eye. You shitting yourself, is that it?

I mentioned the name of a dead actress who often appeared in my dreams but it made not a dint in his confidence.

I only need you here as a witness, he said. If you don't have the bottle, fine. I'll manage. He shook his shoulders, a man limbering up. He went to the window. All three of us in the car on the motorway, he said, and the steering wheel is banjaxed. Skippy is trying to get out of the seatbelt and I'm shouting at Gemmel, hold him down, hold him down. Then I wake up. And the first thing I think about is my father and those bloody endless Sunday walks across the Sally Gap.

And we began to wait seriously now, grimly, out of our depth. Even the sun went in and there followed a period of time during which every face glancing in the window wished it hadn't. The first customer to brave the tiles, a posh kid with a floppy fringe, was given short shrift, told to come back later. The second received the same treatment. Valentine seemed to be familiar with the next one, however, an elderly man who knew his mother, and so he was forced to do some work. He worked quickly. He didn't rush it either, despite the nerves. Next, a man with a perfect horseshoe hairline, followed by one with a story about an incident at a polling booth that on any other day would have deserved a second hearing. And now another man breached the lintel, and it clearly wasn't his first time either because he not only knew the barber's name but believed he had some kind of right to explore the area beyond the till. A journalist, it transpired, stringy orange hair, the jacket too big for him. And soon enough there was acrimony between the barber and the journalist. Valentine caught my eye in the mirror in a way that suggested he feared again the cat must be out of the bag, that others suspected Gemmel was heading our way. Valentine let the man talk on for a few minutes. Then he interrupted him to say, I'm surprised to see you here actually with your woman arriving back into Dublin at the airport—what do you call her, the model, the one with the legs—and they're shipping her right off to rehab in Wicklow. So I heard, anyway. Didn't we hear that earlier? he said, roping me in. Was that this morning or was it yesterday morning? I backed him up. And Valentine continued with, Sure anyway, who can you believe any more? They were probably talking through their hole. People like to feel important. Fame's a bitch though, if you ask me. Fool's gold.

 He wanted a high-five after the journalist had left. Then he stood at the door and had a smoke, scanning the street, down towards the river and up towards the Parnell Street bend. And he smoked another one. He had barely turned back into the shop when Ultan followed him in like a shadow.

For fuck's sake, Ultan. Where did you drop out of—the crowded sky above?

Would you have a minute or two for a chat? said the old Yogi.

A chat? Actually, Ultan, I don't. Not now. I am in the middle of some serious shit here. Something as big as you that day floating in the air. This is my day. This is Valentine S. Rice seizing his moment. I was born for this day. So will every skinny-arsed cunt just get the hell out of my way.

He felt bad about it later, our Valentine did. This was after a few pints in Crusoe's, after we had waited and watched and turned people and their money away from the shop and nothing at all had happened, no one even slightly perverse, or extravagantly superfluous, after we had delayed lowering the shutters until we had seen the lights go out in Coogan's Camping with our own eyes, and finally extinguished any hope that this was the day Valentine would outclass Tintin. We did what you do, and made the bar staff work for their wages. Some drank with us and some departed towards mattresses both hard and soft, single and king size, ascetic, bitterly divided, and paradisiacal. One man from Skibbereen was bedding down in his car. The lock-in came as no surprise. At some stage, Valentine told me about a peculiar episode he had observed in his mother's house involving Ultan and his nephew Skippy. Yes, it seemed Valentine had taken him home to Crumlin the other evening; the old man looked like he could do with a proper meal and Tintin and his denimy northsider pals were pulling the legs off him like an insect.

Muriel was glad of the company, he said. Ultan had been at her table before. She cooked her best pork chops, reminisced and gave out about the war. Then she sang an old CND song. Ultan got to his feet and recited a poem. Valentine opened a bottle of wine. They were interrupted by a knock at the front window. Only one person would announce themselves in that way. The look on Sabrina's face when she saw what she must have thought was a tramp in the kitchen; but she rose above it. She was there to mend some bridges after all, to increase the peace. And the evening continued, and sheltered them, studded with small kindnesses and woven out of sheets of laughter. And Tomas stuck like a frog to his favourite uncle.

The peculiar episode happened near the end. Muriel and Sabrina had gone into the living room for a private conversation, leaving Skippy in the care of his uncle and Ultan. Gasping for a smoke, Valentine had stepped outside the back door. He happened to glance in through the kitchen window. Ultan was sitting on the floor with Tomas and the kid seemed to be giving him a detailed lecture, wagging a finger in the old man's wine-flushed face, and, it was hard to describe, Valentine said, but Ultan was nodding fervently like he understood his orders.

~

Maybe not often enough, but often, when you're down, and fed up, there's someone who will hear your sighs. Up they will rise these sighs and there are ones that make it through the defensive cloud barrier, rising further up beyond the earth's atmosphere, to float around in space in a choir of soft moans and groans and sighs, and often, not too often, one of them gets bumped against a satellite and begins its journey back to earth and into the secret ear of someone who, without knowing why, suddenly has an urge to do a nice thing for you. This is what Valentine was thinking as he drove around the quieter roads of the Phoenix Park in his new car.

You see, what had happened was Sabrina had called her little brother out of the blue to say if he wanted her car he could have it. For good, too. Yes, for keeps. Her and her ex-detective husband were buying a new one, and since her car, a tan-coloured Vauxhall Astra, which by the way she liked to call Marty, after somebody in a band, her first crush, since Marty had been so good and reliable for all those years she had owned him, ten years it was, she could remember the exact date—a date that Valentine didn't hear because her phone cut out at that point but which came rushing back to him anyway, a moment from the past as fresh now as it would have been then, the day she had bought the car and sailed past the window of the shop on Capel Street punching her horn, Sabrina the triumphant, her long bare arms, Sabrina the star, her heavy curls fanning out behind her, gold in her ears, and how he had a kid under his hands at the time, holding a photograph torn out of a football magazine, Celtic it was, he could remember the green and white stripes, a footballer this kid wanted to look like, and it was right then at that moment, back then in the shop, Sabrina driving past, Valentine remembered a walk with his father, one of their Sunday hikes, so many forced Sunday hikes in Wicklow with the silent morose man, and how they had got lost, and more lost, and the night seemed to rise up out of the ground, out of the stones until they were goners, and his father, that shy awkward silent ex-Jewish man, made them both kneel and pray and pray until, after hours of beseeching, they heard the blades of the rescue helicopter high above in the darkness, and Valentine dropped his comb in the shop and he was knocked back on the bed in his room in his mother's house in Crumlin at the very same time, years later, and his phone was ringing and it was Sabrina calling back, only moments later, with Tomas on her arm now, giving his instructions across the airwaves.

 At the park gates now, the wipers on at slow, before him the North Circular Road stretching all the way through Phibsborough, our Valentine gripped the wheel, and said, Marty, it's just me and you now. You be good to me and I'll spoil you in ways you never even dreamed of. Slave to your

LEVITATION

every whim I'll be. Whatever floats your boat. Deal? Let us begin our illustrious second wind together.

And away they went, the barber within his new car, his first ever car, windows up against the mizzle, and they joined the orderly line of traffic.

And their progress was sweet. With ease, they kept a safe distance behind the car in front, they passed through junctions, they waited behind buses, they let other vehicles enter the line, they gave cyclists plenty of room, they signalled clearly their intentions to the car behind, and at Dorset Street, he turned left, and crossed the other canal, and man and machine were sailing through Drumcondra.

We could go all the way to Belfast on this, Marty. What do you think? The M1. We're on the M1.

He took the turn for the airport instead. A plane was taking off, a flying advert, heading for the Irish Sea. From the depths of a multi-storey car park, he rang Lauren and left a message, telling her where he was. He rang Mr Wells. He rang a guy he hadn't spoken to in years and complained in passing that he was out at the airport waiting to pick somebody up in the new motor. He even rang Tintin but hung up before there was an answer.

Let's go home, he said to Marty. I think I deserve a few pints tonight. And tomorrow we're going to the garage and you can have whatever you want. Shampoo, waxing, how about a new air freshener? What's your favourite flavour?

Well inside the speed limit, in the slow lane again, no need for the wipers now, the sun setting over the city, he came back in towards the centre and there, just before Drumcondra, at a pedestrian crossing, where not a person crossed, waiting opposite a purple Datsun, he froze again. Sweat filled his eyes but his hands were locked on the wheel. His breath wouldn't leave his chest. The seat began to sink away under him, down through the chassis. And word spread from car to car along the motorway, from machine to machine until even the toaster in his mother's kitchen was blowing a fuse at the embarrassment.

We think the answer may lie in the colour, said the Couple in Crusoe's that same night.

What? I'm allergic to purple now? I'm purple-intolerant? Will I tell that to the examiner when I do my test, if we see any cars of a particular shade of maroon or plum or violet, is it all right if I just close my eyes?

Don't shoot the messenger, they said almost in unison.

Whatever happened to my real friends, the intelligent ones? Valentine shouted down the bar. I used to have knowledgeable friends, uplifting friends, smart people. Now look at me. Here with you lot. What happened? Is there anyone among you crowd of losers and wannabes who can tell me what happened?

And the next day in the shop, he was asking the same thing of a guy in the chair who he used to know.

What was I like back then? I was good-looking, wasn't I? I had no shortage of attention. Girls. Men. Old and young. I had my pick, didn't I?

What were you like? Hard to work out. Zany. Up for a good time. Weren't you making a film?

Unlike most, I've learned to embrace failure, Valentine said. Let your dream go free, that takes courage too. Real courage. Set it free. That's the mark of a real man. What you give up. What you don't let happen.

I'd say you're pretty much the same.

And I'd say you never knew me anyway.

Yes, everyone sees it now, that day Valentine was in particularly prickly form. Customer after customer, those who he deemed worthy, under the bib in front of the mirror, was pressed to explain why they weren't a hypocrite. Or just a gobshite. Maybe it was all an attempt to push Tintin to breaking point. Coogan got a mouthful also from the door as he was coming up the street. Valentine turned on me at one point too, telling a shopful of strangers what I had done to seven years of work, that I had to fuck my agent to get published in the first place.

All of you, he said, pointing to every man in the shop, all of you are hypocrites and panhandlers and leading a double life. Go on, one of you try to deny it.

Tintin said he'd had it, and removing his belt of scissors, he decamped, the first time I've ever seen it go that far. The remaining barber then ordered the stunned customers, four in total, to leave him be. Yes, leave me be, he said, grandiose, misunderstood, only me left in his kingdom.

You're making lots of friends today, I said, keeping it light and he said, Fuck you too, poseur. You know nothing about me either.

Is this because the shop might be sold?

Feeble.

What then? More driving problems? What's up?

Nothing's up, he said, offended. What do you want me to tell you? What is it you want to hear? My secrets? Well, I don't have any secrets. Can you wrap your head around that by any chance? I don't have any secrets.

For a moment, I thought he was right, and maybe not only about himself, but about all of us, and we were to a man dead obvious, and weighed down by non-existent depths, and pasts which never happened.

I watched him light a cigarette, lean an elbow on the back of one of the big chairs, blow a satisfied gust of smoke up at the old broken fan. In the mirror, I could see the other side of his face, and the juicy round smile.

So how's Lauren? I asked, forgetting everything I had just been thinking. It was the meds. I couldn't hold a thought for long.

Get your own fucken life, he told me. And I took this as a sign to follow the others out onto the pavement. And that's why I wasn't in the shop when, around three o'clock, Gemmel returned to Capel Street and put his shoulder against the glass door of Wylie's.

PART TWO

All of us know, deep down, that life is not a dream. Like some crude monster in the daylight, reality is sustained by our disbelief in it. Maybe this is why not much seems to change, not really. We teach our children that actions have consequences, but we hope for their sake that it isn't true. Now and again, somebody might actually do something that changes their own life, deliberately or not, and it's always a massive shock, and we, the reluctant audience, may react badly to the convulsion. Some take it as a personal insult, a slap in the face to decency, and some turn the other cheek. Some scoff at its motivation and others hope that at least now that it has happened, nothing like it can ever happen again, and are strangely awed. Some admire the simplicity of the act, the ordinariness behind every wonderful retaliation. Some will claim it is a sign of worse to come. And some, of course, will feel guilty and culpable. All of which, more or less, is what happened when word got out in Dublin that a certain barber in a certain shop on Capel Street had gone ahead and done something he was absolutely free not to do.

In one fell swoop, with a flutter of scissors and a bang of talc, Valentine Rice had managed to become persona non grata.

At first, he really couldn't understand what all the fuss was about. A man had come into the shop and he had given his baby soft hair a trim, which it was badly in need of. Wasn't that his job, to tend to the customer's wishes so long as they behaved themselves in the shop? The man, no matter what he had done, had served his time. The State was the entity responsible for his release, and the manner of it, clandestine, a sleight of hand. Some happy-socked minister or other signs the release papers, but who gets it in the neck? A barber who was just doing what he is paid to do. And anyway, what type of barbershop would it be if it ran background checks on every man who darkened the door? The place wouldn't last five minutes. A good barber gives the same attention to the man he respects as to the man he's glad is not serenading his daughter, or his son. Every man is equal on the tiles, in the big chairs, before the mirrors framed by light bulbs, and under the blade. Over the years on Capel Street, Valentine had dragged the teeth of his comb across the scalps of plenty of men whose eyes in the mirror he couldn't bring himself to meet—and they were just the ones who had never been caught. Maybe he should make a list of them, he began to think, that ballet dancer for example who hiccupped every time the word chimney was mentioned, the judge he was certain he had seen pretending to be a junkie on Cuffe Street, the amount of tourists with PTSD, the diabetics trying to sell him Viagra, the floggers of passports, animals, soiled ladies' underwear, blow, phones, cutlery sets, backstage theatre passes, love potions—even a man from Louth who hinted he knew how to get his hands on the shoes Brendan Behan was buried in.

Maybe he should make a list, Valentine was thinking, and stick it in the window of his mother's house. Maybe he would give the list to that journalist who kept ringing. People were ringing who he hadn't seen in years, old flames, old friends.

You've gone too far this time, they said in the main.

Naturally, to begin with, he tried to defend himself: Did you never have someone you work with you couldn't stand any more? A know-it-all, chews gum all day and winks and nods like one of those things stuck on a dashboard.

You crossed the line there man, they said.

It was a joke. Remember them! Remember how we used to laugh. If it wasn't funny, it wasn't worth a damn.

Or when they tried to offer an olive branch: Of course I knew who it was. Of course I knew what he'd done and what he's supposed to have done. Do you think I'm an emu—or whatever they're called? My head's held high.

Or when nobody seemed to understand: Damn right I would do it again. I would tie that bib on him again and rest my hands on his shoulders and smile and give him your fucken address.

Or: I'm more of an artist than any of you will ever be.

Or in the end: Valentine cannot come to the phone right now. This is his hot bodyguard. He is drinking champagne right now in the company of the real A-listers.

Then he gave up answering the damned thing.

Coogan was the one to blame. Pretentious, soul-patched Coogan was out on the pavement having his four o'clock smoke and, despite the traffic, spotted Gemmel in the chair by the window. Valentine, trying to swap the head on the trimmer, his hands shaking so much he couldn't get it attached, happened to glance across the street at the same time, any place but at the mirror out of the depths of which Gemmel's eyes seemed to be off-roading straight for him. The fag dropped out of Coogan's mouth, his hand went to the breast pocket of his Hawaiian shirt for the mobile. It was Coogan who got on the blower to his mate in the media. The barber, he would tell them, and everybody else perverse enough to listen, waved across at him and laughed like he was enjoying himself, like Valentine and the murderer, a multiple murderer perhaps, a serial killer, were having a bowl of snap, crackle and pop together.

That never happened, Valentine swore, I've never waved to him in my life and I certainly wasn't laughing either. When I clocked Coogan gawping in from across the street I was trying to get a grip on myself, hoping some fucker would arrive in, anybody. Gemmel had just told me he had been in the shop before, and not only the once either in the hands of Tintin, who, by the way, had been less than impressive in his scissors work and blow-drying skills, there had been another time before that, years back, and the crazy bastard was certain he recognised Valentine from that day, although he had put on some weight and his skin had lost its glow, and that the two of them had had an enjoyable conversation about Orson Welles. You want the truth? Well that's the moment Coogan saw. But he was too busy getting on his sentimental high horse and ringing the shock jocks.

The first inkling that what he had done had robbed people of their equanimity was the telephone call from a very emotional Tintin. He had nearly been lynched, he said, there was a mob outside the shop, chanting, throwing eggs at the window. To give him his due, Tintin believed it must be a huge misunderstanding, not even the likes of Valentine would dare do such a thing. And he seemed to be genuinely concerned for his colleague's safety, advising him to lay low until he could sort out who was stirring shit.

Don't worry. I'll sort this business out and let you know when the coast is clear, he said.

That's very decent of you, Valentine said, surprisingly decent even. But let me shine a light into your confusion. Gemmel came in yesterday afternoon after you all ran away with your tails between your legs because you can't handle the truth, and yes, I gave him a haircut. So you won't be

Levitation

holding court any more with your favourite story of the killer who slipped through your little fingers, it'll be me they come to listen to.

In the silence on the other end Valentine could hear the fists banging on the window. What Tintin said, once he had got over the shock, is unrepeatable here.

~

Muriel was waiting for him on the landing again, right outside the bathroom door. She had heard a curious bulletin about a ruckus outside a barbershop on the radio and she was demanding an explanation. In his bathrobe, Valentine followed her downstairs and through the living room and into the kitchen. Her list for the day was on the table, a prescription, and her car keys. He sat. Arms folded, Muriel assumed a defensive position in front of the door. The window by the sink was open and it was sunny outside. He heard gulls high over the house.

You were always scared of your own shadow, Muriel said after he had told her what he knew.

Valentine shook his head. No, Mammy, it wasn't that. I wasn't afraid. Well, not in the way you think.

Sure you were, Muriel said. You could never fight your own battles. The truth is you were caught in there by yourself and you wilted. Like your father before you. Run a mile from conflict the two of you.

I did it on purpose, Mammy.

Always the peacemaker. Always the goody two-shoes. See what it gets you now? Keep your nose out of other people's business.

You're blind, Muriel.

I wish that were true, his mother said tragically. May this be a lesson to you. The path of least resistance is a thorny ideological weapon.

She cooked him scrambled eggs and toast and tried to cheer her son up with tales of early faint-heartedness. Before she left for another anti-war meeting, she kissed him hard on the forehead and told him to be brave. Maybe she had a point, he thought, as he heard the car drive away. He was crippled with shyness. A shrinking violet. No, he wouldn't hide away in the house and let them think he was scared of them. He would stand up for himself. Fuck the lot of you, he declared, put his plate in the sink, and went upstairs to get himself dressed. He left the house in a pair of new black trousers and a silver bomber jacket, and got into his own car. For the first time in his life he was going to drive to work. The belt went on, the key slid in and the handbrake was released from its deadlock, but that was as far he got. He simply couldn't move an inch. He wanted to but he couldn't. Marty was calling to him, rearing to go, come on, Valentino, there's nothing to be afraid of, the law of large numbers, come on, brother…

Instead the barber made his way on foot into town. He stopped for a coffee and a smoke at a table outside a café, but he felt he was getting under the feet of the pedestrians. Then somebody he knew was coming along the street, and he gave them the nod, but it was deliberately not returned. The same happened twice more, blanked, by the time he reached the river, and the hump of the Ha'penny bridge. He had a mind for a chat with Ultan on the other side but there was no levitation being practised on Strand Street Great. He sat himself down on Ultan's pallet and smoked another cigarette, composing his thoughts.

Where's himself? A man wanted to know from the back window of a grey Merc. He had a driver and a low hairline and three chins.

Valentine raised his eyes to the sky and winked.

A little later, from a safe distance, he counted eight people outside the shop, both men and women.

~

Mister Funny Valentine!

It was Lauren's voice. She pulled the car up to the high granite curb and threw open the passenger door. She had taken the day off and been shopping, bought an antique iron candelabra, which was on the back seat on top of her papers. As they chatted about this and that, he decided the lady looked younger in her civvies, a brown cord skirt and a white jumper with a loose roll neck, her hair tied back and less make-up. Then, with a glance in her mirror, she mentioned the commotion she had seen outside the shop.

A disgruntled customer, is it?

No, the customer was happy, even left a tip, Valentine said.

Full disclosure? I've a fear of falling asleep in the hairdresser's and waking up a completely different person so I keep blabbing on the whole time. Whatever comes into my mind. They must know everything about me, from what I eat for breakfast to—it just spills out of my mouth. No censor, that's my problem.

You obviously don't listen to the news.

Why, is it someone important who's inside? As if I cared? Don't mention politics to me, she said. Zero interest at all. I have two soaps I follow on the box, but apart from that it's a film and a glass of wine. I'm very ordinary really.

If you're ordinary, Lauren, then I'm...

Up Capel Street, Valentine saw Tintin appear at the door of the shop and attempt to remonstrate with the protesters. Then the Boss stepped out too. Wylie was back.

If I'm ordinary? Go on. You can't keep a girl hanging like this.

He looked at her and then at the candelabra like a big crown on the back seat, and asked, Do you want a hand with that?

Every woman's dream question, Lauren said.

His phone began to ring, and it rang constantly on the way, across Capel Street Bridge, around Christ Church and into the Liberties. It continued to ring in his pocket as he carried the candelabra into Lauren's house, an iron diadem for an ancient god in his arms. He brought it upstairs into the spare room. Her boudoir she called it. A full-length mirror, boxes of shoes, dresses hanging from the high wainscoting. She had a glass of wine waiting for him below. He contemplated the people and horses in the frames along the marbled shelf of her fireplace, many of them dead and gone. Some local children ran laughing by the front window where she kept a vase of flowers.

You seem quiet today, Mister Valentine, she said, from the sofa. Have I kidnapped you maybe?

He smiled and took a sip of the cold wine. You can take me hostage whenever you want, he said.

Lauren fluttered her eyes in a way that suggested she found his reply to be unnecessarily something or other.

Would it be okay, the barber asked, if I just stay here and not talk for an hour?

Lauren agreed. She topped up his glass and, saying she had a few emails to send, she went upstairs. His phone rang again. He put it on mute. Then he took out the SIM card and sat exactly where she had sat on the sofa. The walls were burgundy, like her car. A painting of a lighthouse. Photographs. Cushions. Dried flowers in the fireplace. The children ran past again, shrieking with delight.

He was in the same position when she came down later, switching on the lights as she came. She had changed into a trouser suit with a white belt.

I should probably go, he said and Lauren said, Stay if you like. I really need to talk to you, Valentine. And, she said, I'm gagging for a curry.

And that's what Valentine did. He stayed and ate with her, and drank her wine, and he told her the same stories he always told women, and when she seemed to grow sad and restless he couldn't blame her. She decided to put some music on. It was the stuff he didn't like. He put down his fork and began to hum a tune. Lauren thought he was being rude. It was a tune his nephew liked to hum, Valentine explained, and it could make cutlery fall off the table. He tried again, despite the fact that Lauren had left the room.

My father, she said on her return, handing him one of those photographs of the departed. A bearded man with a gate behind him. Jeans cut into shorts.

They forget us so quickly, Valentine said. Was he brave?

How funny you should ask that. I used to think he was. The bravest man on earth, she said. And then one day...

How dare you? Valentine said, to put a stop to her. Don't speak ill of them. You don't even know me. Let's keep it light. Tell me about your favourite horse.

And I'm a bigger coward, she said, and fled the room. Chewing on some naan bread, he thought of Marty, parked outside the house, filled with silence and darkness. He got up, went into the living room. Lauren was lying on her back on the sofa, her belt undone. Valentine lunged at her, tried to kiss her. She pushed him off.

They sat there, side by side, panting. They hadn't pulled the curtains.

Lauren was the first to speak. Do you ever wish people would just keep their secrets to themselves?

I'm sick and tired of people's secrets, said the embarrassed barber.

It's not your fault, she said. I haven't been honest with you. I've been trying so hard. You know my therapist told me to stay away from you?

There's a therapist comes into the shop and he tells me the cops raided him and took all his notes. And the safe he kept them in.

That's terrible, she said. The poor man.

Stupid place to hide them though. Hiding things takes thought.

I've been giving you mixed signals. I know I have.

You know people hide a lot of stuff in their cars, he said, and Lauren took his hand in hers. It was cold, her hand. She explained she had bad circulation.

I think I may have done something really fucken stupid, he said.

You will probably never speak to me again, she said. But I just can't. Not with this terrible thing between us. Did you ever feel like something was hanging over you and no matter how much you avoid it—

Yes. This Gonzo guy, Valentine said, jumping to his feet. I know all about him. How can you work for somebody like that? It's been driving me mad. He'll start another famine to get what he wants. A famine, Lauren. Trying to control our food. The seeds. He owns all the seeds.

They began to argue. Neither of them would back down. After midnight, he slammed the front door behind him and began to push and elbow and his way through the crowds towards his stool in Crusoe's.

For the first time ever, there was a bouncer on the door. He spoke into his radio and Crusoe himself appeared.

You're not only barred, he told Valentine, you're banned.

~

It seemed for a time that the only thing standing between Valentine and the mob was Gemmel himself. For a few days at least, you would see people in packs running from one end of the city to the other, chasing a whisper of the killer, from the Pope's high cross to the fool's long throne in Merrion Square.

Valentine, meantime, insisted he had stayed at home,

watching old films Muriel rented out for him, and practising his moves in his Astra around Crumlin.

What's Mr Wells's opinion on what happened then? I asked when I was finally granted the opportunity to see him. Instead he told me how he had fucked up the driving test. A story that began with an encounter with his mother outside the bathroom door. Muriel thought he should know that she had spent the previous day at the gates of the Dáil waving a placard with her arthritic arm and yet the pain and the chants weren't enough to drown out the sound of people talking about her son and what he had done. It will all blow over, he tried to reassure her, and reminded her of the brevity of all the best outcries and hoo-has, Michael Jackson, Princess Diana's pile-up, the troubles in the North. Muriel, however, wasn't easily swayed. Wylie had called her. They had a big talk on the phone, she said. He was worried the shop would be blacklisted now, and she was beginning to see his point. She demanded to know, there and then, if this was all a way of him getting back at his brother-in-law.

Graham had been on the case of some of the missing women for five whole minutes at most before he had another breakdown. Valentine told Muriel she was being ridiculous, grasping at straws, when what she needed to do was see it as a joke, a bad joke maybe, but only time would tell.

History will be my judge, he said and realised his mother was still talking about Graham.

It's my own business if I don't like the man. Few and far between are the women who have any reason at all to respect their sons-in-law. I can fight my own battles. I always have and I always will. I don't need you or any man to be standing up for me. I see what you're doing. I see right through you, Valentine Rice. When you were a child—

The one and only way to stop her talking that he could think of was to let his dressing-gown slip from his shoulders to the carpet, and this is what he chose to do. And it became forever more a deed in time. An event in his life. He stood stark naked before his mother.

Next he decided it was high time for a cup of tea. He went down the stairs, Muriel right behind him, slapping him across the shoulders. On the living room carpet he stopped and swung around to face her. She slapped his cheek. He turned the other.

Mammy, he said, speaking calmly over the noise she was making, yes, you have a good heart. But most people do. It's not that big a deal. There are good hearts everywhere. You don't get a prize for having one. There's an interesting man who comes into the shop every Christmas Eve and…

Muriel slapped him again.

I have my driving test shortly, he continued, but before I go I have something to get off my chest. I want to forgive you. I want to forgive you for Daddy's death. So what, you kicked him out. So what, you threatened to divorce him. So what, he tried to drown his sorrows in the pub and got mowed down in the street.

A new voice entered the fray. All it said was his name like he had fallen asleep at the wheel. Sabrina was standing in the kitchen doorway, Skippy in her arms.

Not many people get to see a look like that, he said to me. Only the chosen few. Only the true artists. Your own sister. Appalled isn't the word. Having a row with your mother in the nip and smelling of her lavender body wash. Needless to say, they kicked me out on the street like my father before me. Sabrina in the room while I got dressed, ranting. I only said what she's always saying. She's the one who calls Muriel a murderer.

The secret café we met in had white sand for a floor, parasols, and an incomplete tropical mural. Valentine, unshaven, dressed in black, sported a pair of plastic sunglasses. He was convinced, he told me, that he knew the man with the clipboard and pencil case who was waiting, eyes shut, in the passenger seat. From the cold house of the North, long pockmarked face, head shaved clean to the skin, a white shirt, opened too low, wooden beads around his neck, square ears, too much aftershave. The man denied it with a swift twitch of the head, too swift, Valentine thought, and he asked if it would be permissible if they talked for a little while together first. The tester checked his big watch and gave him five minutes. Valentine began with the train bombings in Madrid, moved on to the new tram tracks being laid, and how great Lauren Bacall was in *Murder on the Orient Express*. The tester said nothing, glanced occasionally at his watch, but otherwise seemed to be watching a man planting flowers in a big tub outside the test centre entrance. Valentine inquired again if the tester was absolutely sure they didn't know each other. I never forget a face, he said. I'm a barber, he said. It's my job never to forget a face. The tester denied it again, more forcefully, and scratched the inside of his thigh. It was a tell, a dead giveaway, Valentine decided. He had him. If he had a moustache, he would have stroked it, Poirot style. And on it went until Valentine got out of the car, demanding to speak to someone in power, and shouting that the test was not only compromised but that he felt intimidated by the manner in which the tester kept scratching his groin.

Laughing about it later, the test form in a ball on the bogus beach floor, Valentine joined his hands behind his head and confided, You know, I've never really liked sex. Not really. I don't mean I think it's disgusting or anything like that. It's not. It can be nice. It can be a nice and intimate thing to do with someone, but that's it. I can take it or leave it. I don't let it dominate me. The way people go on about it, you would think they'd suffocate if they didn't have their five or ten sweaty minutes or however long it takes. Don't get me wrong: I'm not mad enough to claim I know why we're all here in space and time on a spinning hunk of rock, but there has to be a better reason than getting your end away. I'm no prude either. I'm just saying I'm not mad about sex and I bet you, and I know this for a fact, I'm not alone either. People are just too scared to say. They're intimidated. We're all supposed to be sex and porn mad and it's all a load of bollocks. A big lie. The ultimate lie. Sex is over, that's what I'm saying. This is the last blast. No sex in the future, that's my prediction. The sooner we are all half muscle and half wires the better. I want to be a robot.

I told him Wylie had given me my marching orders. I had come back into the flat and found him there, sitting in the old chair, one of the originals, and it took him a few seconds to recognise me and remember what I was doing there. Wylie had asked me, I told Valentine, if I thought it was about him, the whole Gemmel saga, if it was revenge. Valentine laughed at the suggestion. That's him all over, he said, the fat impotent queen. He's bribing you, don't you see? Be nice to me and I'll let you stay. Tell me what I want to hear. You should have agreed with him. I don't care what people think anymore. It's idolatry.

A waitress who had appeared at our table, flinched at the word, and then politely informed us smoking was prohibited in Ireland now. We were under the impression we were outside, we argued, gesturing at the sand and parasols, the wattle roof. It was false advertising. Bored, she held out a bucket with sand in the bottom.

Well, honky, we're both on skid row now, Valentine said then. And I had to tell him that F had rung and told me to come home. His nostrils flared under the scuffed cat-eye frames. He waited, letting the silence do its work. Then he said, in his opinion, I had been kidding myself all along anyway.

She loves you, he said. Give up the booze like she wants.

Forget about pigtails. Give it all up for her. I suppose she hates me now too.

She's very curious to know what you talked about with him, I said. With Gemmel, I meant. I could see by Valentine's reaction that he was thinking this was the only reason I wanted to see him, the morbid grist of the story for the price of a Tequila Mockingbird.

And then a second one. And a third.

Cars, Valentine said. Can you believe it? Another one obsessed with cars. He had a car magazine in his pocket. What he missed most in jail was driving. He used to lie on his bed at night and dream about driving, night driving, how to get from Skerries to Delgany, every bend, every light. And he tried to guess what kind of car I had. The man may be proud of his hair, but he's also proud of his ability to guess what car a man drives by looking at his palms. I'm serious. I had to show him my palms. Have you ever shown a serial killer your palms? And me not even having my test. I thought he would rape me. Five attempts he made and then I pretended he had got it. Do you know what I drive? A fucken Honda Civic.

His phone rang. He looked at the caller ID, shook his head, scratched at the blacked-out tattoo on his arm.

I'm ashamed of that, he continued. Pandering to him like that. What about women? I asked him. Can you guess what a woman drives? And out comes the usual aul guff about women drivers. These people are fucken boring, I'm telling you. Deadly boring. My father was a shit driver, I told him. It was a nightmare being in the car with him. Lose his temper over the slightest thing, the car in front, the car behind, a leaf on the fucken windscreen. Rage. Pure rage. We weren't allowed to make a sound. There was a few times he stopped the car altogether and got out and Muriel had to get out too by the side of the road and calm him down. And then he gets hit by one, isn't that fucken weird? Gemmel was angry now.

LEVITATION

You could see it. A film of sweat. A greasy sheen. And so, you know what I did? The day of my daddy's funeral? I told him about that. Driving to the cemetery. Hearse in front. Us behind in the funeral car, in the back seat, me in the middle of Muriel and Sabrina, holding a hand of each of them. And then turning into the gates somebody steps out in front of the hearse and it stops and we go into the back of it. A bump really, nothing major, but it threw me forward and I burst my nose. Streams and streams of blood. It wouldn't stop. I was standing at my father's grave with my head thrown back, Muriel's lavender-soaked handkerchief against my nose, I had to keep looking up at the sky, there wasn't even a cloud up there.

~

In the days that followed, there were various sightings of Valentine Rice around the city, many of them improbable, and some wistful. Whoever the man was he knew from the shop, a hotel manager somewhere, was clearly no help to him because he spent that first night in a cheap bed and breakfast on Gardiner Street. The next night he seemed to have shifted to the other side of the river, to a bunk bed off Pearse Street, and Baggot Street after that, a shabby Georgian house with a crack up the middle of the steps to a sated blue door. Maybe he had the nightmare again in that house—the motorway, the endless motorway, the cars coming straight at him, pairs of the same mechanical yellow eyes, Gemmel eating a toffee apple, and Skippy, breaking free from the belt, shouting, Uncle, I have come all this way to find you, because the next day he booked into a five-star hotel.

Lauren says she spoke to him on the phone, she could hear the ice in the champagne bucket and he was certainly drunk. He ranted to her about Doctor Gonzo, who he had seen on the television over the bath. He was claiming the camera was suspiciously kind to the man, very suspiciously, because he had spoken to the man in person in the back of his car, seen the triple chins up close, and the rash the lasers left along his hairline, and his genetically modified chauffeur, and they weren't getting away with it, their big plan to do away with the fields, and the poor crops, no way, he was rounding up a gang to put a stop to it.

She begged to see him, asked at the front desk of some of the hotels after a euphoric barber. Wylie claims not to have tried to contact him during those days, but I'd say it's a fair bet he left long, stoned messages casting himself as the captain of a sinking ship.

The first definite sighting of our Valentine was his flight down the fire escape from the hotel room fire. There is no evidence whatsoever that Valentine was responsible for starting the fire, a minor incident anyway, a smouldering pillow, from what I heard. With so many other people in the room at the time, many of them homeless and mentally ill, drug addicts, and some just along for the ride, it's impossible to attribute blame to anyone. Ultan may be right or he may be lying that the beggar's banquet was his idea; having quit his eyrie on Strand Street Great, he had returned to his life as a raging alcoholic when Valentine found him and took him back to the hotel. Valentine was wearing a yarmulke and a kilt, he claims.

The same night as the fire, Lauren's next-door neighbour says there was a knock at his door and a man in a linen bathrobe asked for the loan of a piece of paper and a pen. He wanted to leave a written message. Some type of argument developed between them and the man left, denied the opportunity to express himself, snapping the mirror off the door of a parked car. Coogan, in another dubious claim, swears he has CCTV footage in his possession that shows a group of living skeletons trying to wedge open the shutters on his shop and what could possibly be our Valentine in the passenger seat of a waiting transit van. He wants money for a private viewing, if you could bear to pay him.

    Footage I have actually seen comes from The Royal Ravi, a Nepalese curry house, one Wednesday night towards the end of April. There are twelve people eating. Eight of them are in one party at a table in the middle of the low-ceilinged room. Another two, men in casual clothes, are in one of the four booths along the wall decorated by prayer flags. In the booth furthest from the camera and nearest the bay window to the street sit a man, grey haired, round heavy shoulders, seen only from the back, and a woman, blonde, a napkin in the neck of her pale blouse. It is Wylie and Lauren. The waiters, in black waistcoats, come and go with silver trays. One of the larger group, a young male, takes the stairs out of shot to find the toilets in the basement presumably. Two more, women, party dresses, bare arms, pass through the street door without their coats, suggesting they are not going far, a cigarette break perhaps. Lauren can be seen using the napkin to dab at her eyes. Wylie seems to be counting on his fingers. The images are silent. It is as though a layer of meaning has been removed, and what is exposed is another world where there is infinite distance between what is about to happen in that restaurant room, unknown of course to the strangely guilty participants, and what has already happened, no matter how many times I watch it. Lauren pouring wine, Wylie turning his head in the direction of the young male who happens to be crossing the restaurant floor at that moment, wiping his hands on his trousers, in an exaggerated fashion, before he resumes his seat; none of this activity is wilful connection to the reappearance of the two girls in party frocks and behind them, someone else, a male, moving quickly, possibly using them to shield his entrance from the restaurant staff. He is wearing a branded hoodie and leather trousers zipped up the side. Lauren, her expression is impossible to read from this distance, sees the man coming towards their booth and seems to time perfectly the moment she slides across the bench. The man takes a seat. Valentine Rice, yes. He doesn't look too bad despite his exaggerated pleasure in joining their company. A waiter approaches cautiously with a menu. Valentine waves it away but he does seem to give the waiter an instruction of some kind, which the waiter acknowledges, but only after turning his head towards Wylie, who throws up his arms in mock despair. The two men in the other booth seem to be querying their bill with another waiter, and the large group are applauding one of their number, a woman wearing big glasses, as she carefully tears the paper concealing what must be some kind of gift, and meanwhile a conversation has begun, as they say, among our three friends in the booth by the window. Valentine, to begin with, seems to be leading the conversation, the one with the most to say, and doing a lot of pointing at Wylie. The waiter returns with a tray on which is a drink, clear, a gin and tonic glass that he sets down for Valentine, accompanied by a small plate of momos, I'd guess, and a bowl of chutney. Wylie's hand can then be seen to grasp hold of Valentine's and with his head he seems to make a signal to Lauren who is tapping her mouth with the tips of her fingers.

There, in the Royal Ravi, a Wednesday, his least favourite night of the week, Valentine learned the identity of the man who had killed his father. Lauren told me how it felt to finally tell him, whether it was for her own sake or his, who can say. On his deathbed, her own father had told her a story of the night he had hit a man with his car and drove away. The man had died and his name was Rice. Lauren's father, tortured by guilt, had gone to the funeral, hanging around at the gates of the cemetery, afraid he would be recognised somehow, wanting it, and nearly caused another accident. Lauren was bequeathed the story. And she chose to do nothing. A year passed. Then another. Until one day on Francis Street she ran into the back of a car driven by Valentine.

And how did he take it? I asked her, although I had already seen the footage. Wylie, who knows everybody in Dublin, including the owners of The Royal Ravi, presented me with a copy.

You can see Valentine listening to her. You can only imagine what is happening inside him. Lauren's hands reach out towards him, once, twice, but he doesn't acknowledge them. There, see that, he touches his nostrils and checks his fingers as if he is expecting to see blood. He seems to be staring at a place high above Lauren's head.

Wylie, when Lauren seems to have said her piece, leans his elbows on the table to speak. He told me what he said. He told Valentine not to worry about money. He had done him a favour, Valentine had. The shop might be closing, but there were other possibilities. He's running for the city council now. He might be the mayor someday.

Valentine, as everybody knows, has taken Ultan's spot on Strand Street Great.

The other day when I was there talking to him, Sabrina stopped on a bicycle. Skippy was in a seat over the back wheel. He can talk now, his hair is very long.

Uncle Valentine, he chants, clapping his hands.

Stop by and say hello if you're passing. Sráid na Trá Mhór. Donate quietly.

You can't keep a good man down.

The Stinging Fly magazine was established in 1997 to seek out, publish and promote the very best new Irish and international writing. We have a particular interest in encouraging new writers, and in promoting the short story form. We now publish two issues of *The Stinging Fly* each year: in April and October. It is available on subscription from our website.

The Stinging Fly Press was launched in May 2005 with the publication of our first title, *Watermark* by Sean O'Reilly. In 2007 we published Kevin Barry's debut short story collection, *There Are Little Kingdoms*; and in 2009 *Life in The Universe* by Michael J. Farrell. *The China Factory*, a collection of stories by Mary Costello, was nominated for The Guardian First Book Award in 2012. *Young Skins* by Colin Barrett won the 2014 Frank O'Connor International Short Story Award, the Rooney Prize for Irish Literature and the Guardian First Book Award. In 2015 we published *Pond* by Claire-Louise Bennett and *Dinosaurs On Other Planets* by Danielle McLaughlin. We have also published a number of anthologies as well as new editions of Maeve Brennan's *The Springs of Affection* and *The Long-Winded Lady*.

All Stinging Fly Press titles can be purchased online from our website. Our books are distributed to the trade by Gill (IRL/UK) and Dufour Editions (USA). The titles listed here are also available as ebooks via the main platforms.

If you experience any difficulty in finding our books, please e-mail us at stingingfly@gmail.com.

visit www.stingingfly.org

Thank you for supporting independent publishing.